The Breakaway

CAMPUS CONFESSIONS
BOOK ONE

CYNTHIA GUNDERSON

BUTTON PRESS

With Gratitude

Editing and Critique
Scott Gunderson

Cover Design
Ink and Veil

Author Note

This book deals with teenage sexual abuse. I've talked with countless women about their assault experiences and shared my own story. While I tried to treat this subject with care and sensitivity, I also didn't shy away from telling the truth. So many of us walk through the world still bearing those scars.

I want to be clear: I don't blame parents from our generation. None of us had the knowledge or skills to handle this seamlessly in the nineties. I'm also incredibly grateful for the work of mental health professionals who have not only given us the tools for healing but have worked to make them accessible.

And words can't express the love I have for the men who find us crying and scoop us up, blankets and all. (xoxo Scott)

xo Cindy

For my 90's teens who love a good cinnamon roll.

CHAPTER
One

I SHOT up from the metal bench, screaming at the top of my lungs with the rest of the fans in the ice rink. The roar of the crowd surged, a symphony of cheers, stomping feet, and clanging cowbells reverberating in my chest.

"Sharla! Did you see that?" Crystal shook my shoulders, nearly spilling my Coke. "I can't believe he made it!" She adjusted her toque, her pink-tinged hair flicking out over her neck and ears.

I laughed, replaying the last thirty seconds like a highlight reel. Logan was a damn good winger, but I'd never seen him pull something like that before. The blue and gold UVC jerseys blurred into a streak as Logan darted through them like a fox in a henhouse in his number eighteen jersey.

"I swear he caught the puck mid-air!" Maddie's dark brown eyes were wide as she leaned in. Her breath smelled faintly of mint gum.

I wanted to pinch myself. Logan had just scored the winning

goal in the last minute of the third period against the number one college team in the country.

"Eat that, TV announcers." Crystal held up her middle finger, and I grabbed her hand, laughing.

"TV announcers? Just lumping them all together?" Maddie laughed, sweeping her dark curls over her shoulder.

I snorted. "There are professors here!"

Crystal shook her head, the tiny jewel in her nose sparkling. "I don't care. Everyone underestimated Outlaws hockey. Do you remember how much crap Logan had to deal with over the summer?"

I blew out a breath. Yes, I absolutely remembered. Logan had been in the pissiest mood ever between July and August.

I would never say it out loud, but I couldn't actually blame the analysts for not believing in this team. With a complete overhaul of the coaching staff and losing three of their top players in the draft, they didn't have much to go off of. Truly, if I were going to blame anybody, it would be our neighbour to the south. All those American schools headhunting with deeper pockets than Canadian universities. It wasn't really a fair playing field.

Logan had given up three other offers by choosing to stay in Calgary, and at least part of that was because of me. He swore I wasn't the only reason. Otherwise, I never could've lived with myself.

But I had two years left before I graduated with my Bachelor of Music degree, majoring in violin performance. Then, I could take that skill anywhere, and I planned to. Logan was headed for the NHL—I was sure of it—and I would be there right by his side.

"Come on." I grabbed onto Crystal and Maddie and rushed to the stairs to try and beat the rest of the crowd. We weren't completely successful, but at least we were heading in the opposite direction.

Logan and I had a secret meeting place. We discovered it the first year he started on the Outlaws, and so far, it still seemed to be our little secret. Well, except that Crystal and Maddie always tagged along with me.

We climbed the stairs and exited to the hall that led to the main lobby then cruised around the corner and headed down. This stairwell didn't seem to lead anywhere specific. It was probably only used for janitorial and maintenance staff. There was a door at the bottom, but a passageway behind the stairs led to a little storage area accessible to the locker rooms.

Of course, I never went into the locker room itself, but before Logan would get in the shower, he always came out to give me a quick kiss after the game. I took up my post, still flushed from the excitement.

Sure enough, a few seconds later, Logan opened the door, bringing shouts and laughter on the air with him. He still wore his maroon and gold jersey.

He darted toward me, scooping me up into his arms. "Baby, did you see that?"

"I saw. It was amazing."

"We won."

"I know." I kissed him, then laughed as he buried his face in my neck. I used to complain about his post-game sweaty hair, but now, I loved that I was the first thing he wanted to see after things went well or poorly. Whether he was angry or elated, I was his person.

He exhaled and slowly lowered me back to the ground. "Logan, seriously, that shot. I don't even know where that came from—"

"I was trying to deke left, but then the puck caught something on the ice and popped up, and my stick was just there, you know?"

"You were basically playing lacrosse," Crystal interjected.

Logan looked up. "Oh hey, ladies."

Crystal and Maddie laughed and waved. "Amazing game," Maddie said.

Logan nodded and brushed the hair from his forehead. "I gotta get back in there."

I nodded, grabbing his face and giving him one more kiss. "I love you, babe."

"Love you too. I think we're all going to Ranchmans after."

I frowned. "I thought we were going home because the game was already so late."

Logan exhaled, giving me an apologetic smile. "I know, but after that? We can't just go home. There has to be some sort of celly. I won't be able to wind down for a bit anyway."

I grinned. "I get it, but I have that practice at eight in the morning—"

"We don't have to stay late. Maybe just an hour? Grab a few beers?" He gave me puppy dog eyes. "I want you there with me. This was probably the best game of my life."

I quirked an eyebrow. "I'm pretty sure you said that two weeks ago when you played—"

"I know. I know. But I'm serious this time."

I laughed. He was so dramatic. But that was what I loved about him. He was a dreamer, just like me, even though his dreams involved ice, pucks, and sticks, and mine involved perfect soaring high G's and handcrafted wooden bridges.

"Fine." I planted a hand on his chest. "But you're changing the sheets tomorrow."

He grinned. "Done. I'll even make you breakfast."

I laughed. "Don't make promises you can't keep."

"Eggs and bacon," he called out as he retreated. I shook my head and walked back to Maddie and Crystal.

"He's making you breakfast? Damn." Crystal turned toward the stairs.

"No, he says that now, but there's no way his ass is out of bed before ten o'clock tomorrow."

Maddie laughed. "At least he wants to. That's better than most guys I know."

"I mean, just the fact that he knows how." Crystal snorted.

We trudged back up the stairs and exited the rink, jumping into Maddie's Rabbit. It was the worst old clunker of a car, but I swear she only had to fill it up with gas once every six months.

I didn't even have to ask if they were coming with me. Crystal only had three classes that semester, and Maddie was a bona fide genius. She studied purely to say she had when she got one hundred percent on her midterms and didn't want to brag.

We drove across campus and parked in the student-permitted lot, then walked the two-and-a-half blocks to the restaurant. It was all street parking in that part of the city, and at this time of night on a Friday, no spots would be open until Seventeenth Avenue. It was a surprisingly warm night, but I still brought my jacket.

The sports bar was a crush of people—students packed together like sardines. Girls in tight jeans and tank tops despite, you know, Canada. Guys with backwards baseball caps and oversized jerseys.

Maddie, Crystal, and I pushed our way through the crowd, exchanging hugs and high-fives with familiar faces as we made a beeline for the back of Ranchmans.

The bar was a shrine to Douglas sports. Framed jerseys and posters of past victories adorned the walls. When they renamed the University two years prior, the colours, maroon and gold, stayed the same. Convenient.

In the back, a long table stretched out, reserved for the team. It was in a prime spot, slightly elevated on a step up from the rest of the bar floor. I always felt like I was on display, especially when I got there before Logan.

Thankfully, we didn't have to wait long. By the time we took off our coats and got settled, the door swung open, and the bar erupted. Cheers went up, and the music was drowned out. I craned my neck as the team flooded in, Logan leading the charge. His grin was wide and infectious, and he waved to the crowd, basking in the adoration.

"Hail the conquering heroes!" Axel, one of the forwards, laughed as he parted the crowd like the Red Sea and grabbed a seat. Tim, the goalie, nodded seriously to the crowd like he'd just been knighted. He sat next to Axel, reaching for the closest pitcher of beer.

And then there was Rob.

He sat down at the far end of the table, and I couldn't have been more grateful. I already had to see him one thousand percent more than I would have chosen to. He was Logan's best friend growing up. Or at least all through high school. The only two things I knew for sure about Rob Thompson were, one, that he hated me and, two, he was our only roommate.

I moved in with Logan at the beginning of summer. His parents had purchased a two-bedroom apartment as a real estate investment, which got Logan out of his crappy six-person shared flat on campus. Since I was in a dumpier flat and we'd been together for over six months at that point, it made sense for us to take the leap. But what Logan had forgotten to tell me was that Rob was jumping in with us.

It just makes sense. Rob can pay half the rent, and then we split the second half. That means it would only be one hundred fifty dollars a month for each of us. That was Logan's argument, and, at the time, it was compelling. Financially, anyway.

But, sanity-wise?

The only rebuttal I could draw on was something I would never say out loud to Logan. Not because Logan didn't already know, but because he didn't know that I knew.

I think you're wrong. Sharla isn't like that.

Logan's words still rang in my head, along with Rob's.

All I'm saying is I think she's gonna take away your focus. She doesn't understand the kind of dedication and commitment this takes, bud.

And that wasn't the first or the last time he made some smarmy comment about me. Rob Thompson hated my guts. Or didn't think I was good enough for Logan. Either way, the day he moved out would be the day I had my own "celly."

Logan found me and scooped me back against his chest, dropping his head next to mine. "I'm so glad you came out tonight."

I ran my fingers over the stubble on his jaw. "You know I'm only here for an hour or so."

He kissed my cheek. I rolled my eyes as he sat down in the chair next to me, shoving his hand into the back pocket of my jeans as far as he could before his fingertips hit the wooden seat. I loved that he loved touching me.

Logan was magnetic on and off the ice. He had a smile that would make you feel elated to pay double the price for some shitty T-shirt just because he'd put his hands on it. Everyone else in the bar seemed to rotate around his gravity. Well, around him *and* Rob, but I tried to ignore the fact that he existed.

They were like two burning suns, sucking everyone else into their orbit. When you put them together, the reaction was almost too cataclysmic to look upon with human eyes. Logan was all sunshine and golden lab energy, and Rob was his dark angel counterpart. His brooding, sarcastic balance in the force.

Someone ordered a round of shots for the table. Logan glanced over at me and already knew I wouldn't be drinking. Not only because I hardly ever did, but because if I brought up my rehearsal in the morning again, it would start to feel like verbal flagellation.

Logan held up a hand in solidarity. "Not tonight, bud."

And then there was Rob, carrying over four shot glasses between his hands. "What he meant to say was he'll take double." Rob placed two in front of Logan.

And thus began our toxic, never-ending ritual. Me, sitting on the chair, glaring at Rob. Logan, laughing and saying things like, "Okay. I guess I can have a little," and Rob, pounding shots with him, with eyes darker and more dead inside than Lucifer's hounds.

I nudged Logan. "You don't have to."

He shrugged. It never took much cajoling. Logan was usually only raising the bar on his behaviour because I was around, which is why every single time something like this happened, it pinched the same nerve.

Sharla doesn't get it. Sharla is bringing you down. Sharla doesn't want you to have a good time and is a distraction from hockey.

Okay, so I expanded on his original statement a bit. But all of that was written in the sneer on his face. Rob thought I wasn't good for Logan, which was ironic since he was the one encouraging him to poison his liver.

I turned back to Crystal and Maddie, joining their conversation, exaggerating my hand gestures, and laughing louder than necessary. Enter phase two, where I pretended that nothing Rob did to influence Logan's decisions mattered to me.

Logan's hand stayed on me for the next forty-five minutes, either in my pocket, tucked into the waistband of my jeans, wrapped around the back of my neck, or running over the fringe of my hair that barely covered my ears.

I'd cut my hair short the previous summer after Crystal did. Logan said he liked it, but all he could talk about was how excited he was for when he could play with it properly again. The only problem? I wasn't sure if I wanted to let it grow out. I loved how easy it was to take care of—how little I had to think about it.

With the tiny pinch of Korean in my genetic code, my hair stayed straight even after a sweaty sleep. With my mother's hearty German stock, it was thick enough to qualify me for a Vidal Sassoon commercial. I also had thighs that could barrel roll a log and barely B-cup boobs, but I was counting my hereditary blessings.

Logan was in the middle of kicking field goals with rolled-up paper straw packaging and his fingers when I leaned over and said, "I'm going to head home."

Logan stopped mid-flick and turned to me with eyes that

could have turned Rosie O'Donnell straight. "But I'm going to miss you."

I melted, running my hands through his hair as he pulled me off my chair to stand next to him. He wrapped his arms around my waist and squeezed, making me feel like I was a paper doll. With one movement, he could tear me in two.

"I'm so proud of you," I whispered.

"Wait up for me?"

I nodded. This interaction ushered in stage three, where he pretended he wasn't going to be home at two in the morning, and I pretended I would be naked in the bed with my CD of Usher playing on the stereo. We both knew it wasn't going to happen, but it felt right to fantasize in the moment.

I left with Crystal and Maddie, and by the time they dropped me off, my eyes already felt like they'd been rubbed out with sandpaper. I went inside, checked that I had my folder of music and violin ready to go for the morning, then sped through my bedtime routine and popped Logan's mix tape into my boombox.

I turned the volume on low and drew in a deep breath. I had the song order memorized by now. *When Can I See You* by Baby-face was first, and just hearing the opening chords lulled me into relaxation. Then it was *Can You Feel the Love Tonight* by Elton John, *I Swear* by All 4 One —I still couldn't decide which version I liked better, this or the original by John Michael Montgomery— and *Breathe Again* by Toni Braxton. Amazingly, the songs only got better from there. Janet Jackson, Mariah Carey, Celine Dion, Bryan Adams, The Pretenders.

To this day, I'm still shocked Logan remembered every single song I obsessed over on the radio that fall semester. Crystal, Maddie, and I hung out with the hockey team nonstop. I can't remember exactly how it started. Crystal had Axel in her class or something? Anyway, they became our social circle. Hanging out on campus, parties on the weekend, games—so many games.

It was exactly what I'd hoped my university experience

would be. Like every American rom-com I'd watched in high school, minus the cheerleading. But when Logan handed me this mix tape at the bonfire that night? He become more than just one of the hot guys I flirted with. Because I did flirt with a lot of them. Rob included.

My jaw tightened. That still didn't make any sense to me either. Rob talked to me back then. We sat together at movies, after parties. One night we'd even stayed up late playing air hockey, laughing our asses off with Logan and Bear.

Logan and I getting together changed everything.

I rolled over, pulling the comforter to my chin. I did take up a lot of Logan's time now. Rob probably just wanted his friend back. I guess I could understand that. A little. But it had been almost a year. When was he going to get used to this new setup?

My thoughts drifted until I finally slept, deep and silent until movement on the bed dragged me up from the depths. I tensed, my heart jumping into my throat. My hands gripped the pillow, clenching so tight my knuckles cracked.

"Oh, hey, babe. Are you awake?"

Logan's voice. It was him. *Endless Love* was playing by Mariah and Luther Van Dross. That meant we were at the end of the mix tape. I was home. *I was safe.*

I drew a deep breath, trying to orient myself. "Hey."

His hands were immediately on me, sliding under my cotton tank top and flattening over my stomach. The sour scent of alcohol wafted over me.

"You're home." I barely got the words out before Logan tugged on the sheets and rolled over me. I wrapped my arms across his waist. "Logan, what time is it?"

"I don't know. I missed you."

"That's sweet, but what time is it? I have to be up at six-thirty."

He exhaled, his breath hot against my neck. "I tried to come home early so I could be with you."

I recognized the sulk in his voice. He got like this. After using all his energy, being raucous with his teammates and everyone else, he came home to me tipsy and drained.

"Logan—"

"I promise I'll be fast. I just need you right now."

And those were the magic words.

His lips dragged over my shoulder, his fingertips reaching up and scrubbing along my scalp. I was too groggy to think straight. But with the heat of his body seeping into me and his legs threading between mine, how could I say no?

I dropped my hands from the bare skin of his back, and he shifted his weight so I could pull off my underwear. He fumbled for a condom in the nightstand drawer, knowing that, despite the fact that I was on the pill, I would not want to get out of bed to clean up.

"Thank you. I love you, Sharla," he mumbled as he tore at the wrapper.

I was already predicting a migraine by eleven o'clock tomorrow morning. But he was worth it. Logan was always worth it.

CHAPTER
Two

WHEN MY ALARM went off at six-thirty, an orchestra was already playing forte inside of my head. Logan was dead to the world, one leg kicked out over the comforter. His smooth, tanned skin looked even darker against the white sheets, his baby blonde hairs glinting in the sliver of street lamp light shining in around the blackout curtains that didn't quite fit the window.

It looked like he'd been at the beach for a month, which was unfair since it was mid-October in Calgary. I dragged myself out of bed and went to the washroom. I hadn't planned on showering, but given the night's events, it was a necessity.

I turned on the water and went into autopilot, quickly washing myself, brushing my teeth, and throwing on a pair of leggings and an oversized sweatshirt. Thankfully, my conductor didn't care what we wore to rehearsals as long as our asses were in the seat fifteen minutes early.

I moved as quietly as possible, even though I doubted anything I did would wake Logan. He'd probably be in the exact same position when I returned at ten-thirty. I slipped out of the room and walked into the galley kitchen to grab a hard-boiled egg and an orange.

I smiled when I saw my water bottle washed out and drying on the rack. It didn't matter how late Logan got home or how terrible he was at remembering to do the actual dishes. He always cleaned out my water bottle for me. He'd done it ever since I moved in—a true act of love since he thought it was ridiculous and used his own hockey water bottle for months at a time without washing.

"It's only touching your mouth," he told me as I cleaned it out after school one day. I told him that my own mouth touched plenty of food and *his* mouth during the day, and the idea of sucking on that nozzle grossed me out.

I shared food from the same fork as Crystal and Maddie and licked wing sauce off my fingers, but for some reason, a water bottle nozzle was where I drew the line. I threw on my coat, grabbed a granola bar and my water bottle, and threw them in the bag with my folder of music. I popped in my morning mix tape with Ace of Bass, Lisa Loeb, and new Bryan Adams— always Bryan Adams. It made me feel like my morning walk through the tundra was a movie soundtrack which fueled my cinematic brain.

I picked up my violin case and exited the townhouse. I walked the two blocks to campus and entered the GRB science building, immediately turning down the first corridor and entering the tunnel that connected to the Rosza Art Center and concert hall. It wasn't snowing, but it was just chilly enough that I preferred finishing my journey inside.

I didn't use the tunnels by myself often—very murdery—but that morning, there was a stream of students with the exact same idea. I found Lily and Caleb immediately by Caleb's rust-orange hair. Lily's brunette waves were pulled up into a messy bun on top of her head, and they were wearing comfy uniforms similar to mine. Caleb's pajama pants had pickles on them, which was especially classy.

"Rehearsals on a Saturday morning should be illegal," Lily groaned.

Caleb took a drink of his coffee. "Six months left, and then you'll have rehearsal every day of the week."

Lily laughed. "You don't know that."

Caleb gave her a look. "You're joining a band, Lily. Learning an entire six albums' worth of music. I know you're good, but you're not *that* good."

Lily scoffed. "I'm already working on it. And when my recital's over, I can set my own schedule—three days a week max."

I laughed, mostly to cover the twinge of jealousy in my gut. Lily was first chair and was asked to audition for Stellaluna, an indie bluegrass band out of Toronto. As of three weeks before, she'd been hired on for their upcoming '95 tour in Canada with the possibility of going international with the group. Playing violin had never been cool, and Lily was about to make it kick-ass.

"Have you heard anything from Franck?" Caleb nudged my elbow.

I shook my head. "I don't think she'll make any decisions yet."

He nodded. "You're probably right. I would expect an invitation by February at the latest."

That had been my prediction as well. Ms. Franck had high standards and borderline hubristic opinions on musicianship. She'd chosen Lily for first chair weeks into fall semester the year prior. After hearing her play twice.

I wasn't offended that I hadn't received the same treatment, even though I knew my playing was up to snuff. But I was starting to get nervous. With Lily graduating, I always assumed I would be next in line, especially since I already had two years under my belt. But a few incoming students this year were good, and her decisions weren't always linear.

"I still can't believe she chose Mabel for that cello solo." Caleb lowered his voice.

"I know," Lily whispered. "She's improvising all over the place, completely bastardizing the integrity of the primary melody."

I, as a rule follower, couldn't have agreed more. And that was also why I was starting to get nervous. I was a damn good violinist, but if Ms. Franck was looking for riffing, that was not in my wheelhouse.

We pushed through the doors and walked through the cavernous entryway, our voices and shoes echoing off the steel and glass of the art center. We found our seats in the concert hall and tuned our instruments. All chatter died when Ms. Franck arrived, looking like she was ready for a Paris runway and not a collection of pajama-clad students at eight o'clock on a Saturday morning.

"Instruments in tune?" she asked in her thick Eastern European accent. "Spirits in tune?" she asked when we all nodded our heads the first time. "Alright. Let's begin."

For the next two hours, we played, we stopped. We listened to her criticisms. We corrected. By ten o'clock, my fingers were burning, my shoulder was aching, and the migraine was creeping up the back of my skull as predicted.

I didn't connect with Caleb and Lily after rehearsal, but that was fine because I'd forgotten to eat my granola bar. All I wanted was to head straight home and fall back into bed for a few hours after popping an unholy amount of NSAIDs.

But when I walked into the house and found Logan sitting shirtless at the kitchen counter, I knew that wouldn't happen. "What's wrong?"

He stared at a letter, his eyes wide. I dropped my bag and violin case, slipped off my shoes, and hurried over to him. He turned the letter toward me.

I scanned it. "This is an email."

"Yeah. I know. I printed it off."

"You printed off an email?"

He nodded and tapped the paper impatiently. I started to read.

Subject: Official Invitation to Hockey Canada November Selection Camp

Dear Logan Kemp,

I am pleased to inform you that you have been selected to participate in Hockey Canada's November Selection Camp as part of the 1994 IIHF World Junior Championship evaluation process. Your outstanding performance throughout the past season has allowed you to compete for a spot on Team Canada.

My heart picked up speed. Team Canada? Logan had been devastated when he hadn't been selected in previous years. Last season, because of a tweaked knee.

I kept reading.

Camp Details

Dates: November 5 - December 3 (upon selection after round one)

Location: Max Bell Centre, Winnipeg, Manitoba

Arrival Date: November 4 (evening check-in)

During this camp, you will be evaluated through:

On-Ice Training: Skill development sessions, tactical scrimmages, and special teams strategy work.

Off-Ice Assessments: Fitness evaluations, team-building exercises, and leadership workshops.

Exhibition Games: Pre-tournament matchups against international junior teams from Finland and Sweden (locations to be determined).

Important Note: While this invitation reflects our confidence in your potential, participation in this camp does not guarantee a spot on the final roster. Final selections will be based on your performance in practices, exhibition games, and your demonstration of character, discipline, and commitment.

If Selected for the Final Roster:

December 4-7: Travel to Europe for acclimatization and exhibition games.

December 8-23: Pre-tournament preparation in Ostrava and Frýdek-Místek, Czech Republic.

December 26 - January 4: 1994 IIHF World Junior Championship Tournament.

I skipped over the expectations and contact info and re-read the dates, then looked up at Logan. "Czech Republic?"

He nodded. "I have to leave in a week for Winnipeg."

Have to? "But what about school? You still have half the semester left."

He held out a hand. "This is what I've been working for, Shar. Who cares about school?"

"Who cares about school?"

He exhaled. "No. I don't mean who cares about school. I'm just saying they'll figure something out. This is why I'm here, to play hockey. They'll probably defer my classes or something. This is huge."

I sat down on the stool next to him. "Yeah. No. It's amazing. I just—sorry. It's a lot to process."

He set the letter on the counter. "Maybe I can take my finals when I get back or something."

"Two months"

He blew out a puff of air. "Yeah."

"You'll miss the holidays."

"Hey, I'll get to see Christmas in freaking Europe."

Fair. I went on a trip to Germany during high school one spring. All anybody could talk about was how amazing the Christmas markets were and how they wished we'd been there over the holidays.

My mind immediately jumped into logistics. Two months and a bit. It wasn't that long. I would finish out finals, go home for Christmas, and then it would only be a couple of weeks before he was back.

Before I could say as much, a door opened at the end of the hallway. Rob sauntered out, his hair standing on end. Shirtless. I swear he did that on purpose. Just to make me uncomfortable.

I gripped Logan's wrist. "What about Rob?" I hissed, suddenly desperate to hear his answer before Dr. Evil made it within earshot.

Logan frowned. "What about Rob?"

"Well, he can't—"

"Morning, shitheads." Rob stalked to the fridge and pulled out a carton of milk with his name scrawled across the side in Sharpie. He had to label all his food since I was definitely going to share his skin cells by touching it.

"I got some news, bud," Logan said.

My grip tightened. "Logan—"

Rob turned, and Logan held up the email. "I'm going to World Juniors."

Rob's eyes widened. He started saying something, but I didn't hear a word of it. Because Logan hadn't answered my question.

CHAPTER
Three

MY ALARM WENT off at nine, the noise drilling into my skull. Ugh. Tuesdays were supposed to be my day off from class, but there was no rest for the wicked, aka the string section in Select Orchestra.

Rolling out of bed, I stumbled to the washroom, avoiding my reflection in the mirror. By the way my eyes seemed to be shrivelling up like raisins, I was well aware I looked like a hot mess. After brushing my teeth and splashing some cold water on my face in a feeble attempt to shock myself awake, I padded out to the living room.

Logan was already gone, off to the gym for his daily dose of lactic acid production before hockey practice later that afternoon. The townhouse was quiet, and this was when I loved it least. Modern grey furniture and abstract art on the walls, all selected by Logan's dad. It felt about as welcoming as a dentist's waiting room.

I plopped down on the cold leather couch with a sigh. The harsh reality had sunk in after talking more with Logan last night. With him leaving, I would be stuck here alone with Rob for two months. Rob, who hated me for stealing his friend. Rob, who excreted disdain from his pores. Rob, who would probably murder me in my sleep if he could get away with it.

Fantastic.

I had to find another option. I could look in the school paper, but it wasn't likely I'd find a seasonal living opportunity. Lily, Caleb, and any orchestra people I knew weren't options. Caleb lived at home, and Lily was in a shared room off campus. I would just have to brainstorm with Crystal and Maddie when we met up for coffee in a half hour.

I started a load of laundry, then threw on jeans and a hoodie and headed out. The ten-minute walk to the campus coffee shop seemed to take an eternity, my mind reeling with worst-case Rob scenarios. He'd start hosting parties instead of going out every night. He'd hang his jock strap on the stools in the kitchen. I shuddered.

Crystal and Maddie were already at our usual corner table when I arrived, steaming lattes in hand. I collapsed into the empty chair with a groan, and Maddie passed me my cup.

"Thank you." I blew out a breath. "I'm so screwed." I'd called them both multiple times since I'd seen Logan's letter, so they were well-versed in my current level of hopelessness.

Crystal grimaced, her pink hair almost neon under the fluorescent lights. "I talked with Lindsey. We don't have anyone moving out at the semester. There aren't any openings in the fourplex across from us either."

Maddie squeezed my hand. Her fingers were warm from her coffee cup. "I mean, I'd be down to share my bed with you for a couple of months, Shar. Mi casa es su casa and all that."

"Your roommates would be okay with that?"

Her curls bounced as she shrugged. "I have my own room. As long as you cleaned up after yourself, they wouldn't bitch about it."

I bit my lip, considering it. Her room was small, but I could probably get a twin mattress in there. Make a cot on the floor.

But Maddie's place was so far from campus. At least a

twenty-minute drive by car, which I didn't have. It would make getting to rehearsals and shows a nightmare since the bus ride would be almost double that.

I glanced up at Crystal, who was staring at her coffee cup. "What?"

She flinched, her eyes widening. "Hmm? Oh, nothing."

I raised an eyebrow. "Just say it." Crystal was doing a new thing where she tried not to blurt out the first thing that came to her mind. After her last relationship ended because she told her boyfriend Matt he "just acted a little feminine sometimes," she'd decided it was time to nurture a filter.

"Uh." She took a drink of her coffee. I waited, not letting her wriggle out of this. "I was just thinking that . . . " She tapped her fingers on the cup.

I exhaled. "Crystal—"

"Fine, I think you're being a baby." I blinked, and she backpedalled. "Not a baby like this doesn't suck, but just—you know. There are a lot of students here that don't have a brand new townhouse to live in with a private washroom."

I pursed my lips. "Yeah. Okay. That's fair."

Crystal glanced at Maddie, then back at me. "I know it's not what you want to hear."

It definitely wasn't. But it didn't mean she was wrong. "So I need to get over it."

Maddie winced. "Maybe? It's two months."

"You'll be home with your family for part of it, right?" Crystal offered.

I drew a deep breath and exhaled. Yes. They were right. I had a great place to live, and I didn't even have to be there that often. "I could spend more time on campus."

"There you go, girl." Maddie leaned back in her chair and took a sip from her cup.

"And maybe . . ." Crystal gave me a look.

"Maybe what?" I braced myself.

She leaned forward, wrapping both hands around her cardboard cozy. "I know you and Rob have this thing—"

"A thing?" I scowled.

"Where you bicker and try to get under each other's skin."

I scoffed. "I don't try. Rob is the one who goes on the offensive. I try to ignore him most of the time."

Crystal waved a hand. "Whatever, all I'm saying is, Rob isn't, like, scary or anything. He's an asshole sometimes, but he's also funny and—"

"Funny?" I reacted like she'd just said Rob was a patron saint. "He's not funny. He thinks he's funny. He thinks he's God's gift to—"

"Okay, forget I said anything. I only meant that you wouldn't need to be . . . you know. Worried."

I took off the lid of my coffee cup and tested the temperature with my pinky finger, then took a drink. "Yeah." Surprisingly, I hadn't even thought about that. About being in a townhouse alone with a guy who wasn't my boyfriend in general.

I didn't trust men, but Crystal was right. Rob was a dick, but he didn't make me feel unsafe. At least not physically. No, unsafe wasn't the right word at all. He made me feel on edge. Like I needed a shield up. But why? Plenty of other people in the world didn't like me. Plenty who pressed my buttons. So why did I go from zero to a hundred when it was him getting in the digs?

I forced a smile. "Enough about my dramatic descent into roommate anxiety hell. What's new with you guys?"

Crystal groaned, slouching back in her chair. "Don't even get me started. This music theory class is kicking my ass. I swear, Professor Gant is out to get me."

Maddie patted her arm sympathetically. "Aww. He probably is."

Crystal laughed and slapped her hand away. Maddie and Crystal were like yin and yang—complete opposites. Crystal was full artist, and Maddie was straight math and science. I was the hybrid brain that bridged the gap.

We'd all met in a required sociology class our first year and bonded over our mutual hatred for the professor's monotone lectures. Now, two years later, they were my besties. The Thelma and Louise to my . . . Well, whoever the third wheel in that movie would've been. The dog? Brad Pitt? Probably the dog.

We chatted for a while longer before they both had to get to class. I walked back home and trudged up the stairs to the house, feeling oddly naked without my violin case. As I fumbled with my keys, I heard the Counting Crows filtering through the door. My heart leaped. Logan was home.

I pushed open the door and there he was, sprawled out on the couch in his post-workout glory. His blond hair was still damp from the shower, and he had a binder and textbook both opened in front of him on the coffee table. He grinned up at me. "Hey, babe. Where were you?"

I slipped off my shoes and raced to him, hopping onto his lap. "With Crystal and Maddie."

Logan wrapped his arms around my waist. "I missed you."

I hesitated for a moment, glancing around the house. "Where's Rob?"

"At class. That or he isn't up yet."

Probably the latter. I kissed him again, but even that couldn't shake the strange shifting in my gut. "Logan, I need to talk to you about something." I pulled back to look at him. "I don't love this. The fact that you're leaving. That I have to live here with Rob."

Logan frowned. "What do you mean? Rob's a good guy, Shar. He won't bother you."

I shook my head, frustration bubbling up inside me. "That's not the point. He—" *He hates me. He tried to get you to break up with me.* "He's negative and grumpy. All the time. Logan. Without you here—"

Logan ran a hand through my hair. "You think he's negative?"

I gaped at him. "Yeah. On Sunday, he greeted us with 'Morning, shitheads.'"

Logan laughed. "That's just Rob."

Kind of my point, but I kept my mouth shut. Logan just didn't get it. He didn't understand how it felt to be constantly on edge, to feel like you were walking on eggshells in your own home.

"What if we came up with some ground rules?" Logan nudged my chin so he could drop his head into the hollow of my neck. "Like, no parties at the house, no bringing random people over. No telling you you're a shithead."

I laughed. "I doubt he'll go for that."

Logan lay back on the couch, pulling me with him. "Rule number four: no coming home wasted." He reached his hands up the back of my shirt. "Number five: no farting in public spaces."

I snorted. "Where were these rules when we moved in together?" Logan feigned offence, and I jabbed my fingers into his ribs. "Rule number six: no leaving the seat up. Number seven: must be fully clothed."

Logan gripped my wrists. "You don't want to see me naked?"

I grunted, trying to twist away from him and failing. "No, I don't want to see Rob. He's always walking around with his shirt off."

Logan's hands relaxed a little, his face becoming more serious. "That bothers you?"

I grinned. "No, not bothers. It's just—he could put a shirt on."

Logan pushed up to lean against the arm of the couch. I sat up, straddling him.

He ran a hand through his now barely damp hair. "Do you notice other guys like that?"

I rolled my eyes. "Logan—"

"No, I'm serious. Rob isn't unattractive."

I raised an eyebrow, trying to disguise the hammering of my heart. "And how would you know that?"

"Because." He gave me a look that said, *isn't it obvious?* No. No, it was not obvious, and I was suddenly itching for him to make his case.

I swallowed hard. "Logan, I don't look at other guys like that. Do you look at other girls?"

He scoffed. "That's different."

My eyes widened. "Different?"

He realized his misstep, his throat working. "No, I just mean, women are beautiful. Works of art. Guys are . . ." He exhaled in a rush. "Never mind. I'll just tell Rob to put on a shirt."

The simmering in my gut had grown to a full, uncomfortable boil. "Great. Thanks." I shifted off him, giving him a peck on the cheek.

"Where are you going?"

I rounded the end of the table and planted my hands on my hips. "I need to get in some practice. Before rehearsal."

Logan stood, adjusting his shirt. "This weekend. Me and you? Before I head out?"

I nodded, exhaling with relief. It was fine. This was just a weird moment because we were both stressed about being apart for the next couple of months.

But I was happy for him. I wanted this for him, and it was another step toward the life we wanted to create together.

I stepped forward, looping my arms around his waist. "Yeah. I'd love that."

CHAPTER

Four

ON FRIDAY, after two days of rare fog, the sun was out again, glinting off the bronze statue of Michelle Douglas as I crossed campus. That was a new addition when they rebranded Douglas in 1992 after she won her court case. Now, two years later, it felt like it had always been there.

Fallen leaves crunched under my feet, the ones still stubbornly clinging to their branches a riot of golds and reds and oranges. The crisp October breeze carried the excited chatter of students discussing their Halloween party plans.

I passed the stone archway leading to the GRB and its tunnel. The university's 1950s architecture was showing its age, but I loved the history imbued in every brick. This campus had seen so much change over the decades. I was told all about it at orientation.

A girl with two lip piercings walked by wearing cat ears, which spurred my memory. I still needed to buy fish nets for the Boos and Booze party tomorrow night with the Outlaws. Parties weren't really my scene, but it was important to Logan. Then we were going to spend the weekend together. He promised me brunch at The Kitchen, and I promised I'd help him pack.

But first . . .

Pulling my jacket tighter, I gritted my teeth and trudged to the north side of campus. I'd walked this route so many times since I moved in over the summer, I was on autopilot. For better or worse, I had Rob's schedule memorized. I was probably more attuned to his day-to-day activities than I was to Logans. Disturbing, to say the least.

On Thursdays he was always back early from class, splaying his notebooks out on the counter and making some concoction involving a hell of a lot of cheese while I tried to study. Which was why I sought refuge in the library or booked a practice room to work through a new piece on my violin. I was very much absent on Thursday afternoons by design.

But not today.

As the house came into view, I drew a deep breath, squared my shoulders, and marched up the path. Logan had been right about ground rules, and initially, I wanted to ask him to present them to Rob. But Logan wouldn't be there to save me for the next two months. I would have to put on my big girl panties and do this myself.

Rob's head snapped up as I entered, his dark eyes narrowing. He was hunched over a notebook at the kitchen counter, textbooks spread around him. The surprise on his face would've been comical if my heart wasn't thrashing in my chest like a fish yanked out of water.

"You're home early." His voice was flat, his expression stony.

"Sorry to ruin your afternoon." I set down my violin case and backpack, then slipped off my shoes and put them on the rack. I circled him warily, grabbing a glass from the cupboard and filling it at the tap. Rob's gaze bored into my back, and my hands wobbled as I took a sip.

"What are you doing?" Rob dropped his pen on his notebook.

I turned, already glaring. I took in his rumpled t-shirt, the furrow between his brows. The sharp angle of his jaw and his current five o'clock shadow. Objectively, I could see why girls would find him attractive. But they didn't know what I knew.

"What does it look like I'm doing?"

He cocked his head to the side, straightening on the stool. "No need to stay hydrated. Logan's not even here to make you sweat." He stretched his arms, resting his hands behind his head.

I raised an eyebrow. "Careful or people might think you're overly invested."

He exhaled in a rush, his smile turning ice cold. "Just do me a favour. When you're crying in your room Tuesday night, don't come knocking on my door."

I laughed out loud. "You know what? Perfect segue." I stomped into my bedroom and grabbed my notebook, wishing I could smother my face in a pillow and let out the string of curses racing through my head. He was just such an *ass*.

I strode back into the kitchen with the air of a Broadway star and slammed my book on the counter between us, then flipped it open to the page titled "Sharla and Rob's Rules for Peaceful Coexistence" with a flourish. Now I wished I'd been more creative.

He blinked. "What the hell is this?"

"Wow. We're really not connecting the dots today, are we?"

He flicked his eyes up to mine. "I already don't bring people home."

I dropped my gaze to the list I'd come up with over the weekend.

1. No bringing friends home without approval. No sleepovers.

2. The couch is Switzerland. Whoever gets there first claims it.

3. *No shirt, no service.*
4. *Be respectful. Don't call me a shithead.*
5. *No studying in the kitchen unless alone.*

I shrugged. "Maybe you don't bring people home because of Logan."

"You think Logan would give a shit?"

I pressed my palms into the counter. "Probably not, but I'm going to be by myself." A tendril of fear slid along my spine. *He's a good guy.* I'd heard that before. Plenty of times. Guys were always good until they weren't.

"What kind of service?" Rob crossed his arms over his chest.

I glared at him. "What?"

"Not connecting the dots are we?" He tapped number three on the list.

I rolled my eyes. "I was trying to be funny. I just meant, wear a damn shirt."

"Hmm. Got it. Did you have a particular one you wanted me to—"

"I don't care what shirt you wear. Just put one on before you come out here!" I straightened, mirroring him to hide the fact that my chest was heaving.

"Careful. Or people might think—"

"Ugh! I'm trying to figure this out, okay? I know neither of us is thrilled about this living situation, and I'm freaking terrified because I *barely* feel safe with Logan sleeping next to me, and once he's gone, anyone you bring in here could just come right on in and—" I sucked in a breath, my cheeks heating. I pulled my hand back from pointing at my doorway.

Rob wasn't smiling anymore. His brow was pinched, his fingers pressing into his biceps so hard, his skin was blanching.

I was shaking too hard to hide it, so I scooped up my notebook and whirled from the counter.

"I'll wear a shirt."

I blinked back tears, pausing but not turning to face him. "Thank you."

CHAPTER
Five

FRIDAY NIGHT, Maddie and Crystal strutted up the pathway to our townhouse, their pleather mini-skirts barely covering their shivering asses. I swung open the door.

"You skanks ready to get wild?" Maddie squealed, flashing me a cheeky grin under her Catwoman mask.

Crystal twirled, showing off her tiny police uniform, night-stick and all. "I'm ready to arrest some naughty boys!"

I couldn't help but laugh. My devil costume felt downright demure in comparison—tight red dress, the fishnets I found at The Bay, my silly horns headband. But hey, if you can't dress like a total slut from the underworld on Halloween, when can you?

Thank the Great Pumpkin that Rob decided to sit this one out. Or at least that he wasn't riding with us. I didn't know or care whether he'd be there later, I was just counting my blessings that I hadn't crossed paths with him much the day before. After our little chat, the last thing I needed was refereeing him and Logan all night.

Speaking of my golden retriever boyfriend, Logan bounded down the hall in his firefighter getup, all glistening bare chest and booty shorts. "Damn ladies, looking hot! Let's show those lacrosse losers how the Outlaws party!"

Okay, so maybe dressing slutty wasn't just for the women. I strode forward, threading my arms under his fireman's jacket. "Where did you get this? It looks real."

"Nah, the real ones weigh a ton." He lowered his head and kissed me. "I can keep this one, though. If you like it."

I grinned. "At least keep it for the weekend."

We piled into Logan's pickup truck, the leather seats freezing against all of our bare thighs. As he roared away from the curb, Logan hollered out the details for Crystal and Maddie.

"Kay, so here's the deal. My boy Brayden has this sick house off-campus he shares with like five other dudes. Hockey, lax, rugby—they're all my bros." He glanced over at me with a goofy smile. "Closest thing we've got to frats up here in Canuckistan."

I rolled my eyes but couldn't suppress a smile. Leave it to Logan to get me out of my mopey mood. With no rehearsals over the weekend, maybe I could let loose and have some fun for once.

Crystal gaped as we pulled up to the sprawling house already throbbing with music. The old brick mansion wasn't a surprise to me, but the cobwebs and strobe lights were.

Maddie clicked her tongue. "Hopefully nobody on this block has epilepsy."

Logan parked and turned in his seat. "Is that a thing?"

Crystal, Maddie, and I burst out laughing. "Yes it's a thing!" I shoved his shoulder and we piled out of the truck. Time to shake off my good girl persona and raise a little hell. I had the horns for moral support.

We tottered on our heels up the leaf-strewn walk. I tugged down the hem of my dress, suddenly self-conscious. I felt fine with Logan and my friends, but maybe I'd gone a little too skimpy for being seen in public.

"Staaahp." Maddie slapped my hand. "You look hot."

"I think my underwear is showing," I muttered.

She winked. "Good. I hope you wore red."

I laughed, and as we stepped inside the packed house, my

nerves evaporated. It was warm, and the air felt almost sticky. Bodies moved and gyrated in the purple and orange lighting, their plastic cups held up while they danced. Rubber masks and feather boas flashed under the strobing lights. The whole place buzzed with an electric energy that sparked something reckless in me.

I wanted Logan to *see* me tonight. To know what he'd be missing in Winnipeg and Europe. I wanted him to want me so bad, he thought about staying.

"Yo, Kemp!" A burly guy in a gorilla suit tackled Logan into a bear hug.

"Sick turnout, bud!" Logan high-fived his way through the crowd, calling out to his endless roster of teammates and friends. I loved watching him in his element. He positively glowed.

"Sharla, hey!" A girl dressed as Cleopatra pulled me into a drunken embrace. "Damn, girl!" She pulled back to look me up and down, then licked her finger and tapped it to my shoulder, pretending it sizzled.

I laughed, buoyed by the compliment. Drinks appeared in my hand as if by magic—shots of glittering green "witch's brew", cups of violently purple jungle juice. The sickly-sweet burn wiped away the last traces of my responsibility meter.

We laughed and chatted. Then I followed Maddie and Crystal as they shimmied their way into the main living room, where all the furniture was pushed against the wall. All three of us were handed glow sticks.

An arm snaked around my waist and I turned to see Logan's face, flushed and smiling. "Having fun, babe?"

Alcohol made Logan a little melancoly, but it made me giddy. Love swelled in my chest, and I nearly pinched his cheeks before pulling him in for a kiss. I tangled my fingers in his hair, arching against him.

I wanted him to look at me differently tonight. Like a girl he'd find in the stands and want to wait for after his shower. Like someone he couldn't wait to pull into a side room.

Logan responded eagerly, his big hands roaming my satin curves, landing on bare thigh. We made out sloppily against the wall, hot and hungry. The room spun, and nothing existed but his lips, his touch, pounding bass and flashing lights.

Until a splash of dark hair made my gaze snag.

I surfaced for air to see Rob skulking into the party, hands shoved in the pockets of his half-assed vampire costume. Our eyes met and I felt a sickening swoop in my stomach.

His jaw clenched, his nostrils flared, and then he was gone. He vanished into the hall. Suddenly everything felt too bright, too loud, too close. I sagged against the wall, the heat oozing out of me like a popped balloon.

"Hey, you okay?" Logan wet his lips, his cheek still against mine.

I nodded. "Yeah, I think I just need some air."

"Do you want me to—"

"No. No, you stay here. I'll be right back." I kissed his cheek, then slipped out of his arms and headed for the back door.

The chill night air was a slap to my flushed cheeks as I stumbled onto the back porch. I gripped the railing, knuckles white, and sucked in lungfuls of crisp oxygen. Tears filled my eyes from the cold, blurring the inky sky and shadowy trees.

I stood there until I started to shiver. Logan didn't come after me. I'd told him to stay, but when I turned and saw him laughing with a few of his teammates, it stung. It was unfair to expect him to read my mind, but how much translation did it really take? He was leaving. Of course I wasn't okay.

I stiffened when Rob turned to fill his cup, and he looked up. His eyes dropped to my bare shoulders, a frown turning down the corners of his mouth. I was about to flip him off when Crystal cut off my view of him.

"There you are." She opened the glass door and stepped out onto the patio with me. "Shit, how long have you been out here?"

I rubbed my arms. "Too long, I think?"

"Uh-huh." Her eyes searched mine, a divot forming between her brows. "Did something happen? With Logan, or—"

"No, I'm just—I don't know. Thinking about Tuesday, I guess."

Crystal grinned, walking closer and throwing her arm over my shoulder. "Parties aren't for thinking, silly."

I scoffed. "It's like you don't even know me."

"No, I do know you, which is why I'm here to drag you back in there. You need to make at least three more bad decisions before we can go home."

I laughed, allowing her to pull me toward the doors.

Logan turned, his eyes lighting up. "Hell yeah. That's my girl!" He took a swig of jungle juice, then pushed through his teammates and planted a kiss on my mouth, prying my lips open and sharing his drink.

"Logan!" I pulled back, wiping my lips with the back of my hand as it dribbled down my chin.

He threw his head back and howled.

The rest of the night passed in a strobe-lit blur of shots and shimmies, culminating in a giggling, stumbling trek back to Logan's truck. Maddie was our designated driver, and before we even pulled away from the curb, Logan's hand was already up my skirt. Which didn't take much effort considering it was only ten centimeters long.

When we got back, I hugged my friends, then we trudged inside and tumbled into bed in a tangle of limbs and boozy breath. For all his handsiness on the drive, Logan was out within seconds, his fireman coat in a crumpled heap on the floor. I forced myself out of bed to brush my teeth, then stripped off my costume and sank into oblivion before my head hit the pillow.

Morning arrived like a sledgehammer to the skull. I groaned and burrowed deeper under the covers, but the mattress lurched as Logan bounded out of bed with disgusting verve.

"Wakey wakey, eggs and bakey," he trilled, ripping open the

curtains. Eye-searing sunlight knifed into my retinas and I whimpered.

"I will murder you," I croaked. "With a spatula. Slowly."

Logan just laughed, tugging the duvet off my limp carcass. "You'll change your tune once you taste my world-famous breakfast. Up and at 'em, sunshine!"

I hauled myself vertical with a pitiful moan, head throbbing like a rotten melon. Logan was already whistling his way into the kitchen. How was he so damn chipper? And since when did he make breakfast?

I pressed my palm to my forehead and threw on sweats and a hoodie, then washed my face and moisturized. My clock said ten. At least I'd gotten a decent amount of sleep.

By the time I slouched into the kitchen, Logan was sitting with a plate full of . . . blueberry pancakes?

"Umm, did you swap souls with someone last night?" It was Hallows Eve. I'd heard of stranger things.

Logan flashed a mysterious smile. "It's my secret special-occasion recipe. Blueberry sour cream pancakes with lemon zest. Prepare to have your mind blown."

I narrowed my eyes at him. "You've literally never mentioned special-occasion pancakes. Or recipes in general." *And hadn't he only been out there for fifteen minutes?*

"Because I was saving it for a special occasion." He pulled out a stool and patted it. I walked over and sat like a good girl even though the scene in front of me wasn't computing. Rob used the kitchen regularly, but Logan? I'd only seen him use the microwave. One time he'd heated up leftover wings in the oven because Rob told him to.

Logan kissed my cheek. "I've been saving this for a day when you really need some comfort food. Figured a killer hangover qualified." He grabbed a plate and fork from the counter and put two pancakes on it, then passed it to me.

Damn him for being so thoughtful. My eyes prickled traitorously as I drowned my pancakes in syrup. "You're too good to me, you know that?"

"Nah, babe. You're too good for me." He winked, digging into his own short stack.

We devoured brunch, nursing cups of strong black coffee and making dumb jokes. For a few cozy hours, I could almost pretend the world outside didn't exist. No nagging worries about the future, no shadow of Rob lurking at the edges. Just me and my blue-eyed boy in our bubble of maple syrup and morning light.

If I could've frozen that moment, bottled it and kept it on my shelf, I would've. Because the rest of the weekend passed by in a blur. We packed, napped, and made love when Rob finally left for the day. Even though we were in our own room, I felt weird knowing he was right outside the door. Yet another reason I didn't want a roommate, especially not one of Logan's friends.

Logan took me out for our fancy dinner, and gave me a thin silver bracelet. It was gorgeous. And something I'd feel guilty about not wearing. I couldn't have anything on my hands or wrists while I played. Some people in orchestra could, but it annoyed the hell out of me to have anything touching my skin.

I wore it to campus on Monday, took it off and kept it in my pocket, then put it back on for the walk home.

And then it was Tuesday.

I tried to give Logan a present to open in Europe on Christmas, but he wanted to wait until he got back. We agreed to exchange gifts as soon as he arrived home. Something to look forward to.

Logan loaded his bags into his truck, and I got in to drop him off at the airport. The drive was quiet. Our hands interlaced over the console, and the bracelet twisted on my wrist. Logan's thumb brushed soothing circles on my skin, but it did little to loosen the knot in my chest.

I blinked hard, determined not to let the tears fall. At least not yet. He didn't need to feel guilty when he was on his way to living the dream he'd been working toward for almost his entire life.

"Hey." Logan's voice was soft as he pulled into the departures lane. "It's only a few weeks. I'll be back before you know it, causing a ruckus and leaving my socks all over the floor."

I choked out a watery laugh.

He pulled to a stop in the unloading zone. "I'll phone you every day. So much you'll get sick of me." He leaned over, pressing a gentle kiss to my forehead.

I just nodded, not trusting myself to speak. He unbuckled, leaving the key in the ignition. I got out and waited with my hands shoved in the pockets of my coat while he unloaded his bags.

One more kiss, one more bone-crushing hug.

"I love you, babe," he whispered.

"Love you, too."

And then he was gone, swallowed up by the automatic doors.

The tears came in earnest as I slid back into the driver's seat, the truck suddenly far too big without Logan in it. I felt like a middle schooler taking my dad's car out for a joy ride. Sobs shook my shoulders, blurring the road as I wound my way back to campus. Back to a house that only felt like home because of who I usually shared it with. Not with who was waiting for me.

Rob.

My stomach twisted at the thought of facing him alone, without Logan as a buffer. Anger lanced through me, hot and bright. It wasn't fair. I shouldn't have to tiptoe around my own home, dreading every interaction with my boyfriend's shitty friend. I shouldn't have to spend Christmas missing Logan like a phantom limb.

I dragged a sleeve across my face, taking vicious pleasure in smearing my mascara. I parked Logan's truck haphazardly, not caring if I took up two spots. Grabbing my purse and keys, I stormed into the townhouse, a whirlwind of smudged eyeliner and snot.

I let the door slam behind me, locked it, then made a beeline for my washroom, desperate for a moment of privacy to collect myself. To splash some cold water on my face and remind myself that I wasn't just Logan's girlfriend. I had other priorities, other commitments. I had my own dreams, and they weren't all wrapped up in a guy.

I dropped Logan's keys on the dresser and flung open the washroom door, ready to collapse on the floor and let myself come disgustingly undone. But instead, I froze, my breath catching in my throat.

Rob stood in front of the toilet, his fly halfway zipped.

CHAPTER

Six

"WHAT THE HELL?" It was a croak, raw and ragged.

He scanned my face, and a muscle in his jaw jumped. Then he shrugged and finished zipping his pants. Infuriatingly nonchalant. "Had to piss."

"You're in my washroom, asshole." Anger surged through me, a welcome distraction from the ache in my chest.

He held up a hand. "Be respectful, remember?"

I wanted to tear his throat out.

"Didn't think you'd be back so soon." He took a step closer, turning on the faucet and grabbing the soap. "Thought you'd be too busy clinging to Kemp's leg, begging him not to leave."

I recoiled as if he'd slapped me. "Screw you."

"You wish." His lip curled.

And that's when I lost it. I already looked like a mess, and I didn't give a rat's ass whether Rob thought I was insane. Or respectful. "Get the *hell* out of my washroom." I flung the door wide. I didn't know what kind of power play he was trying to pull, but I was not having it. I would not allow him to intimidate me and—

"I couldn't use mine because there's a leak." He dried his hands on my towel.

My mouth was already open to hurl curse words that would've made my grandfather proud, when I processed what he'd just said. My jaw snapped shut, and I sucked in a breath.

He turned as if he wasn't staring at a splotchy, smeared mess of makeup and tears, leaning his hip against the counter. "There was a puddle on my floor. A big one. I couldn't tell where it was coming from, so I called Logan's dad. He told me not to use anything in there until they could come check it out."

My shoulders slumped as the rage fire and adrenaline began to ebb away, leaving behind a throbbing headache and a sadness that seemed to coat my bones. Rob grabbed a box of tissues from the counter and thrust them at me. I snatched them and stepped back into the room, dropping onto my bed. I blew my nose, the reality of the situation sinking in. "So, we're going to have to share a washroom until it's fixed?"

Rob walked out after me, shoving his hands in his pockets. "Looks like it." He glanced back at the washroom. "Do I have to wear a shirt while I shower, too?"

I rolled my eyes, too drained to come up with a witty retort. Of course this would happen. Seconds after dropping Logan off at the airport, and already the shit was hitting the fan. My body felt like a wrung-out dishrag, and the prospect of navigating a shared washroom with Rob made me want to scream into a pillow.

I jumped when the phone started to ring from the kitchen.

"Bet that's the plumber now." Rob stalked out of my room, and I sagged, dropping sideways onto the mattress. I groaned involuntarily and allowed myself to wallow for fifteen seconds before forcing myself up and into the washroom.

I replaced the tissues and washed my face, taking in my red-rimmed eyes and puffy cheeks and lips. Fantastic. I looked like I'd run face first into a beehive.

I dried my skin and braved the kitchen. It didn't really matter. Rob had already seen me. I found him leaning over the counter, the phone cord stretching from the wall as he scribbled on a notepad.

He glanced up as I entered, his dark eyes unreadable. "Uh-huh. Yeah, got it. Thanks." *So he could be amiable when he wanted to be.* He hung up and tossed the notepad onto the counter. "A guy's coming tomorrow to assess the damage."

"Okay."

"And... he's not sure how long it'll take to fix." Rob leaned back against the counter, crossing his arms. "Could be a couple of days, could be a week. Depending on if he has the right parts."

I deflated like a punctured balloon. *A week?* Sharing a washroom with Rob for a whole week? It may be worth sharing a bed with Maddie. I wasn't insured on Logan's truck, and he hadn't exactly offered it to me for general use. But he wouldn't mind too much, would he? But if I got in an accident—

"I leave after you do for class. Shouldn't be that big of a deal." Rob knocked his knuckles on the counter.

That was . . . actually a good point. I nodded. "Okay." I could survive this. I didn't really have a choice, so I was going to have to suck it up and deal. It wasn't his fault that his washroom wasn't working even if it sucked balls.

Rob ran a hand through his hair, then walked the opposite way around the island so we wouldn't accidentally share the same air. "Okay." His steps slowed so minutely as he passed me, I wondered if I imagined it.

When the door clicked shut to his room, I finally let myself fall apart.

————

After two hours and three cycles through the mix tape, I was all cried out. I wanted to commandeer the couch and watch reruns of Degrassi or Maury. Really anything that would remind me that my life was, in fact, not the worst. But the idea of Rob walking past and seeing me being pathetic was enough for me to stay locked in my room until rehearsal.

By then, my face was mostly back to normal. I looked tired, but with concealer and blush, I at least passed as not a corpse.

Caleb and Lily knew what day it was. They brought me a box of Timbits, which brightened my afternoon more than they could've imagined, and when I walked out the front doors of the Rosza Arts Centre, Maddie and Crystal were there waiting for me.

My jaw dropped, but before I could say anything, their arms were linked through mine and they were dragging me the opposite direction of home.

"We're going for burgers," Maddie informed me. "I parked in the student lot."

Somehow, new tears pricked my eyes. "You guys—"

"We know. We're the best friends in the world."

I laughed and cried, telling them everything about Logan's departure, including the leaking washroom and the current hellscape of sharing a toilet with Rob.

"Wait, is he leaving his toothbrush in there? You could dip it in salt or something." Crystal took a drink of her shake.

My eyes widened. "I'm not going to mess with his toothbrush. He'd know exactly who did it, and who knows what he'd do to mine?"

"Rub it in the toilet." Maddie grabbed a fry.

I pretended to dry heave. "Exactly. No pranks. I can't afford that kind of anxiety."

Crystal leaned over the table. "Plumber comes tomorrow?" I nodded. "I'll pray he has the right parts."

"Yes, please." I crumpled up my trash and piled it on the tray, then let out a slow breath. "Thank you. This was exactly what I needed."

Maddie grinned. "We know."

We piled into her car, and she drove me back to my place, her car jumping and jolting with every pebble on the road.

I reached over the seats and squeezed their shoulders. "I'm slammed with rehearsals and recital workshops until Friday, but can we meet up then?"

Crystal nodded. "I have to submit my tracks by the weekend, so as long as I get them finished—"

"She'll get them finished." Maddie grinned. "I'm in labs until four. Free after that."

I drew a breath and exhaled. "Perfect. Thanks again." I grabbed my violin and bag, then exited the vehicle and waved as they skidded off down the street.

Inside was blissfully empty. No Rob, which meant I probably wouldn't see him at all for twenty-four hours. He'd be out doing whatever he did until all hours of the night, and then I'd be gone before he got up in the morning.

Perfect. This could work.

I wrote out more of my composition for my advanced harmonies class, finished a poetry assessment for literature, checked my email to see if I'd missed anything from Logan, then cleaned up and got ready for bed.

I took off Logan's bracelet and set it on the thin glass shelf below the medicine cabinet in my washroom, then walked into my room and hopped into bed. I rolled onto my back and stared at the ceiling. And that's when missing him became a physical ache.

Logan was already off the plane by now, but I didn't blame him for not calling yet. He was probably overwhelmed. Getting to know his new coaches, checking into his hotel. He might even have practice tonight. *Maybe if I stayed up a little later . . .*

With a groan, I hauled myself off the bed and padded to the kitchen. I made some herbal tea and headed back to my room, then pulled out the novel I'd barely looked at since reading to page forty-two. It had been so long, I had to go back to the beginning and start again.

Finally, after re-reading the same page three times with zero comprehension, I turned off my lamp and tried to sleep. *No call.* Logan was busy. He'd phone when he could.

I tossed and turned, imagining what he was doing at that moment. I ran through scenarios in my head. Mostly ending with him curled up in bed cradling the non-functioning phone to his chest as he longed to hear my voice.

I must have dropped off mid-fantasy because it was pitch black when I woke with a start.

A creak. The scraping of a door.

My heart seized, the sound far too close. *In my room.* I held my breath, my heart jumping into my throat.

No. Not again.

CHAPTER
Seven

JUST LIKE THOSE times in my Grandma's spare bedroom, my entire body seized, fear sinking its claws into any rational thought and refusing to release. I couldn't move. Couldn't think.

I just had to be quiet, and then—

Another creak and a whimper slipped from my lips.

Adrenaline flooded my veins as a dark silhouette shifted near the doorway. It was happening again. My lungs constricted, refusing to expand. Trapped. *I was trapped.*

Panic clawed at my throat, and I was paralyzed by the sickening sense of déjà vu—heavy breathing, rough hands—

A choked cry ripped from my throat as the shadow moved closer. *No, no, no!* A scream built in my chest but lodged there, blocked by sheer terror until I blurted, "Don't touch me! I won't let you touch me again!" I hurled the words out into the blackness, my senses scrambling to make sense of what I was hearing, the shadow slowly creeping along the wall toward me.

"Sharla?"

A hand landed on my shoulder, and I flinched. It was so dark, I couldn't see anything, but the contact brought my body violently to life, breaking the spell. I tried to strike out with the palm of my hand like I'd learned in the self-defense class I took last semester, then yelped when my arm tangled in the sheets. I gasped for breath, trying to extricate myself.

Before I could, I was scooped up, blankets and all, and crushed against a warm chest.

"It's me. Hey, shhhh. I didn't mean to scare you. I'm so sorry."

I worked to fill my lungs, my mind spinning. My head immediately defaulted to Logan, but that was impossible. He was across the country, which meant—

"I know I'm the last person in the world you want here right now. I'm sorry. I'm not going to hurt you." He was rambling so fast, I could barely place his voice.

"Rob?" His name came out hoarse, and his arms tightened around me.

"Shh, Shar. I've got you."

I forced a ragged breath into my lungs, blinking as my chest heaved. I was in my bedroom. It was Rob, not *him*. He wasn't trying to touch me. He wasn't going to hurt me.

I repeated those last two sentences like prayers, and the panic began to subside.

As soon as my head stopped spinning, reality draped over me like a thick blanket. *It was Rob.* Why was Rob in my bedroom?

The day before crashed into my consciousness—the leak in the washroom. *He was just coming in to use the washroom.*

"What time is it?" I whispered.

Rob cleared his throat. "I don't know. I think around three?"

I dragged in greedy breaths, the vertigo beginning to subside as all of my other senses came online. Rob's heartbeat beneath my ear. His arms linked around me. No fabric between my cheek and his skin.

I should've been pissed. Should've shoved him away, but exhaustion sank into me like body lotion. "You said you would wear a shirt."

Rob blew out a breath, and I thought I caught a hint of a chuckle. "You were asleep. I didn't think you'd see anything."

That was nice. Not snarky or sarcastic, not pretending I wanted him or that I was a prude for telling him to put on clothes. *Why was he being nice to me?*

I needed to push away, to get the scent of his body wash or deodorant or whatever warm spice I was smelling out of my nostrils, but I couldn't move. My arms were limp noodles and my whole body felt like it was smothered under a candle snuffer.

I mustered the only fight I had in me. I needed to balance the force. "You seriously couldn't come home at a decent time when you knew you were going to have to come in here?"

"I tried to be quiet."

My heart thundered in my ears. Rob. Rob was sitting on my bed. His arms were around me, and he sounded lucid. Heat flashed through me. That, along with the adrenaline spike at the memory of Logan being in Winnipeg, allowed me to push myself out of Rob's arms.

I curled around myself, moving away from him. "Don't you think you could *not* party for two nights until your washroom is fixed?" How could he be so selfish? The audacity to come home at all hours of the night and just assume that it was acceptable to walk into someone's bedroom.

Rob didn't answer, and the silence stretched between us like an elastic band ready to snap. I wrapped my arms around my knees, finally able to at least make out the outline of his head and shoulders.

"You think I was partying?" His voice was low, terse. Almost sad. It lobbed a bucket of cold water over the snarky reply I had waiting on the tip of my tongue, sparking doubt. *Was he partying?* I'd been right next to him and hadn't smelled any alcohol or smoke.

"I come home late every night," he said.

"Yeah. I'm aware." I swallowed hard.

"And that's what you thought ever since you moved in?"

My pulse kicked up a notch. I didn't know where he was

going with this, but I didn't like it. "Can we just—Can you just—"

"I have a job, Sharla."

I bit my lip, my thoughts draining like water through a colander. "What kind of job?"

"I'm on the janitorial staff," he grunted. "I work the night shift, so it doesn't conflict with my classes." He shifted to the edge of the bed. "Unlike Logan, I don't have daddy's money to cover everything."

My throat worked, but I couldn't form words. Janitorial staff? A night shift? Why had Logan never mentioned that to me before?

Truthfully, I hadn't ever brought up the annoyance I felt at Rob's hours. Logan didn't like when I criticized him, as evidenced by his reaction to me bringing up the whole bare chest situation. It was better if I pretended Rob didn't exist. For my sake and his. But still. After six months, it was odd that a full-on job hadn't come up.

I locked onto Rob's silhouette rising and moving along the wall toward the washroom. The door creaked, and light flooded into the room as he flicked the switch. He walked in and closed the door behind him, leaving a rectangular, glowing outline.

I tried not to listen. Tried not to imagine him unzipping his pants, relieving himself, and washing his hands in my sink. Drying his hands again on my towel. But it was impossible not to.

The sweat on my skin started to cool, and I shivered. I hurriedly straightened the sheets and comforter, pulling it up to my chest just as he opened the door again. I wasn't wearing a bra, just my cotton camisole, and I suddenly felt self-conscious.

Rob opened the door and his eyes met mine. "You're not wearing the bracelet he gave you."

I blinked and glanced at the nightstand. No, I'd left it in the washroom. On the glass shelf. "I don't wear jewelry at night."

"Huh." Rob wet his lips, then dropped his eyes. "I'm sorry I woke you."

I was plunged into darkness as he flicked off the light and exited into the hall.

———

He called me Shar. That realization flashed in my head like a neon sign when I woke with my alarm the following day. Rob had been in my room. He'd held me in his arms. And he'd called me Shar.

Logan called me Shar. Crystal and Maddie called me Shar. But Rob?

Had last night been some jacked up fever dream? Some hallucination my brain made up to process Logan leaving?

The phone rang in the kitchen, shattering the early morning quiet. We really needed to invest in a cordless. I fumbled out of bed, hopping on one foot as I frantically pulled on a pair of sweatpants.

"Hello?" I whispered, stumbling into the kitchen and snatching the phone before it could wake Rob.

"Shar!" There was that name again. "Did I wake you?" Logan's chipper voice boomed through the speaker. I could hear whooping and hollering in the background. *What the hell time was it?*

"No it's fine. I was getting up anyway." I glanced at the clock. It was only seven, but—right. He was two hours ahead of me. I crept toward my room, stretching the cord and easing the door shut behind me. I slumped to the floor and leaned back. "I'm so glad you called. What are you doing?"

"Not much, just breakfast before training." More laughter rang out, and I rolled my eyes. I could already tell that getting

Logan alone would be like herding a cat. "They've got this huge buffet, like everything you can imagine. Sausages—"

"*I'll give you sausages!*" someone cried out.

Logan laughed, his breath crackling in the speaker. "Sorry, pancakes, fruit, whipped cream, it's insane. Ooh and chocolate milk. The best chocolate milk."

I couldn't help but grin even though it felt like my insides were being yanked through my stomach. I was so happy for him. Of course I was. But there was a part of me that hoped he would've called missing me. Heartsick. Even a little.

I yawned. "That's amazing, I—"

A loud crash interrupted me, followed by guffaws and shouts. "Sorry babe, Coop just ate it hard. What were you saying?"

I sighed. This was a losing battle. "Nothing. I just—I miss you."

"Aww, miss you, too! Love you. Phone you later?"

"Mm. Yep, I'll be back at—"

The line went dead.

I held the phone for a minute, listening to the dial tone before peeling myself off the floor and exiting the room to unstretch the cord. I wanted to ask about his flight. To tell him about the washroom disaster. Probably not about what happened last night . . .

The realization that I hadn't intended to tell Logan about that gave me pause. I replaced the receiver on its cradle. *Nothing had happened.* Rob was helping me calm down. In the light of day, I could see it for what it was. A trauma response. I had been startled at night, and since that reflected what had happened when I was a teenager, I was sucked right back to those nights.

It wasn't my fault that I freaked out.

It wasn't Rob's fault that the washroom was unusable.

It was nobody's fault. Logan would understand that.

I started hot water for tea, then began getting ready for orchestra. Logan's carefree attitude grated on my nerves like a bow against unrosined strings. At least Tchaikovsky never flaked

on me. Dating Logan sometimes felt as dramatic as the 1812 Overture—all sound and fury. Intense emotion, and that was an understatement.

That was why I loved him, though, wasn't it? He was always balls deep in whatever moment presented itself. The problem was, *I* wasn't in his moments currently. For two months he was living a plethora of moments that were decidedly Sharla free, and the fact that he wasn't thinking about me or missing our life here burrowed into me like a tick.

I exhaled and rubbed my temple. It was fine. This was his first day with new teammates. I wanted him to dive in, to fully embrace this experience. I was just sad, and the night before had been a total trash fire. This was probably a me issue.

I threw on a clean pair of dark jeans and a cozy burgundy sweater, not even bothering with makeup. Grabbing my violin case, I rushed out of the dorm room, careful not to slam the door.

Once outside, I took my first full breath of the morning. Even though Rob was in his room, his existence filled the house like air freshener. Especially after last night. What if he just showed up again? Walked in when I wasn't expecting it? Put his arms around me. Pulled me against his chest . . .

I ignored the heat lifting to my cheeks and worked to shake the memory of him in my bed as I hurried through the winding tunnels connecting the Douglas buildings. Still, my mind raced faster than my feet.

I should've been relieved to discover that there was a beating heart under the layers of asshole Rob usually presented. He could see I was upset, and he knew he'd caused it. He wasn't a complete narcissist, so it made sense that he'd want to help. To apologize.

But those rationalizations didn't strangle the brand new thoughts—emotions? Possibilities?—that had bloomed in my mind after that moment. I'd *liked* his touch. And then I felt annoyed with Logan, which never happened.

I was so lost in thought, I nearly collided with a group of

students heading in the opposite direction. I mumbled an apology and quickened my pace. I surfaced in the arts centre and entered the rehearsal room early.

I took my time tuning up, listening to the creak of the wood, the hiss of my rosin against my bow.

"Since when do you beat me here?" Caleb slid into his seat.

I grinned. "Since my boyfriend calls me on Winnipeg time."

Caleb laughed and Ms. Franck started in with instructions. I listened fully, grateful to have a respite from my own thoughts. We started with warmups, and when we began our first piece, I took a deep breath and let the music wash over me—Vivaldi's "Winter" from *The Four Seasons*. The frenzied sixteenth notes flurried from my fingers, each note dragging me further outside of myself.

As my bow danced across the strings, I floated, lilting with the resonance. The world faded away—no more worries about Logan, the washroom, or bad memories. In that moment, it was just me, my violin, and the music.

As we reached the end of the first movement, Lily stood for her solo. Her slender fingers caressed the fingerboard, coaxing out the plaintive melody with effortless grace. She was so damn good, I couldn't even muster envy.

I would get there. She had a year and a half on me, and I knew I was on the short list for that spot once she moved on. I had to hope Franck would notice what I had to offer. Maybe Logan's call this morning would turn out to provide a boost. Getting there early couldn't be a bad thing.

At the end of rehearsal, chairs scraped as everyone in the orchestra packed up their instruments. I carefully loosened my bow and nestled my violin into its case. I stood and walked toward the back exit. Just as I pushed through the door, Lily bounded over to me, ponytail swishing.

Caleb loped along behind her. "Want to grab a coffee and knock out that music history essay?"

I hesitated. Part of me longed to rush back to the house, to

see if Rob was there. To have him break my rules and call me a shithead so the universe could start spinning on its correct axis again. Another part dreaded a second awkward encounter after last night. *What if he was nice? Again?* "Sure, sounds good."

The three of us claimed a table in the arts lounge and spread out our notebooks and textbooks. I stared at my notes, but the words wouldn't come. I doodled for a bit, read a little more on Mendehlson since he was the composer I'd chosen to research. After an hour, it was obvious I wasn't going to make much headway.

I closed my textbook. "I'm going to head for lunch." I already knew both their classes were in this building in another forty-five minutes, so I didn't bother inviting them along. "See you tomorrow?"

"Sure, see you then." Lily smiled. Caleb put out a hand for a fist bump.

Slinging my violin case over my shoulder, I headed for the bookstore. They had pre-made salads and cookies there—the lunch of champions.

After grabbing my food, I headed for the library. Food wasn't allowed in the general areas, but snacks were okay in reserved study rooms. I walked in and filled out the sign in sheet, then settled in for the next few hours. I couldn't avoid the house forever, but damn, if I wouldn't try to stay away as long as possible.

I worked on my essay, my composition homework, then left the study room to do some internet searching and check my email. Crystal and Maddie had sent a few about the upcoming hockey invitational.

The Outlaws were defending home champs three years running, but without Logan, did they stand a chance? The tournament was a highlight of the year at Douglas U. The snowy tailgate parties, the packed stands, the epic post-game celebrations . . .

I smiled wistfully, remembering last year. Logan scoring the

game-winning goal in overtime. The bonfire by the pond where we drank spiked hot chocolate and laughed until our voices were hoarse. That was what started all of this. Me and him. It was the night he gave me the playlist.

This year promised to be even bigger, but without Logan, it all seemed pointless. What was the fun in sledding down Pratt Hill on cafeteria trays without him? In shotgunning beers in the parking lot before sneaking into the arena? In slow dancing to Journey at the closing banquet?

By the time I walked home, the house was dark and quiet. I flicked on the light, half expecting Rob to be sprawled on the couch even though I knew from past experience that he should be gone by now.

The door to his room was open. No sounds. I took off my shoes and hung my jacket, straightening my poppy pin on the lapel, and wandered into the kitchen. There was a note on the counter.

Plumber came by. Needs to order a part for the washroom. Won't be fixed for a while. I'll use the washroom on campus before I come home.

CHAPTER
Eight

THE PHONE RANG JUST as I was slathering a thick pat of butter on my toasted English muffin, and my heart leaped. Logan hadn't called the night before, and I was hoping this time he'd be less distracted.

"Hello?"

"Good morning, Sharla." Mom's voice sang through the speaker, and my stomach sank. What if he tried to call? We didn't have call waiting,

"Morning Mom." I tried to keep my voice down. "What's up?"

"Oh, just calling to firm up plans for your Christmas visit home. We can't wait to see you. When should Dad and I come pick you up from campus? We were thinking the Friday—your classes end on the sixth, right?"

I nibbled the edge of my muffin, considering. A whole month back home felt like . . . a lot. I loved my family, but being under their roof again, in my old bedroom with the N'SYNC posters still tacked to the walls, sounded stifling. Plus, if I left right when classes ended, I'd miss the invitational. Not an option. If I said there was a tournament, Mom would suggest they all come. Again, not an option.

"Actually Mom, I have some responsibilities for an invitational on campus that weekend," I fibbed, the white lie rolling easily off my tongue. I purposely left out the "hockey" part of that statement. "Could you pick me up Monday morning, the ninth, instead?"

Even though Red Deer was only an hour away, it might as well have been an alternate universe. Three weeks of Mom's doting, Dad's awkward jokes, and bumping into people from high school at the grocery store sounded like more than enough. This way, I could ring in the New Year back at Douglas with my friends and, more importantly, be here when Logan returned.

"Well, I'll have to rearrange some plans, but. Okay. Monday the ninth it is." She only sounded mildly annoyed. I couldn't ask for more.

We exchanged "love you"'s and I hung up, relieved to have successfully negotiated for some breathing room. I polished off the last buttery bite of muffin and strode over to the sink, feeling quite pleased with myself. Until I looked up and froze.

"Morning, sunshine."

Sunshine. I groaned internally. That was worse. So much worse. I never thought I'd find a day when I preferred the term "shithead," but lo and behold, it had arrived. I thought I would appreciate him changing his ways and trying to get along, but now it felt like it meant something. Like he was doing it *for me.*

Which I knew wasn't true. He could've done plenty for me over the past six months, and he hadn't. Nothing had changed. It was probably just pity.

Rob slouched against the hallway wall, arms crossed, dark hair sticking up at odd angles like some brooding anime character. *How long had he been standing there?*

I self-consciously patted my own mop of bedhead as he pushed off the wall and stalked into the kitchen, zeroing in on the coffee maker like a heat-seeking missile. "Responsibilities, eh?" He threw me a knowing smirk over his shoulder as he measured out the grounds. "Funny, I don't remember you mentioning working with the invitational before."

My face heated. "Mmm, I forgot. You're an angel who would never lie to his parents." I busied myself wiping down the spotless counter to avoid making eye contact.

Rob hummed noncommittally and punched the brew button. The gurgle of percolating coffee filled the silence between us as we circled the tiny kitchen in a strange dance.

He was wearing a shirt. It was inside out and looked like it had been haphazardly yanked on, but still. My brain took in every detail like I was cramming for an exam. *Don't forget to memorize those low-slung sweats and bare feet, they'll be on the final!*

Rob turned and leaned on the counter. He blew out a breath, then glanced at my bedroom door. "Could I, uh . . . "

It took me a second, but finally, his words computed. He needed to use the washroom. "Oh, yeah. Of course. It's all yours."

A flicker of something—relief?—crossed his face before he schooled it into indifference. "Thanks." The word came out like a grunt. Like it physically pained him to be polite.

As he brushed by me, a knot formed in my stomach. What if I'd left something embarrassing in there? I mentally scanned my memory of the room from last night. No tampons or panty liners. Hopefully.

Each second that ticked by felt like an eternity. I poured myself coffee now that the pot was full, then grabbed the creamer from the fridge, my stomach churning. When he finally emerged, looking unfairly refreshed, my eye caught on his toothbrush and toothpaste sitting on the kitchen counter next to the sink.

A pang of guilt prodded my conscience. I needed to rip off the Band-Aid. Just acknowledge the awkwardness and move on. I eased into it. "Sorry for waking you up so early with that phone call." I took a fortifying gulp of coffee, then forced out the words lodged in my throat. "And, um, also . . . sorry about the other night."

My pulse kicked up, and a cold sweat prickled my skin. Anxiety squirmed in my gut like a live eel. Rob stepped forward, and I moved out of the way so he could pour himself a cup of coffee. He leaned against the counter, appraising me over the rim of his mug.

My ears started to buzz. I squirmed on my stool, feeling about as exposed as a nudist at a nunnery. The urge to flee to my room with my half-English muffin and coffee built up until I couldn't stand it anymore. I was halfway off my seat when his voice stopped me cold.

"What happened to make you so afraid?"

I froze, muscles locking up like an engine seized with rust. That was his question? Like a dart hitting a bullseye, my mind landed on the summer I turned thirteen. Dead center. Straight to the heart.

I cleared my throat. "Uh, nothing. Just a bad dream." I stared at the crumbs scattered across my plate. The weight of his stare bore into me, but mercifully, he didn't press. I shoveled a bite of muffin into my mouth, the once fluffy bread now dry as sawdust on my tongue.

Desperate to turn the spotlight off of myself, I blurted, "So, you heading home for the holidays?"

A shadow passed over Rob's face. He gave a curt nod. "Yeah. After the invitational."

"Cool, me too." I bobbed my head, feeling like one of those toy-drinking birds. Rising on wobbly legs, I dumped my plate in the sink. "I got your note about the plumber."

Rob ran a hand over the back of his neck. "They're going to phone when the part comes in."

"Okay." I picked up my mug, blood rushing in my ears. I did not know what to do with this version of him. I was alone, and he'd watched me have a mental breakdown. He was Logan's friend, after all. I may have misjudged him. A little—*a tad*. He had to have some redeeming qualities or Logan never would've given him the spare room in the first place.

"Well, um, sorry again for the rude awakening. I guess we're even, hey?" I backed toward my room. "I'll just let you . . . " I made a vague gesture at his rumpled appearance even though the truth was, he could walk out on campus like that, and every girl he passed would do a double take.

Before he could respond, I darted into my bedroom and shut the door, sagging against it with a gusty exhale. Smooth, Sharla. Real smooth.

CHAPTER
Nine

THE NEXT WEEK flew by in a blur of classes and pre-Christmas concert rehearsals. My violin became an extension of my body as I poured myself into the music. Even though we technically had Monday off for Remembrance Day, the orchestra played at the memorial in the morning, and then I was asked to join a smaller group of musicians to play for a private event and a dinner honouring veterans that evening across town.

I was glad to participate, but adding that to my regular schedule meant I barely had time to think, let alone go grocery shopping or see anyone outside the arts centre. Including Crystal and Maddie.

Logan called three times. Not enough that I got sick of him like he promised. From the sounds of it, they were working him hard. The second time we talked, he was drunk. Sad drunk. All I wanted to do was get on a plane and go to him. To crawl into bed with him and make him feel better. But then yesterday, he'd been his happy normal self.

All the emotional whiplash left me begging for Friday evening until I remembered I couldn't sit at home with Logan like normal. The weekend before, Rob was gone most of the weekend for an away tournament, and I'd been too busy to enjoy it. I mentally cursed the scheduling gods.

I couldn't veg at home this weekend, which meant these few days felt more like a prison sentence than a break. At least Crystal, Maddie, and I already had plans to go to the Outlaws game Saturday afternoon. That was something.

I finished up rehearsal and moved through my routine of packing up, then slung my backpack over my shoulders and grabbed the handle of my violin case. I left the building, my boots crunching on the slushy sidewalks.

"Hey, perfect timing!"

I turned my head to find Caleb leaning against the lamp post. He tucked his Gameboy into his backpack and walked toward me.

I laughed. "How did you beat me out of there?" No wonder I hadn't noticed him when I left.

"I had to meet with my advisor."

I narrowed my eyes. "And you came back over here because . . ."

"I was looking for you." He grinned.

I planted a hand on my hip. "Caleb, if you need a fake date for—"

"No, no, nothing like that." He clapped a hand on my shoulder. "I told you about this, don't you remember?"

I frowned, scanning through my memory for recent conversations. "I have no idea what you're talking about."

He sighed dramatically. "I got my new Nintendo set up! Convinced the 'rents to give me my Christmas present early. Super Nintendo with Super Bomberman 2. Up to five players at once!" His eyes gleamed with excitement. "Lily's in."

I laughed out loud. "Okay, I do remember you telling me about this, but you didn't say you were getting it early."

He waved off my comment. "Neither here nor there. The important question is: Are you free tonight?"

I hesitated. Normally, I'd politely decline Caleb's game

invites. This wasn't the first time he'd invited me over, but I had zero experience. However . . . the thought of a solitary evening in the house with Rob made my stomach twist.

Crystal and Maddie were both busy tonight, so there wasn't a chance I was giving up better plans. Not that Caleb was a fall back, just the video games portion of the evening.

"You know what? I'm in." I adjusted my violin case on my shoulder. "Let me just drop this off and change. Meet you at the bookstore in thirty?"

Caleb pumped his fist. "Yes! Awesome. Lily's gonna flip her shit. See you soon!" He took off down the walkway, practically skipping. How could I say no to that?

I walked home with an extra bounce in my step, helped along by *Don't Turn Around* by Ace of Bass through my headphones. I burst into the house in a flurry, cold air nipping at my heels. I tossed my keys on the entry table and was already unzipping my coat when I saw him.

Rob sat hunched over the kitchen island, notebooks and binders spread before him like an academic buffet. He watched me, his dark brows raised. His hair was mussed. He was not wearing a shirt. "Oh. Hey."

"Hey," I mumbled, lingering awkwardly in the doorway.

"Sorry, I didn't think you'd be home."

I raised an eyebrow. "You're apologizing now?" I dropped my coat next to my shoes. I was going to put it back on in point five seconds.

"Don't get used to it."

The corner of my mouth quirked without my permission. I kept my eyes on the couch, the TV stand, anything but the tattoo on his left shoulder or the muscles in his back. "Aren't you cold?" The fact that he and Logan walked around half-undressed was a mystery to me. I needed a sweatshirt and socks, even with the thermostat cranked to twenty-four degrees.

Rob cleared his throat, scooping up his study materials. "I don't get cold."

Figured. "You don't need to move. I'm heading out again in a sec anyway."

"Oh yeah?" His gaze followed me to the bedroom. I ducked in and dropped my bag and violin case. I thought about changing but settled on brushing my teeth and grabbing a toque. I grabbed my water bottle, too, and rushed back out into the kitchen. I'd told Caleb thirty minutes, and I was already going to be late.

"Where to?" Rob's brow was pinched as he stared at his textbook.

None of your business, I wanted to snap. But I bit my tongue, reaching for the shredded cabbage and leftover rotisserie chicken. "Out." I dumped the ingredients on the counter. Tacos would have to do—quick and easy.

I assembled my makeshift dinner, my senses heightened. I could feel Rob's judgment radiating across the kitchen. He'd made enough comments over the months about my lack of cooking. Probably another reason he thought Logan could do so much better.

It wasn't that I didn't know how to cook. My mom made us dinner every night growing up. It was just easier to have my weekly taco ingredients, a few quick breakfast items, and grab-and-go snacks. Especially since Logan was rarely home for dinner anyway.

Truthfully, having Logan gone was going to save me money. That was one micro silver lining. I wouldn't be tempted to go out to eat all the time with him and his friends. He was always willing to pay, but unless we were on an actual date, I felt guilty bumming off of him constantly.

It was good timing. I'd squirrelled away every penny from my summer job, allocating the bare minimum each month. November's portion sat in my account, and I needed as much as possible to be able to buy Christmas gifts for family and friends.

Scooping the cabbage and chicken onto corn tortillas, I

ignored Rob's stare burning holes in my back. I took a bite of my taco, not bothering with a plate and keeping my back turned.

"I don't bite." Rob spoke up behind me. "Unless you're into that sort of thing."

I nearly choked on a piece of chicken. Coughing, I grabbed a glass from the cupboard and filled it with water. Rob had cleared the counter space in front of the second stool. Okaaaaay.

When I could breathe normally, I took my plate and cup over and sat down, scooting it as far from him as possible without being obvious. As I settled onto the seat, his scent—the clean body wash or deodorant he used—tinged the air.

Unbidden, the memory of that night surfaced. Not pictures in my head since it had been dark. Just feelings. Sounds. The rush of his breath, the solid warmth of his chest. *I don't get cold.*

My cheeks flamed as I jammed another bite of taco in my mouth. This wasn't okay. Whatever was happening in my head felt like an absolute betrayal. Shouldn't I be thinking about Logan? Imagining his hands? His chest?

I frowned, trying to draw from the hundreds of moments I had with him, scrambling for a moment to redirect the heat and ache building in my lower belly. Desperate for a distraction, I glanced at the textbook spread open on the counter. Complex equations and diagrams filled the pages, and my frown deepened.

"What's this?" I asked, unable to contain my curiosity. "I didn't think hockey players bothered with anything beyond the basics." At least Logan didn't. His priority was getting on the ice, and when he wasn't lacing up, it was building muscle and agility to support his game. Textbook cracking was not a regular activity in his book.

Rob's gaze flicked to mine, his dark eyes unreadable. "You're right. Us hockey players. Carbon copies."

I rolled my eyes. "You know what I meant."

He shrugged, his tattoo drawing my eyes like a magnet. "I'm

not planning on being a hockey player forever. Gotta have a backup plan."

I raised an eyebrow. "You don't think you're good enough to go pro?"

Rob scoffed. "Doesn't matter what I think."

I gave him a look. "Okay. What does that mean?"

Rob's jaw clenched. "It's competitive."

"Yeah. So are most things."

He turned, putting his lean muscles on full display. "You're not taking a business minor? Just putting all your eggs in the orchestra basket?"

I blinked, my half a taco frozen on its path to my mouth. "Did Logan tell you I was doing that?"

A shutter seemed to draw over his eyes. He turned back to his books. "Logan has opportunities," he said, his tone clipped. "I need to be realistic."

I took a bite, chewing slowly, and then took a drink from my water glass. "Everyone should have a backup plan."

Rob tapped the end of his pencil on his notebook. "So you're Logan's, then?"

My jaw dropped. White-hot anger surged through me. "Nice." I picked up my plate and glass, rounding the countertop.

"What. I'm serious."

I shot him a look, my eyes flashing. I wasn't going to dignify that with a response. But Rob didn't stop there.

"You're right, I'm being ridiculous. Logan Kemp always gets what he wants."

I set my dishes in the sink and slammed on the faucet. "At least he isn't a coward who's too afraid to work for his dreams."

Rob recoiled as if I'd slapped him, his eyes widening. For a moment, we stared at each other, the air between us crackling.

"You know, this whole roommate thing would be a lot easier if you didn't hate my guts," I snapped.

Rob's eyes narrowed. "What?"

My fingers trembled as I rinsed the dishes a second time. "I don't know what I ever did to you. Besides take time with Logan, which I'm sure got your panties in a bunch, but seriously. I tried to be nice when I moved in and—"

"I don't hate you."

I turned off the water and dried my hands. "What is it then? Am I just not *dedicated* or *committed* enough for you? Do I not understand the focus hockey takes, am I a distraction to Logan? Because right now, you don't seem like you give a shit about his career."

Rob's brow furrowed. "I don't know what the hell you're talking about."

I shoved away from the counter, rounding it. "I heard what you said to him. Last year. So what did I do to deserve it?"

Rob's nostrils flared. He took a step back, then turned and stalked toward his room.

"Mm. Good idea. Just walk away because—"

Rob spun back to face me, and I froze. His breathing was heavy, his eyes dark. "I'm walking away so I don't do something I regret."

My throat worked, his gaze pinning me in place like a bug on a corkboard. I willed my legs to move. "I have to go." I shoved my feet into my shoes and grabbed my coat.

"Where are you going?" Rob demanded again, his voice rough.

"Why the hell do you care?"

Rob clenched his pencil so tight I thought it might break. "Because you're going out alone. We have a game tomorrow. You know how people get."

I snatched my toque from the counter and stalked to the door, grabbing my coat. "I'm not going to a party. I'm just hanging out with my dorky orchestra friends. We're playing Super Nintendo. I doubt it'll get crazy. Probably home around eleven, so if you could finish up in the washroom before then."

With that, I stormed out of the house, slamming the door behind me with a satisfying bang. The cool night air hit my face, and I sucked in a deep breath, trying to calm the storm of emotions raging inside me.

I was halfway down the steps when the door opened behind me. "Sharla!" I didn't turn around, even though Rob's footsteps pounded on the pavement.

"What do you want?" I quickened my pace.

He caught up to me easily, his long legs eating up the distance between us. "Logan called," he said, slightly out of breath. "He has a game tonight. Said he won't be able to talk until the morning."

I stopped short, my heart stuttering in my chest as I turned to face him. "Couldn't have told me that ten minutes ago?" Rob shoved his hands in his pockets. "How did he sound?" I asked, hating the way my voice trembled.

Rob shrugged. "How does Logan always sound? Like everything's just peachy keen."

That clawing started up again in my stomach. I swallowed hard, blinking back the sudden tears that pricked at the corners of my eyes.

"Jealousy isn't a good look on you," I snapped, then turned on my heel and stalked away.

CHAPTER
Ten

I MASHED the buttons on the Super Nintendo controller as my Bomberman character raced around the maze-like stage, laying bombs and trying to blow up the other players. The 16-bit music and sound effects blared from Caleb's 20-inch CRT TV.

"Ha, got you, Shar!" Caleb laughed as his white Bomberman exploded my pink one. Pixels burst across the screen.

I groaned and shoved him playfully. "Damn it, I almost had you." I adjusted the bracelet on my wrist. It slipped around, and I was trying not to let it annoy me.

Caleb, his roommate Evan, and a couple of other orchestra friends were crammed on the ratty couch in their grungy apartment, empty cans of PBR and half-eaten bags of Doritos scattered on the coffee table. Not my usual Friday night scene, but I was having fun.

"Evan, quit camping in the corner, you wuss," Breanna called out. She played clarinet and had streaks of purple in her frizzy brown hair.

"All's fair in love and Bomberman," Evan retorted.

We played a few more rounds, yelling, trash-talking, and passing around more beers. The room buzzed with warmth—not just from the alcohol but from the familiar comfort of being with people who got each other. I surprised myself by getting into it, even doing a ridiculous victory dance when I finally won. It was goofy and over-the-top, but for once, I didn't care.

Lily flopped onto the battered couch beside me, her long, dark braid falling over her shoulder as she cracked open a soda instead of a beer. Lily always had this quiet, steady energy, like she was anchored while the rest of us drifted.

"You're weirdly competitive," she said with a grin, nudging me with her elbow.

I laughed. "I didn't know I had it in me."

She tilted her head thoughtfully. "You sure about that?"

I blushed. Okay, so maybe I wasn't as opaque as I thought. I never said anything about wanting her chair in orchestra, but maybe not saying something was a giveaway of how desperate I was to earn it. I opened my mouth to respond, but she'd already turned back toward the TV, engrossed in the next round.

"Just like band camp. Slip it in behind the bleachers." Evan laughed maniacally as he sneak attacked Caleb.

I laughed, my mind drifting to my one and only band camp experiences. Late-night shenanigans with Tyler, a cocky sax player whose dimples looked like belly buttons under the hazy campfire glow. We'd snuck behind the cabins, not the bleachers. His breath tasted like the cheap vodka someone had smuggled in Gatorade bottles. The kiss had been sloppy but so hot. Forbidden.

I'd never been a "band geek," not really. Music had always been something more to me—something serious, something sacred. While others swapped inside jokes about marching band disasters or made weird pacts with their wind instruments, I was the girl running scales until my fingers ached. Music was home —but musicians? I wasn't sure where I fit among them. Maybe only pieces of me did. Just like pieces fit with my Outlaws family. Almost all my pieces fit with Crystal and Maddie. And Logan. Of course, with Logan.

Lily let out a triumphant shout, snapping me back to the

present. Breanna groaned dramatically as her character exploded in pixelated flames.

"Victory is mine!" Lily crowed, pointing like a Roman emperor in triumph.

I laughed, settling deeper into the worn cushions. Rob's snide comment from earlier about having a "backup plan" popped into my head, souring my good mood. Where did he get off trying to comment on my relationship with Logan when he wouldn't know a relationship if it bit him in the face?

It especially pissed me off considering how loyal Logan had been, letting Rob crash at our place when he needed somewhere to stay. Some friend he was. The more I stewed on it, the angrier I got.

"Hey Sharla, you still in the game or what?" Caleb's voice snapped me out of my bitter thoughts.

"Sorry, just got distracted for a sec." I glanced up at the clock on the wall, and my eyes widened. It was already eleven. "I think I'm going to call it a night, though." I put my controller down and stood up to a chorus of groans and lighthearted boos. It wasn't that I needed to get home at a certain time, but I didn't love walking across campus too late. Especially not alone.

"Me, too." Lily grinned as if reading my mind.

I exhaled with relief and slipped on my shoes. The November air was crisp and bracing. The sky stretched dark and infinite, dotted with stars shimmering faintly through thin clouds. Our shoes crunched over a thin layer of frost covering the campus pathways.

We walked side by side, shoulders brushing occasionally, our breath forming soft clouds in the cold night air.

"I'm so glad we have this weekend off." Lily stuffed her hands into her coat pockets. "That Christmas concert rehearsal schedule is murder."

I nodded. "Seriously. If I have to play the violin obbligato from 'Jesu, Joy of Man's Desiring' one more time, I'm going to lose it."

She laughed. "What, you don't like perpetual tight-rope walking?"

I laughed, kicking a stray pebble down the path. Lily slowed as we approached the fork by the bookstore. "Thanks for walking with me." I gave her a quick hug.

She nodded, tucking her hands back in the pockets of her coat. "Sharla, if you want first chair, you need to *own* it. Stop waiting for someone to hand it to you." Her voice was calm but firm. I swallowed, unsure how to respond. "You're good enough," she added. "You've always been good enough."

Warmth crept into my chest, chasing away the November chill for a moment. I managed a small smile. "Thanks. I guess I don't want to push, you know?"

She grinned. "Musicians? Pushy?"

I laughed, my breath blooming between us.

"Franck will appreciate it. She likes people who know what they want."

I rocked on my heels. "Okay. I'll think about it."

"Good." She gave a small wave and turned down the path as I continued on. The crisp night air felt good as I headed north past the bookstore, the alcohol buzz wearing off.

I heard voices before I saw anything. But then, cutting through the quad, I spotted some movement by the Charlotte Douglas statue. Getting closer, I realized it was a group of guys, clearly drunk off their asses. One was climbing on the statue while the others hooted and hollered crude remarks.

"Woo, you tell 'em, Charlie!"

"You won't take me, you Outlaw fags!"

I stopped in my tracks, blood boiling as I watched them pull out a can of spray paint. *What the actual hell?* I didn't think, just broke into a jog.

"Hey jackasses! Get the hell away from that statue!" I yelled, fists clenched at my sides. They whipped around to face me, the ringleader nearly toppling off his perch.

I don't know what I expected. For them to startle and run?

Honestly, that was what my brain had put together as the most probable outcome. It was only when the three guys on the ground turned to face me that I realized I'd vastly miscalculated.

"Well, well, boys, looks like we got ourselves a little hero!" one of them slurred, swaggering toward me. He had dirty blond hair that curled around his ears. A handsome face. He was tall, strong. His eyes were red-rimmed, his cheeks flushed. "I hear Canadian girls are nice and compliant."

My stomach dropped as the reality of the situation sank in. I was alone, facing down a pack of wasted hockey players built like brick shithouses. This was a mistake. I stumbled back, and he cackled.

"Aw c'mon baby, we're just having some fun," he leered, eyes raking over my body. Even with my coat on, I felt stripped down. "Why don't you come have some fun with us? We don't know anyone in town yet."

The other guys snickered as they walked closer. My heart hammered in my chest. I had to get out of here. Now.

I didn't turn my back, thinking he wouldn't have the balls to do anything while I was watching him. Another mistake.

He lunged forward, and I couldn't run backward. He caught my arm, yanking me. "Don't be like that sweetheart. I'll show you a real good time," he breathed in my ear, his other hand pawing at my waist.

I slapped his hands away, trying to wrestle out of his grip. "Get off me!"

But he just laughed, hold tightening as he pressed himself against me. Panic threatened to choke me. I was only two blocks from home, but it may as well have been Airdrie. *Scream.* I needed to—

There was a blur of motion, and suddenly the creep went flying backwards, slamming against the ground with a sickening crunch. There were no words. No shouts. Just grunts and low thuds as someone in a T-shirt with dark hair landed on top of him, his fists pounding into his stomach.

I knew that hair.
I knew those shoulders.

CHAPTER
Eleven

THE OTHER GUYS stumbled back in surprise, their brains responding with appropriate speed given the substances they'd most likely consumed.

"Rob!" I ran forward, grabbing his arm. He was going to seriously injure this guy, and not only that, if he got caught, he could be suspended for the season. It had already happened once with their right winger, Cody Simmons, who'd punched a guy for grabbing his girlfriend's butt at Ranchmans. The evaluation committee didn't seem to care who started the altercation. There was no fighting on campus. Period.

"Rob, I'm fine. You can't get suspended." I pulled harder without making much headway. His muscles were tight, his body so rigid, I thought he might snap.

Finally, my words sank in. He pulled back, pushing to his feet next to me. His knuckles were ripped and bloody. The whole thing had taken less than twenty seconds, but the guy on the ground was a bruised and bloody mess.

Rob scanned the other guys who were barely getting their shit together to move in and help their friend. "Back the hell off or I'll put you all in an ambulance." He caught the symbol on one of their jackets and laughed. "Are you shitting me?

Nah, I'll just phone your coach." That stopped them in their tracks.

They exchanged nervous glances, their fearless leader struggling to his feet with a groan. "Whatever, man, crazy bitch ain't worth it," he spat, slinking away.

"You think you can come to our campus and pull this shit?" Rob shouted after them, and the last few seconds were finally processed in my brain. This was the visiting hockey team. The guys we were playing tomorrow.

I stood frozen, trembling as the adrenaline drained away, then reached for Rob's still bleeding hands. "Are you—"

He didn't let me finish my sentence. He was touching my face, my neck, checking every inch of skin that was visible. "Did he hurt you? If he hurt you, I swear, I'll kill him, Shar."

"No. He didn't hurt me." Rob's hands trembled on my shoulders, and I stared at him. He was only wearing a damn T-shirt. "What are you doing out here like that? It's freezing and—"

Rob's hand clamped onto my shoulder, his grip firm as he steered me away from the courtyard. We walked in tense silence, the crunch of snow beneath our feet the only sound echoing through the cold night air.

I couldn't stop shaking. Adrenaline still surged through my veins, my heart hammering against my ribcage. I clenched my jaw, trying to will my body to relax. It refused to obey.

"How did you know where I was?" I asked, my teeth chattering.

His dark eyes flicked to mine then away again, his mouth set in a grim line. "Doesn't matter. You shouldn't be out alone this late. It's not safe."

I bristled at his patronizing tone. "I walked most of the way with a friend."

"Seems like that worked well for you."

I clamped my mouth shut. He'd just saved me, and I wanted to slap him. I wanted to do a lot of things. Scream. Cry.

How was it not okay for me to walk across my own University campus without being afraid? How was I ever going to feel safe again after this?

Emotion choked my throat, and I stared straight ahead, Rob still guiding me toward our house. His breathing was heavy, his eyes murderous in the amber glow of the street lamps.

Finally the townhouse appeared before us. Rob dropped his hands from my shoulders, and I sagged. He reached past me and turned the knob. The door swung open—he'd left it unlocked.

As soon as we stepped inside, blessed warmth enveloped me. I kicked off my shoes, trying to pretend that nothing was wrong. I was fine. I wasn't physically hurt, but my traitorous body refused to stop trembling.

Suddenly, something heavy and warm draped over my shoulders. That clean scent filled my nostrils. Rob's jacket. I whirled to face him, an automatic protest on my lips, but he cut me off.

"Don't even try, Shar. You're shaking like a damn leaf."

"I'm fine," I insisted through gritted teeth, shrugging off the jacket. "I don't need your—"

"You're not fine!" he snapped, those onyx eyes flashing. "You almost just got assaulted! If you're going to insist on walking home alone at ungodly hours, then I'm coming with you from now on. End of story."

I gaped at him, indignation rising in my throat like bile. "You're not my boyfriend." I regretted it the second it left my lips. Rob ran a hand through his hair, and I caught sight of his bruised and bleeding fingers. "Rob—"

"Don't." He strode past me, heading for his bedroom.

"Rob!" I stomped after him. "I'm sorry, I don't know why I said that. I—"

"Don't!" He whirled, and the sight of his glassy eyes choked the words from my mouth. His eyes scanned my face, darting over my features like a cat watching a mosquito. He opened his mouth, then closed it, his throat working.

"Did you wait up for me?" I asked, my voice a whisper.

Rob's lips twitched. This close, I could see the stubble on his jaw. The scar that nicked the edge of his lower lip. "Lock the door." He turned and disappeared into his room, closing the door behind him.

I stepped forward, pressing a hand to the wood. My body was still, no longer shaking. Instead, something hot and sharp unfurled low in my belly like a curl of smoke. I shivered and stepped back, then walked mechanically back to the entry. I hung up both our coats. The silence pressed in on me, making my ears ring.

I turned toward the kitchen and froze, my eyes snagging on the flash of teal.

My water bottle. It was turned upside down. Washed and drying on the rack.

CHAPTER
Twelve

I WOKE WITH A START, my heart racing. I shouldn't have been surprised that I dreamed about a break-in after everything that happened the night before. I didn't need a dream interpreter to figure that one out.

I lay there for a while, letting my mind wander as I stared at the popcorn-textured ceiling. So strange. Everything inside me felt foreign, like I'd picked up an instrument that wasn't mine. Still familiar, but I didn't know its quirks.

As much as I wanted to stay there forever and not risk running into Rob, I did have to get ready for the day. I cursed my past self for not thinking far enough ahead to grab some of my snacks from the cupboard. That and my . . . water bottle.

What the hell? It was only me and Rob in this house. He was the only person who could've washed it out, but why would he do that? It was in the exact same place as where Logan typically left it, and that was the most disturbing piece of information.

My head throbbed as I rose from the mattress like a corpse from a grave. Tylenol was going to be my friend today. I threw my legs over the side of the bed and walked to the door, cracking it and listening for any signs of life. When all I heard was the hum of the refrigerator, I threw on a hoodie and braved the short hall.

I strode to the island and leaned forward to peek in the other direction. Rob's bedroom door was open. I drew a deep breath and exhaled in relief. He must have left already for the rink.

I grabbed a banana and some yogurt from the fridge, then booted up the computer to check my emails. The dial-up modem screeched and crackled as it connected. I walked back into the kitchen and ate while I waited.

I glanced at my water bottle still sitting upside down on the counter. What. The. Hell.

By the time I finished my banana, the internet finally connected with a chime. I sat down on the chair, curling my leg under me, and set my half-eaten yogurt on the desk.

I scrolled through a few messages from my mom, one from my little sister who I needed to be better about writing. She was in grade ten, and we probably had plenty in common now. I was legitimately excited to see her over the holiday, which had certainly not always been the case. Being out of the house made me view a lot of things differently.

The shrill ring of the phone made me jump. I leaped from the chair and ran to the kitchen, grabbing the receiver.

"Hello?"

"Hey, babe."

I grinned, leaning back against the counter. No shouting. No clattering dishes. "Hey."

"You getting ready for the game today?"

"Of course. Not the same without you here, though." I twisted the cord around my finger. "What are you doing this weekend?"

He blew out a breath. "Rest morning."

"Well, that's nice." I tensed, already sensing his mood. I couldn't hear the smile in his voice. He was too quiet. I wanted to throw something out there, something new we could talk about to take his mind off whatever was bothering him, but came up empty. Every single thing on my mind was either depressing, disturbing, or both. None of it was what Logan needed.

"Sharla, I don't know what I'm doing out here." He paused, then drew another long breath. "I'm letting the team down. I missed an easy shot on goal last night, and then I totally botched a pass. Coach reamed me out."

My heart ached for him. "Hey, everyone has off days—"

"I just feel like I have to be better. If I want to make the final team—"

"Wait, you're not on the final team?"

He grunted, and there was a scuffle of fabric. I imagined him dropping onto the couch or lying back in his bed. "No, they make final selections right before the tournament."

"So . . . it's like you're auditioning."

"Yep. Every day. Practice, games, off the ice."

I let go of the cord, letting it drape over the counter. "Sounds exhausting." He sniffed, and I wondered if he was crying or close to it. Ugh, I hated that we were so far apart. "But, you're Logan freaking Kemp. I think you might be forgetting that."

He chuckled weakly. "Yeah."

I chewed my bottom lip. "I know you really want this. I one hundred percent believe in you."

He groaned. "I miss you."

My heart skipped a beat. Finally. It had been weeks, and that was the first time he'd said those words. "I miss you, too. So much." It was then that I wanted to blurt everything out. Tell him about the weird night with Rob, about the altercation with that asshole on the Montana team, about my weird dreams. But the closest I could get was, "Rob washed my water bottle."

Logan paused a second. "Huh."

"Did you . . . I don't know, tell him to look out for me or something? While you were gone?" The question sounded worse out loud than in my head. Stupid, and cheesy.

Logan laughed. "Uh, of course I did. I told him not to be a dickwad otherwise I'd kick his ass to the curb." I laughed with him, noting that he hadn't exactly answered my question. "I didn't think he'd take it that far, though."

"That far, how?" I grinned, picking up my water bottle so I could fill it.

"Washing a bottle that doesn't need to be washed." He laughed again, but that time, I didn't join in. "I guess he got sick of waiting for you to do it. My girl. So particular. I love it."

My stomach dropped to my knees. I set the bottle back on the counter. Those were not the words of someone who washed my water bottles.

The last six months flashed in my mind. The mornings I woke up and found it there drying on the side of the sink. *Last night when I found it there.*

I started to feel nauseous. "Hey, I should probably get going."

"Yeah, okay. Well, say hi to everyone for me."

I nodded. "For sure."

"They gave us our flight info. We leave for Europe December third instead of the fourth."

I exhaled in a rush. "Wow. Coming up quick."

"We need to get acclimated. Jet lag and all that."

"Well, hopefully it all works out." I stretched the phone cord so I could look at my calendar hanging next to the computer across the room. Today was the sixteenth of November. "So we can talk for the next two weeks on the phone. Then email?" Logan was terrible at email. And who knew how often he'd have access to a computer?

"Yep. Maybe I'll have to do some typing practice." He chuckled.

"You know, in all your spare time." Here we were, fantasizing again.

"Love you, Shar."

"Love you, Logan." I hung up the phone.

Not wanting to think too much about the wildly confusing

conversation we just had, I finished my yogurt, then blasted the radio and got in the shower. I washed my hair, grateful for the thousandth time that it was short, then shaved my legs for absolutely zero reason—I wasn't going to the pool anytime soon and the only person who would notice my smooth skin was in another province—and got out.

The steamy washroom mirror greeted me, and I swiped a hand across the glass. It was go time. Game day makeup was a ritual. Really only for Maddie, Crystal, and me, but that counted. Winged black eyeliner with gold shadow, mascara, and a bold red lip. It was close enough to our school colours without it looking like our lipstick had expired.

I glanced down at the bracelet on the shelf and picked it up. It was beautiful. Delicate. I slipped it around my wrist and tightened the clasp, then dried my hair and left it a little spiky with product. Once I threw on my Outlaws jersey, I headed out to meet Maddie.

By the time we arrived at the parking lot, it was already buzzing with pregame energy. Tailgates down, music blasting, the scent of charcoal grilled burgers and beer wafting through the air. This was college hockey at its finest.

"Hey!" Crystal's pink hair bobbed through the crowd as she waved me over. "About time, girl. We were about to send out a search party."

Maddie grinned, handing me a red Solo cup. "Drink up. It's game time."

I took a sip, the cheap beer cold and bitter on my tongue. We laughed and joked with the other Outlaws fans, the camaraderie electric. But as the minutes ticked by, I noticed Maddie and Crystal exchanging glances, their eyes darting to me with poorly concealed concern.

"What?" I finally asked, exasperated. "Do I have something on my face?"

Crystal shook her head. "No, you just seem a bit off today. Everything okay?"

I forced a smile. "Yeah, totally. This is just weird without Logan, you know?"

It was a good enough excuse, they let it drop. I considered telling them everything swirling in my head. They wouldn't have judged me. But I couldn't speak any of it yet since I wasn't finished judging myself.

Why couldn't I just be excited for Logan? Why had I put myself in that stupid situation in the courtyard? And why did my chest resonate like someone was dragging a bow over an upright bass anytime I thought about Rob?

I put more energy into looking like I was having a good time, which meant I was the star of the show. Hilarious! Charming! Full of anecdotes! The Sharla everyone knew and loved.

I needed a nap by the time we made our way into the rink, but parking ourselves on the benches directly under the heaters was almost enough of a reward for my efforts. The stands were a sea of maroon and gold, Outlaws fans out in full force. On the opposite side, a small but vocal cluster of Rocky College of Montana fans sat waving a blue flag.

Crystal unfurled our own massive banner reading "GO OUTLAWS!" in glittery letters while Maddie pulled out a stack of posters she'd made with each player's number. "Aw, guess we don't need this one." She held up a number eighteen, then slid it back into her folder.

Something about that hit me like a bucket of cold water. I was suddenly back in the hall, listening to Rob and Logan. *She doesn't understand the kind of dedication and commitment this takes, bud.*

Was this what he meant? That I didn't get how hockey would take Logan away from me? How hard it would be to stay home while he was off having grand adventures in the US or Europe or wherever else they wanted him to play?

I clenched my fists. I was nothing if not dedicated and committed. I could do this for two months, and then Logan and I could talk about everything. Distance was the problem here, not *us*.

The Outlaws took the ice for warmups, and the ache in my chest eased. These boys were family, a band of brothers I'd come to love over the past year. From the first line to the fourth, the starting goalie to the backup, they were my boys. And tonight, I'd cheer them on with everything I had, even if my heart wasn't fully in it.

We chatted and laughed until the lights dimmed, and we all rose for the national anthems. The choir sang both the Canadian and American since the visiting team was from Montana. I already wanted to throat-punch them, which didn't bode well for the shit-talking that was about to come out of my mouth during the game.

"Here we go!" Crystal grabbed onto my arm and squeezed. The buzzer sounded, signalling the start of the game. I leaned forward, my eyes locked on the ice.

Rob took the face-off. I shouldn't have been surprised, but it was still jarring to see him in Logan's place. As the puck dropped, I tried to figure out which player was opposite him. The guy who'd grabbed my arm? One of his friends?

Their sticks clashed. Rob won, kicking the puck across to Axel. And then he was crushed against the boards.

"Interference!" Maddie cried out. The ref didn't see it. He was already down the ice. "That's bull!"

The crowd booed, and my pulse rushed, heat flooding to my cheeks. This was because of the courtyard. I knew it before Rob sprinted to catch up with the other guys and got nailed by another player as he went for a pass from Bear.

The Montana team had it out for him through the entire first period, slamming into him at every opportunity. Each hit was harder than the last. Brutal. Punishing. The first period was a mess of dirty plays and cheap shots. Montana racked up penalty after penalty, but it didn't seem to deter them. Rob was taking the brunt of it, his frustration mounting with each hit.

I winced as Rob was checked into the boards near the blue line, his head snapping back from the force.

"What the hell is going on?" Crystal muttered, her brow furrowed. "They're targeting him."

I nodded, my stomach twisting as another Montana player slammed Rob into the glass. He staggered, slapping a glove to his helmet.

Maddie let out a low hiss beside me, her fingers clenching around her poster. And then, with just seconds left on the clock, it happened. Rob snapped. When the player from last night collided into him at center ice, he shoved him back. Hard.

"This is my fault." I groaned, clapping my hands over my mouth.

"What?" Crystal turned to look at me, but I couldn't stop staring. The Montana player dropped his stick to the ice, and Rob's gloves were already next to it. He tore at his jersey, and both their helmets went flying. They were throwing punches, a blur of maroon and blue.

The refs descended, prying them apart and escorting them to the penalty box. As Rob yanked off his helmet, I got a clear look at his opponent. It was him, the drunk douchebag from the courtyard. Rage boiled in my veins as they hurled insults at each other, slamming their fists against the glass.

"I've never seen Rob lose it like that," Maddie said, her eyes wide. "He's usually so controlled."

Crystal nodded, her pink hair glinting under the lights. "What happened, Shar?"

I bit my lip. "Long story." The buzzer sounded, signalling the end of the period. I slumped back in my seat.

Crystal raised an eyebrow. "Start talking."

"Holy hell." Maddie straightened in her seat, saving me from answering for the moment. Crystal and I both followed her gaze to the Outlaws bench.

"What?" I asked. I didn't see anything noteworthy.

She curled into me, pointing toward the end of the bench. "That guy. Who is he?"

I searched and found the only face I didn't recognize. "I don't know. New coaching staff?" They were all new this year, but Logan hadn't mentioned someone coming in mid-semester. But then again, Logan wasn't here.

Maddie's face was drawn, her eyes wide. "I think that's my step brother."

CHAPTER
Thirteen

"STEP BROTHER WINS." Crystal put a chip slathered in queso into her mouth. The victorious energy surged around us at Ranchmans after the game, but we were in our own world, huddled together in the back corner.

"Yes!" Maddie crossed her arms over her chest, a smug grin on her face.

"What? How does that win? I was in literal physical and emotional danger, and then Rob swooped in like a vigilante. Wearing a T-shirt at minus fifteen. That totally wins."

Crystal reached for her glass of ice water. "I would never minimize what you went through, Shar. For real. But hot step brother who used to walk around in your house in basketball shorts? Then shows up out of nowhere across the rink from you? What are the chances of that?"

"I mean, he's from Calgary, and he played pro hockey," I muttered, reaching for a jalapeño popper. "It's not that unrealistic."

"Jealousy's not a good look on you," Maddie teased.

I grinned, not wanting to show where my head went with that phrase. I scanned the crowd for Rob, but only saw a few Outlaws sauntering in, getting high fives and cheers from all directions. I didn't need to be on the lookout. Ranchmans was going to flip its lid when Rob arrived. He'd scored the winning goal—making the score three to two—in the last minute of the third. The hits he'd taken only bonded the fans, and by the time the game ended, I wondered if the visiting team would get jumped in the parking lot.

Maddie's head snapped toward us as she swivelled on her chair and hunched her shoulders. "He's here."

"What?" Crystal squeaked, craning her head.

"*No!* Don't look!" Maddie hissed.

I couldn't help myself. I peered over her shoulder and caught sight of her taboo crush. He was tall, athletic build. He had wavy, dirty blond hair and— "Dude, he has a moustache."

Maddie wrinkled her nose. "Yeah. I don't know how I feel about that."

"It's kind of hot," Crystal whispered, and Maddie smacked her arm.

"How much older is he than you?" I asked, reaching for a chip.

Maddie exhaled, still trying to make herself invisible, which was impossible. Her hair alone took up two of my facial footprints. "My mom married his dad when I was thirteen. Total Brady Bunch fail. He's four years older than me and back then . . ." She sighed. "I don't know. He was just crazy cool. The girls at school, all my friends, were obsessed with him. There was this rumour that he slept with our biology teacher."

"What?" I hissed, and Maddie nearly spit out her water in her rush to clarify.

"Like *after* he graduated. But he was out of the house by then."

Crystal frowned. "He moved out before he finished high school?"

Maddie nodded. "He had some big blow-up with his dad. I never saw him after that. My mom and his dad split by the time I left."

"Geez." Crystal swooped her hand through her hair, knocking it to one side, making her look like a rock star. She leaned in. "Are you going to go talk to him?"

"Hell, no!" Maddie's eyes popped out of her head. "He probably doesn't even remember me."

I scoffed. "What, you don't look the same as you did at thirteen?"

She shot me a look. "I didn't have boobs at thirteen. I was basically a stick figure with an afro."

Crystal snorted. "Babe, I've seen pictures of you in high school. You were spicy."

Maddie rolled her eyes, then turned to me. "Okay. I'm stress sweating. Back to you."

"Nope, I'm good talking about your step brother fixation." I pursed my lips.

Crystal shook her head. "Not getting off that easy. How did Rob know where to find you?"

That was a fantastic question. One Rob hadn't given me the answer to. "Logan asked him to look after me. I think he was waiting up." My conversation with Logan could've explained all of Rob's behaviour. His checking in on me, him washing my water bottle. But I couldn't stop picking at the way Logan had responded about that. Logan definitely hadn't asked Rob to take me under his wing *before* he left. Why would Rob have been doing that for me? Especially when every damn word out of his mouth was a jab?

Before Maddie and Crystal could comment, the bar erupted. Rob had finally arrived, hands shoved in his pockets as he shouldered through the crowd. My heart launched itself into my throat.

He had a bruise blooming over his right cheekbone. A cut on his eyebrow. A swollen lip. *My fault.*

He nodded to his cheering teammates, waved a hand in gratitude for the fans all crowding in to clap him on the back, then slid onto a chair, his shoulders tense. *You're not my boyfriend.*

The memory of those words soured my stomach. I groaned, dropping my chin into my hands. "I was such a jerk to him."

Crystal leaned in. "When? Last night?"

I nodded. "I was shaken up, and he was all riled up. Treating me like a child. He basically told me I had to hold his hand while I crossed the street."

Maddie smirked. "I wouldn't mind holding his hand."

"Not the point!"

Crystal considered this. "I guess I don't get what the big deal is. He was worried about you."

"Rob?" I shot her a look. "Do you even remember everything he said to me since I moved in? This wasn't worry. He thinks I'm a ditz. Like I'm incapable of taking care of myself. Or Logan, which—"

"Ladies! Why are you hiding back here?" Axel swooped in, throwing his arms over Maddie and Crystal's shoulders.

Crystal laughed and leaned into him. "Just giving you an extra challenge."

"Accepted." He nodded like he was accepting a secret mission. "Since I've hopefully passed your test, I'd like to extend an invitation. As you can see, our boy Rob feels a tad bit like shit." He gestured behind him. "His head isn't loving the noise and neon signs in this joint. We're going to take this party to my apartment and would be honoured if you'd join us."

Maddie eyed him. "What are we going to do at said apartment?"

Axel bowed slightly. "So happy you asked. My roommates and I recently procured a thrift store foosball table which we smuggled into the basement. Nick got the code from the building manager. I think he had to trade a pair of your under-wear, but—"

Maddie laughed out loud and slapped a hand on his chest. "I didn't sleep with Nick! Is he still telling people that?"

Axel pulled his arm off Crystal's shoulder and put his hand over his heart. "Just grateful for your contribution." Maddie swiped for his hair, and he dodged, grinning from ear to ear. "So that's a yes?"

Crystal was already shrugging on her jacket. "Let the games begin."

Maddie hesitated, sneaking another glance at her stepbrother.

I squeezed her hand. "You sure?" I asked quietly. "We can stay if you want."

She drew a deep breath. "No, let's go."

They both handed me cash, and I tracked down our server to settle our bill, then the three of us followed Axel, Bear, and Nick outside. Where Rob was standing next to a friend as he smoked a cigarette.

Blood rushed to my middle as they both fell into step with us. Rob was coming. Of course he was coming. He, Axel, and Logan were close. The whole Outlaws team was like a brotherhood, but those three were inseparable.

I tried to act normal on the walk to Axel's apartment on the other side of campus, but my mind felt like a shaken kaleidoscope. Rob didn't say hello. Didn't turn to look at me or acknowledge my existence. Though, that could've been on account of his bruised face and hands.

I shuddered, thinking about the game. I ached for him, though I knew I couldn't say anything. I'd made that mistake with Logan, and I didn't have an excuse for worrying over Rob.

As we climbed the steps to their building, the bass thumping from one of the first-floor flats vibrated the soles of my sneakers. We walked into the entry and took the stairs to the second floor.

Rory Harmon, a stocky redheaded defender, jumped off the couch with a whoop of delight when he saw us. "Eyy, you brought ladies!" He ruffled my hair as we pushed past him into the packed living room. Apparently, half the team hadn't made it to Ranchmans.

I ducked away with a laugh, and Axel shoved him. "Hands off, bud, or Logan'll whoop your ass."

My eyes flicked up, locking with Rob's. I quickly glanced away, my cheeks flushing, and Rory handed me a plastic cup with some kind of concoction. He bumped his cup against it. "Here's to almost finals week."

I laughed. "Why are we toasting that?"

He grinned as if to say *I toast everything, remember?* Then whooped and headed toward the door. "We ain't staying here, so don't get comfy." He pulled the door wide and motioned for us to walk out into the hall.

He led the whole slew of us to the stairwell. We followed him through the heavy metal door like baby ducks, our voices echoing off the concrete.

"This is the day," Crystal murmured.

"When Axel and Rory use us as human sacrifices?" Maddie grabbed onto the railing when she almost missed a step. Crystal and I died laughing.

"Geez, you're going to make me spill!" Crystal held her cup over her head.

I snorted. "Because that will make you more stable."

We finally made it to the basement, and Rory charged over to where Mark was setting up the foosball table, a battered old thing that looked like it had seen its share of teenage brawls.

"First match." Crystal cracked her knuckles, stepping up next to me. "You and me, babe. Let's show 'em how it's done."

"Not me?" Maddie frowned.

Crystal put a hand on her shoulder. "You're smart. You can't have all the skills."

I grinned and joined her at one end of the table, flicking the goal counters on their metal rod. "What do you say? Girls against boys?"

Axel puffed out his chest. "A challenge has been issued!"

Mark exhaled. "The path of the righteous man is beset on all sides."

I rolled my eyes at the dramatic Pulp Fiction quote and took up a position on the goalie and defender bars. "You care if I take these?"

Crystal shook her head. "Please. I want striker."

Maddie perched on the arm of a threadbare couch to cheer us on, safely away from the rowdy group of guys already arguing over who got to face the winners.

Rory dropped the ball, and the rest of the room, besides my handles and spinning men, ceased to exist.

Axel flicked his wrists like his life depended on it. "Mark, cover the midfield! You're letting them penetrate."

Mark snorted. "They can penetrate me anytime."

Crystal smirked. "I hope you like it deep."

Maddie made a sound in her throat. "Crystal! Gross!"

"What! They started it!" Crystal missed a ball and swore under her breath.

"All part of my master plan." Axel clenched his teeth in concentration. "Just distract them with innuendo and—"

"Yes!" Mark's arms shot up as the ball dropped into our goal.

I pulled the ball out of the box and set it at the entry slide. "Don't get comfy."

We battled it out, trading goals until Crystal whipped one into their goal, putting us at ten to nine. "Suck it!" Crystal laughed in their faces, and Axel didn't seem to mind. If I were to hazard a guess, based on the way he was watching Crystal, he would've been happy to lose again and again to get that kind of reaction out of her.

"Alright, alright," Rory called out, shouldering his way to the table with a cocky grin. "My turn to defend the house's honour."

He turned to scan the room, eyes alighting on Rob lurking in the corner, nursing a beer. "Thompson!" he barked. "Get your ass over here and help me school these girls."

For a moment, Rob looked like he might refuse, his expression darkening. But then he shrugged, putting something in his pocket and sauntering over with a smirk that looked more practiced than indicative of any real emotion.

"You get a page or something?" Rory asked. Rob nodded. "Who from?"

He wet his lips. "It only gives a number. It's not like you can send a novel."

"You're not going to call it?" Rory's eyes widened.

Maddie leaned in. "You have a pager?"

Rob shrugged. "Yes I have a pager, and no. I don't recognize the number."

"Can I see it?" Maddie held out her hand as if she couldn't imagine a world where a guy wouldn't just hand something over to her because she asked.

Rob solidified that theory. He reached into his pocket and pulled out a beeper with the footprint of a debit card. Maddie plucked it from his hands and pressed a button to make the display light up.

She grinned. "What's your number?"

Rob opened his mouth, but Rory was faster. "403-772-7272."

I gave him a look. "Who'd you bribe to get that number?"

Rob didn't answer, just wrapped his fingers around the handles as Maddie took his pager with her back to the couch. His knuckles were already scabbing. New bruises bloomed over the green-tinged ones. The image of him screaming past me and knocking that guy to the ground was cued up and ready to roll.

My chest settled like someone had draped a heated blanket over me. Safe. A word I never would've thought to use with Rob Thompson, but there it was. I felt safe with him. He had protected me. Thrown himself in harm's way. I'd tried to protect a hunk of bronze, and Rob . . . He'd run out into the November night in a T-shirt and punched the hell out of a hockey player. For me.

"Ready?" Rory scanned our faces. Rob grunted. Crystal nodded and tucked her hair behind her ear. I stared a little too hard at the plastic uni-footed men in front of me to keep my eyes from wandering over Rob's hands a second time. Or possibly migrating up his forearms to the place where his T-shirt sleeve bisected his biceps.

And then we were off, the ball ricocheting between us like a tiny missile. Rob played hard and fast with sharp angles and vicious spins that sent me scrambling.

"Did you bring in a ringer?" Crystal teased when Rob scored first.

Rory winked. "Rob comes over every night to practice. We've been planning this for weeks."

I laughed and chanced a glance up at Rob. Nothing. He looked anywhere else but not at my face. Crystal dropped the ball in, and we continued on, shrieking and cursing our way to fives. Maddie, Mark, Nick, Axel, and a few of the other guys stood behind us, far enough not to get elbowed but close enough they could commentate on the game and shit talk.

"Weak!" Mark cupped his hand to his mouth since we definitely couldn't hear him from a foot away.

"You girls need to get the ball on *this* side of the table. Rob's getting all the action," Rory teased.

"Heeey, just like in real life." Axel held up a hand, and Rob reached up to slap it.

"Oh yeah?" I blurted before I could stop myself. Maddie passed me my cup and I took a drink.

Rob finally looked up, meeting my eyes. "You know me. Out every night."

I pursed my lips. So. I hadn't lived that down. "You always go to their house?"

Rob raised an eyebrow. "You wouldn't know if I brought them home. You and Logan are always spirited away in your bedroom."

I scoffed. "We are not."

He reached back to the window sill where he'd set his beer and took a swig. "That's how Logan likes it, so that's what Logan gets."

My insides twisted. "It's what I like."

Rob set the bottle back on the sill. "Ah. Right. Thrilling."

The Outlaws laughed, and my cheeks flushed. I clenched my jaw. "It just takes time when a man can last more than thirty seconds."

Rory clutched his chest, throwing his head back and laughing, but I was locked on Rob. His eyes hardened, and his shoulders tensed. "Without mentioning himself? Absolutely."

My eyes flashed. What exactly was he trying to accomplish? He acted like he hadn't cradled me in his arms in my bed or broken the skin on his knuckles because a douchebag grabbed my wrist.

A thought crashed over me, fanning across my skin. What if he would do that for anyone? What if I just happened to be the girl having a panic attack, the girl who was stupid enough to walk across campus alone after dark?

"I have to go." I let go of the handles and stepped back. Maddie frowned, standing from the couch.

Crystal might have been following, but I wasn't sure. I was so sick to my stomach, my vision blurred.

I wanted to be special to Rob. Part of me, not so deep down anymore it seemed, wanted him to notice me. To care enough to hold, to protect, *because* it was me. Not just some girl.

And the fact that I wanted that—that I hoped for it—made me a despicable human being.

I was dating Logan. I shouldn't give a damn what his roommate thought of me or whether he noticed that I'd worn my tight jeans today or that my underwear was still sitting in the dryer.

"What's wrong?" Maddie grabbed her purse and followed me to the door.

"Can I stay at your place tonight?" I asked, reaching out for the door handle.

She frowned. "Yeah, but—"

"Thanks." I pulled the door open and strode toward the stairs.

CHAPTER
Fourteen

I STRETCHED out on Maddie's bed, trying not to take up too much space. She'd been kind enough to drive me home to pick up my toiletries, my violin, and my music so I wouldn't have to go home until Sunday night.

"Are you a messy sleeper?" Maddie hopped in next to me, flicking off her lamp and pulling the covers over herself. Her sheets were soft cotton. Clean and crisp despite the fact that she didn't know she'd be having company.

"Messy? I don't pee the bed, if that's what you're wondering."

Maddie laughed. "No. I mean, are the covers all messed up and twisted when you wake up?"

I shook my head. "Nope. It pretty much looks the same as when I went to bed, besides a body imprint on the mattress."

Maddie turned to face me, propping her head on her hand. She paused for a moment, then said, "I told you, you can stay here as long as you want."

"You offered before you even knew if I was going to kick you in the middle of the night."

She sighed. "That's true friendship right there." She dropped her head on the pillow. "Are you going to tell me what prompted this?"

I chewed on my lower lip. "I thought it would be a good weekend for a sleepover." I knew that wasn't going to cut it, but any other explanation wouldn't move from my brain to my lips. *Oh, well, I've been wanting to touch Rob's abs lately, so I thought it was time for a break.*

Maddie raised an eyebrow. "Did something happen with Rob?"

I blew out a breath and tucked my hand behind my head. "No." *Yes. Absolutely, yes.* "I don't know what's wrong with me. I think I'm just really missing Logan." I stared up at the ceiling, at the thin stripes of light pushing through the blinds on her window.

"Okay, let's break that down. Are you missing talking with Logan, being with Logan . . . or are you just missing sex with Logan?"

I laughed out loud. Had Maddie just asked that? Sex wasn't a taboo topic in our trio, but it was typically Crystal who brought it up. "All of the above?" It was what I was supposed to say. Part of it was true. I did miss those things, but being without him was making me more and more aware that there may be a dark underbelly to each point that I didn't want to face.

Did I miss being with Logan, or did I miss him wanting to be with me? Did I miss talking with Logan, or did I miss him needing to talk with me? Did I miss sex with Logan, or did I miss the way he looked at me? The way he desired me? How sure he was that I would be the one to make him feel good?

My heart started to race, a pit opening up inside of me.

"How is sex with Logan?" Maddie's voice was softer, more tentative.

I turned to face her, even though I could barely see the outline of her curls in the dark. "What do you mean?"

She let out a breath. "Okay, I know we joke about sex all the time, but honestly, I don't get what all the fuss is about."

My ears perked up. Talking about Maddie's sex life sounded

like way more fun than anything swirling in my brain at the moment. "Tell me more."

Maddie gave a nervous laugh. "You know I dated that guy, Colin? Right before you and Logan got together?"

"Yeah, I remember." How could I not remember? Maddie told us that he was her first. "You said it was great. I remember being a little bit jealous."

Maddie groaned. "It was *not* great. At least, not what I think 'great' is supposed to be." She rolled onto her back, dropping her hands next to her sides. "How are we even supposed to know what great is? I mean, I read a few articles in Cosmopolitan and all of those women sounded like they freaking loved it. That it was the best experience of their lives. They listed all those hot things their boyfriends like to do—"

"Oh, yeah. I'm pretty sure we read the same article."

"Well, that is not what Colin did."

I pushed up, propping myself on my arm. "Umm, what did he do?"

"Like—" she paused, searching for the words. "I don't know, thirty seconds of thrusting?"

I groaned and fell back to the bed. "Yikes."

"That's not what it's supposed to be, right?" Maddie sounded so hopeful it made my heart hurt.

"Definitely not."

Maddie shifted to her side. "You don't have to tell me what Logan does if you don't want to. But I'm just wondering what I should say next time. How do you even bring that up? For me and Colin, there was, like, no talking. He just did his thing."

I snorted. "Yeah, that's pretty much how it was with Logan at first, too."

"Was?"

"I mean, we've talked about some things . . . not everything." Maddie was being so open with me, but she wasn't with Colin anymore. I didn't want to say anything that would paint Logan in a bad light.

"Because you don't want to talk to him or because he doesn't want to hear it?" Maddie asked.

I ran a hand through my hair. "I'm pretty sure this one's on me. I feel too nervous."

"Yes, exactly. Like, what is he going to do if I tell him that's not what feels good?"

"Oh my gosh. Seriously."

Maddie sat up, gesticulating with her hands. "He was, like, jamming his thumb down there. Like kneading bread dough or something. I felt like he was either tenderizing meat or doing an autopsy."

That made me laugh so hard, I got the hiccups.

Maddie continued. "At least I knew what an orgasm was supposed to sound like because of When Harry Met Sally, so I just did that."

I gasped for air. "You did that exactly like her?"

Maddie chortled. "I mean, as close as I could manage. I just wanted him to stop."

I wiped tears from my eyes. "Oh my gosh, Maddie. I'm so sorry. Logan has never been that bad." I clutched my stomach, dragging air into my lungs.

Maddie flopped back down to her pillow. "So you actually, you know . . . get there?"

I sighed. "I know *how* to get there. I don't necessarily get there with Logan." The admission popped out of me. "Not because of him," I amended. "I think that's a me problem."

"Why is it a 'you' problem? Isn't it his job to figure it out?"

I pondered that a moment, wondering how much I wanted to share. "There are some things that happened when I was a kid, and now it's really hard for me to just relax."

Maddie let out a slow breath. It didn't take her long to connect the dots. When a female friend says "some things that happened," we all know what that means, even if we don't have the details. "Oh, Sharla. I'm so sorry."

"No, it's fine." It wasn't fine. It was very not fine. "It was a long time ago. It's just I haven't quite figured that out yet, which is why I don't talk to Logan about it because I don't even know what I want or how my body should work. You know?"

We lay there in silence for a moment, thinking.

"I want to know what good sex is like," Maddie said finally.

I didn't answer because the words I wanted to say lodged in my throat. *Maybe it happens when you can talk about anything.* Logan and I were supposed to have that. But clearly, there were a lot of things I wasn't saying.

"It'll happen." I reached out and rubbed her shoulder, then turned toward the wall and pretended to settle in for sleep.

———

On Sunday, I trudged through the slushy snow, violin case in hand, toward the arts centre. The glass and steel structure looked cold and uninviting against the grey November sky. I stepped into the quiet lobby, my footsteps echoing on the polished concrete floor, and waved to a couple of violinists I recognized in the hallway as I made my way downstairs to the practice rooms.

Having time away from the house and Rob was a good thing. Especially since all I could think about since our conversation was sex. The not having it. The wondering if I was too broken to ever make it good.

I emailed Logan, telling him everything I missed about him and informing him I'd be at Maddie's for the weekend. It was a bit over the top and more than once, I'd checked to see if there was any way to take it back and rewrite my message. Hopefully he wouldn't look at it in public.

Inside the cramped room, I unpacked my violin, tightened the bow, and began slowly warming up with scales. The motions were familiar and comforting, like slipping on a favourite old sweatshirt. I flipped through some sheet music I hadn't played in ages, pieces from high school that used to be my go-to's when I needed an escape. My eyes landed on Tchaikovsky's Violin Concerto in D Major. A rush of memories washed over me.

Ms. Petrova, my violin teacher back then, had insisted I learn it, even though it was far above my skill level at the time. "This piece has fire and passion," she'd said in her thick Russian accent. "Like you. You will grow into it." I'd rolled my eyes but was so secretly flattered, I practiced for months, determined to master the challenging techniques and lightning-fast passages.

Now, as I started the familiar opening melody, the notes danced off the strings, my fingers finding the positions like no time had passed. Pieces like this were my personal rubric. Time stamps to judge my skill by. I'd improved so much, and it was good to remember that when I was surrounded by musicians who I felt far exceeded my level of musicianship.

I thought I would only play one section, but I couldn't stop. The music dragged me along, its hand fisted in my shirt, drowning me in memories. As I launched into the frenetic, emotional second movement, something cracked open inside me.

This song. I'd forgotten. I'd started it before *that summer.* The emotions I'd stuffed down at Maddie's the night before resurfaced with a vengeance. Hot tears pricked my eyes, then blurred my vision so completely, I couldn't see the notes.

Fragments of those awful nights at my Grandma's house flickered through my mind—the sound of the door creaking open, the shadow crossing the floor, my cousin's heavy breathing. His hand sliding into my underwear. I squeezed my eyes shut out of habit, trying to block it out, but the music wouldn't let me. It opened a door I refused to, and suddenly I was caught in the torrent of memory.

How I'd tried to tell my doctor what happened weeks afterward when the nightmares and panic attacks got too bad to hide.

She referred me to a therapist who insisted on looping in my parents.

That excruciating conversation was seared into my brain. Stuttering out the terrible details to my mom and dad. Their shocked faces. The way doubt and pity crept into their expressions.

I did my best to package it away, throw myself into violin and school and pretend to be the old Sharla. But there were cracks then. Just like there were now. After all my patching, they still showed.

Logan being gone exposed them more than usual. I hated sleeping alone. Hated how insecure I felt, always wondering if he was thinking about me. Or if he wished he had a girlfriend who was more . . . free. Who could be one of those women in Cosmopolitan. More go with the flow. More like him.

I couldn't hold it in any longer. Any of it. The fear, the worry, the guilt, the aching loneliness, the shame of being so pathetically attached, and the overwhelm of keeping up appearances like everything was fine. Would I ever feel whole? Or at least less broken?

I played something brand new. Notes that made no musical sense, that didn't follow a melody. I let the grief and anger pour out through my fingers and bow, filling the small room with heartwrenching strains and the sound of my own choked breaths and sniffles.

When my arms ached, and the tears ran dry, I ended in an inelegant screech as I lifted the bow with a shaking hand. I took a few deep breaths, trying to regain my composure.

Well. That was . . . something I'd never done before. I wiped my face with my sleeve. Maybe that was what it meant to be a true artist. To have something inside of you that was so massive, the only way to let it out, to describe it or communicate it, was through music.

I laughed at myself. How melodramatic. If the orchestra thing didn't work out, maybe I had a future doing poetry readings or posing on MySpace. I carefully packed up my instrument, feeling raw and wrung out but lighter. Like I'd released a pressure valve, just a little.

As I emerged from the practice room, I nearly collided with Caleb.

"Whoa, girl!" He grinned, then eyed my blotchy face with concern. "You okay?"

"Yeah, no, I'm good," I lied, averting my gaze.

Caleb held up a hand for a high five. "Music, amiright?"

I laughed. And this was what it was like to have artist friends. They understood parts of your brain that nobody else did. I gave him a one-armed hug instead of a hand slap. "You practicing?"

He glanced down the hall. "Nope. Just picking up chicks."

I snorted. "Sorry, I'm probably ruining your opportunities."

"I wasn't going to say anything, but . . ." He gave me a look, then smiled. "You could be my wingwoman."

"What would that look like?"

"Uh, basically asking me pre-approved questions so I can answer loudly and impress anyone who walks by."

"Hmm. As fun as that sounds . . . "

He ran a hand through his red hair. "You don't happen to have a kitten or a baby I could borrow?"

I nudged his arm. "See you tomorrow?"

"Yup." He tried to ruffle my hair, but I stepped away too quickly. What was it with guys wanting to touch my hair now that it was short?

"Bye!" I waved and walked down the hall, my mind already hovering over the worries I'd tried to exorcise through music. The best way I could describe it was that I was higher up. Not drowning, but not fully escaping them either.

As I walked across the chilly campus back to the house, I wondered about him. Not Logan. Him. My cousin who was two years older than me. Who I had to see at family reunions in the summer.

I never stayed overnight where he was, but his family only lived a few hours away. Thank the heavens he wasn't at home anymore. I didn't actually give a shit where he was or what he was doing, but I did wonder sometimes. Wishing I would've done more. Said more. Forced my parents to do something other than tell me it would be okay.

The walk home seemed to take forever, my mind replaying the devastating memories on a sickening loop. When I finally reached the house, Rob's door was firmly shut. A huge relief. I couldn't even imagine trying to act normal around him right now. Hopefully he'd already used the washroom. *When was that part coming in?*

In the kitchen, I made myself a sandwich and retreated to my room. I ate mechanically, not tasting a thing, then curled up under the covers without even changing out of my clothes.

I stared ahead at the dark wall, chewing my lip. Being back in my bed—our bed—peeled back another layer from my thoughts. Those cracks in my armour were more visible with Logan gone . . . and Rob had seen them.

Had Logan?

I'd never told him what happened. He'd never asked. Even when he felt me flinch away or when I had to take time to breathe. I gave him the basics.

Rob had straight up asked in the kitchen.

I lied to him.

But he asked.

CHAPTER
Fifteen

AS I SIPPED my morning coffee, I waited for the internet to connect. I finished my oatmeal by the time my inbox opened. No messages from Logan.

It stung less than usual, and that only slathered on another layer of worry. I was losing it. I'd been on my own for three weeks, and I was going bat-shit crazy.

I filled my clean water bottle, grabbed my violin, and headed out to rehearsal. It was fine. I wasn't going to implode my life because of some momentary psychological crisis.

I *could* open up to Logan, couldn't I? Maybe that was why I needed to go through all of this. So I could figure out why I was holding us back.

The familiar smell of old wood and sheet music filled my nose as I entered the hall. Lily waved at me from her spot, her usual perky self. "How was your weekend?"

I plastered on a smile. "I spent it with Maddie."

Caleb scoffed. "You're not going to even mention our moment in the practice hall?"

"Ah, yes. Caleb and I had an intense conversation about picking up women outside my practice room."

"Way to out me," he muttered.

Lily told me about a new-to-her restaurant downtown as we rosined our bows and tuned our instruments. For a minute, I almost felt normal. Then, as Ms. Franck strode to the podium and raised her baton, I focused on the one thing I currently had control over.

As we launched into a sprightly rendition of "Sleigh Ride," I let muscle memory take over, my fingers dancing across the fingerboard. Franck stopped us halfway through and took a moment to correct the woodwinds.

Caleb leaned over. "Another Nintendo night this week?"

I blinked. Right. Nintendo. We'd done that together. My walk home had almost completely erased the fun earlier that night. Rob showing up out of nowhere. His hands on my shoulders. *I swear, if he touched you, I'll kill him, Shar.*

I shivered. "Hmm. Yeah. Maybe not this week, but raincheck?" Caleb looked satisfied with that response.

While most of the events of that night made me squirm, there was one thing that jumped to my memory. Lily. What had she said on the walk home? Something about fighting for my chance at first chair?

Own it . . . Franck likes people who know what they want.

The rest of the hour passed in a blur of Christmas carols. As the final notes of "Silent Night" faded away, my hands grew clammy. Own it? How the hell was I supposed to own it? It would've been nice if Lily gave me some sort of instruction manual.

My heart battered against my ribcage, and I jumped up from my chair before I knew what I was going to do next. Ms. Franck cut an imposing figure as she gathered her scores with her severe black bob and sharp features.

Squaring my shoulders, I marched up to the podium before I could lose my nerve. "Ms. Franck?" My voice came out embarrassingly squeaky. I cleared my throat and tried again. "I was wondering what I could do to be considered for first chair next year. After Lily graduates."

She looked up, her piercing blue eyes seeming to see straight through me. "Ah." She took me in, appraising. "I appreciate your initiative." She reached into her briefcase and pulled out a black folder, opened it, then licked her finger and scrolled through the papers inside. "Here. Prepare this and play for me on Wednesday. Eight-fifteen on stage."

Relief crashed over me in a wave. I took the paper from her. "Okay. Perfect, thank you."

I practically floated back to my seat and packed up my violin with shaking hands. Caleb and Lily were waiting for me by the door, twin expressions of curiosity on their faces.

"What was that about?" Caleb asked as we made our way to the open study area.

I couldn't keep the grin off my face. "I asked Ms. Franck what I could do to be considered for first chair next year."

Lily's eyes widened. "It's about time." She pulled me into a quick hug, her lavender perfume enveloping me. "Did she give you anything?"

I nodded, showing her the score. Lily grinned. "I played the same thing. It's tough. I think she likes it because of these intervals at the end."

We claimed our usual spot, a cluster of overstuffed armchairs tucked into a corner. I pulled out my music theory homework, determined to focus despite the butterflies in my stomach. I was just getting into the groove, scribbling away at chord progressions when a shock of pink near the entrance made me look up.

"There she is!" Crystal's hair was like a beacon as she zeroed in on me. She and Maddie rushed over.

"Shar, we need to go. Now." Crystal's smile was manic.

I blinked at them, confused. "What? Why? Is everything okay?"

"No time to explain." Crystal grabbed my arm, hauling me to my feet. "Just trust us, okay?"

Bewildered, I shoved my papers into my backpack, barely zipping it closed before they were dragging me toward the door.

Outside, crystalline flakes drifted from the steely sky, dusting the campus like powdered sugar.

"Crystal, what—"

"Shh, I have the most amazing surprise!" Crystal cut me off, bouncing on her toes. "You guys are going to die!"

"Dead." Maddie mimed a stake to the heart. "Spit it out before we freeze to death out here."

"Okay, okay, so you know my roommate Jenna? Her friend works at that beauty school a few blocks from South Campus, and they had a bunch of cancellations. Guess who scored us free facials for the next hour and a half?" Crystal sing-songed.

"Shut up!" I squealed. Spa treatments were not in my budget, so this felt like an early Christmas.

"Yes, please." Maddie beamed at her.

We rushed along the sidewalk, the towers of South Campus rising around us—stately brick buildings that had been standing there since before our parents were born. I had class later, but for now, all thoughts of school flitted away, replaced by visions of creamy masks and aromatherapy. Maybe this is just what I needed. To be a little irresponsible. I still had tonight and all day tomorrow to prepare for Wednesday.

Crystal tugged her coat tighter around her as we walked, her breath puffing in frosty clouds. "I can't wait to be done with finals. Just a few more days and then it's nothing but powdery slopes and hot cocoa."

I laughed. "You're starting to sound like a travel commercial."

"Hey, my parents booked the chalet," she shot back with a grin. "Fireplace, mountain views . . . it's basically a movie waiting to happen."

"Maybe you'll meet a handsome guy on ski patrol," Maddie said in a husky voice. "I'll be soaking up the sun in Hawaii while you're freezing on the slopes. No snow gear required."

Crystal gasped in mock outrage. "Yeah, Shar, you think I'm living a dream?" She turned to Maddie. "You better send me a postcard—or at least the ass of a hot surfer."

"His actual ass?" Maddie grinned.

"A picture!" Crystal said over her.

I snorted. "Well, I know you're both jealous that I'll be at home. Just me, my cat, my sister and parents. Lots of Blockbuster visits for cheesy romcoms."

"That sounds kind of amazing," Maddie admitted. "No airports, no schedules. Just peace and quiet."

"Parental judgement, childhood bedrooms," I deadpanned. "I'm going to bake cookies, wear fuzzy socks, and ignore humanity for two solid weeks."

Crystal smirked. "Careful, you might relax too much and forget how to be stressed."

"One can only hope."

———

The spa smelled like flowers and teenage sleepovers, that mix of nail polish and hair products. This was a school, so there weren't cushy arm chairs and fluffy towels, but we didn't care in the least. Factory line facials? As Maddie said, yes, please.

Crystal found Jenna, and they ushered us in. We settled onto massage tables next to each other and were treated to steaming towels around our necks as slow Zen chords played from the speakers. The aesthetician cleansed my face with a solution on a cotton pad, then slathered a cool mask over my face, tingly and soothing all at once.

The calm seeped down to my bones, languid and soft as honey. If only I could bottle this feeling and carry it with me. But for now, I let myself drift. Let the eucalyptus-scented steam blur the edges of my worries until they floated up and away.

The mask hardened, making me feel like my skin was going to crack, and as the aesthetician wiped it away, I felt shiny and new. She prompted me to sit, and I turned to find that Crystal and Maddie looked dewy and content.

"I'm the best, right?" Crystal held out her hands, and Maddie and I nodded our approval.

We floated out of the spa on a cloud of bliss and walked back to the north side of campus. After thanking Crystal profusely, I detoured to the cafeteria, snagging a slightly wilted salad that had seen better days and an iced tea. I ate quickly, then headed across the square. The library beckoned. I needed to study past quizzes before my music harmony free write.

But first, email. The computers glowed in invitation, and I plopped down at a free one, the plasticky seat squealing in protest. I jabbed at the power button, drumming my fingers as the screen flickered to life, and I signed in with my student ID.

I blinked at Logan's name at the top of my inbox, the subject line screaming, "YOU WON'T BELIEVE THIS!"

I clicked.

Sharla holy shit you'll never guess who I just met at training camp only JARED HALL, can you believe? He's like a literal legend scouts are basically drooling over him says he might put in a good word for me with some of his NHL buddies if I keep killing it out here not to brag but coach says I'm 'really impressing' him with my work ethic and natural talent so ya know not to big of a deal or anything

I pieced together the sentences despite his lack of punctuation and grinned from ear to ear. That was amazing news, and I was so proud of him. He'd worked his ass off to get here, and if anyone deserved a shot at the big leagues, it was him.

That's incredible! SO happy for you, babe!

My fingers hovered over the keys. What next? More gushing? That was what he would want, undoubtedly. And what else could I say, really?

Over here things are pretty same old same old. I'm still hunting down first chair in the orchestra, ooh! And I'm on the verge of a mental breakdown. I almost got assaulted in the square and Rob came to my rescue. Also, funny story, I thought you were washing my water bottle for me these past months but it was actually him. For no reason. He held me one night when I was having a panic attack, and now I can't stop thinking about that either, especially since I haven't ever let you do something like that. I spent the weekend with my friend so I didn't have to look him in the eyes. Phew! Looks like we're both having a great week!

I stared at the screen, hypnotized by my blinking cursor. My fingers started typing.

I knew you'd take the hockey world by storm! I'll be cheering you on from home! Keep sending me updates!

So. Many. Exclamation points.

I hit send, hoping the swooping in my stomach was because of the questionable salad.

An hour later, I emerged from the library in a daze, chords and intervals swirling in my head. I attended my class, finished my free write early, and made my way back to the townhouse on autopilot, ready to collapse into bed and not think for the next twelve hours.

But when I swung the door open, I froze. There was Rob,

lounging on the couch like some kind of off-duty model, his hair all artfully tousled.

Right. Exactly what I'd been actively avoiding.

He glanced up as I walked in, lips twitching. "You're not dead."

I rolled my eyes, ignoring the traitorous flutter in my stomach. "Disappointed?"

Rob didn't move, just watched me as I took off my shoes and hung my coat. "You stayed with Maddie all weekend?"

I pretended to fix something on my bag. "Yeah. Did you guys have a game?" I knew they didn't, but I couldn't think of anything else to say, and it felt important to make him think I wasn't thinking about him or his team all weekend. Since the opposite was most definitely true.

I glanced up as I passed through the kitchen and living area. How, in one split second, did my brain register the way his t-shirt clung to his shoulders and the sinewy muscles of his forearms as he gripped the TV remote?

I nodded once and escaped to my room before I could do something idiotic like run my fingers through that perfect mess of hair or trace the angle of his jawline with my tongue. I wouldn't do it. But the fact that it crossed my mind sent my heart into palpitations.

Violin. That's what I needed. It was only seven, so the neighbors wouldn't get pissy if I played. I reached for my case and—

Wait. Where was my case? I always left it tucked into the corner, but now there was only empty space staring back at me.

Daaamn it. Normally I brought my violin home in the afternoon before class, so it hadn't even registered that I didn't have it.

I backtracked, retracing my day and landed on my answer. Crystal dragging me and Maddie out of the arts center, giddy with excitement over our impromptu spa day. I'd been so distracted that I must have left my violin under the table.

Panic propelled me out of my room and into the kitchen. Rob

stood at the counter making a cup of coffee. Work. Right. He was about to head out for his night shift.

"Hey." He leaned against the counter, his brow furrowing. He didn't have to ask what was wrong, his concern was written all over his face.

I ignored the flutter in my stomach. "My violin. I left it at the arts center, and I need it for my audition on Wednesday."

His jaw worked. "The building's closed."

I'd been preparing to explain that fact. "There's not a show tonight." I paced, rubbing my temples. "I could go over. Maybe there's someone—" I turned back to him. "On the janitorial staff."

This wasn't literal life or death. I knew that. I had tomorrow to practice, but I also understood that brains synthesized music better overnight. If I only had one day, I wouldn't feel as prepared. That felt like enough of an emergency to me.

Rob wet his lips, his thumb dragging over the counter's edge. "I'm assigned to the GRB."

The science building. "But you have a key?"

"I do."

My heart sped in my chest. "But?" His eyes flicked down, then back up to mine. "Rob—"

"Help me with my shift." His jaw ticked, his hand now clenching the countertop. I opened my mouth and closed it. "I have a conditioning assessment tomorrow and a physics exam. If we work together, we could be done by eleven or so. Then we can go get your violin."

I raised an eyebrow. "Are you blackmailing me?"

He blew out a breath. "I'm . . . asking a favour."

Something in my chest flipped. His shoulders were tight, his breathing quick. Rob was stressed. I'd been so focused on myself when I walked in, I hadn't noticed.

"Yeah, okay. Just let me change."

"Wear something you don't mind getting piss on."

I flipped him off and strode to my bedroom.

CHAPTER
Sixteen

I PULLED on a ratty T-shirt and faded jeans, the uniform of the glamorous janitor's assistant. Rob waited by the door, his foot tapping an annoyed staccato on the tile. He smirked when he saw my expression.

He held the door open, and I swept past him into the frigid night air. It wasn't until we were a block away that I realized I hadn't eaten dinner.

We trekked across the quiet campus, street lamps casting gentle halos on the brick buildings of Douglas. The scent of ginger and soy sauce tickled my nose as we passed a little noodle shop kiddy corner to the bookstore, its neon sign buzzing "open." My hunger pangs grew claws.

"Pit stop," I announced, veering toward the shop. Rob rolled his eyes but followed me inside. I paused. "Is this going to make you late?"

"I'm flexible."

The cramped interior was a steamy cocoon of savoury aromas and clattering dishes. I slid into a booth and ordered a bowl of ramen. It came blessedly quickly, the broth fragrant with star anise and chilli oil. Rob slouched across from me, arms crossed. "You realize this detour is cutting into valuable practice time."

I slurped down noodles. "Hey, I need sustenance to clean all night." I motioned to the counter. "Are you sure you don't want anything?"

Rob fidgeted with a loose thread on his sleeve. "I already ate."

I narrowed my eyes. I hadn't seen any dishes. Another mouthful of rich umami broth. Heaven. "Is school stressful for you this semester?"

He dragged a hand over his jaw. "It's not not stressful. Why?"

I shrugged. "I don't know. You always seem calm. In control."

"We hardly ever cross paths."

I dabbed my chin with my napkin. There was no way to eat this gracefully. "Yeah, well, up until a couple of weeks ago, I thought you wanted me to crawl into a hole and die."

He huffed out a breath, staring at his hands on the table.

I twirled my noodles with my chopsticks. "I heard what you said. When you told Logan I wasn't good for him. What did I do to make you think that?"

Rob considered for a moment. "Not sure what you're talking about."

"In the hall. Outside the rink. When we first started dating."

Rob stiffened. "I didn't know anyone was listening."

"Does that really matter?" I drank broth from my spoon. "I just—you said you didn't hate me. But then you were mean—"

"I wasn't mean."

I looked up, my eyes wide. "You were a total asshole to me. Are you serious?"

A muscle in Rob's jaw flexed. "Can we not talk about this right now?"

I shrugged, not able to hide my annoyance. "I don't know. Will you give me an answer at some point?" I played it off like my heart wasn't jackhammering in my chest.

"Sure."

"For Christmas. It can be my present."

The corner of Rob's mouth lifted. "Who says I was planning to get you anything?"

The pounding of my heart transformed into a flutter. "See? Asshole."

Rob shook his head. "Are you almost done?"

I nodded and pointed at my bowl. "You sure you don't want any?"

"You drooled in that."

My jaw dropped. "I did not drool!"

"You were licking the noodles."

I barked a laugh and lifted my tray, transporting it to the bin of dirty dishes over the trash. I wiped my hands on my soon-to-be piss-covered jeans, then gave him a salute. "Alright. At your service."

Rob reached out and smacked my hand away from my forehead. "You're making a scene."

I sucked in a breath, resisting the urge to grab my hand and feel the skin where he'd touched. Make sure it wasn't on literal fire.

I followed Rob outside and we continued on toward the GRB. When we got to the side door, Rob pulled out his keyring and unlocked it. He held the door open with a mocking bow.

"Now who's making a scene?"

He grunted. "There's nobody here."

"There were, like, two people in the noodle place."

"Huge scene." He led me down a hallway and stopped in front of a door marked 'Janitorial'. "Washrooms first. Hope you're not too delicate for that."

"Dude, you promised piss. Don't get all soft on me now."

He smirked and tossed me a pair of rubber gloves. Armed with mops, buckets, and a truly alarming array of cleaning products, we set to work.

It was every bit as disgusting as I'd feared. Stall by stall, we scrubbed toilets, wiped down sinks, and mopped floors that had seen unspeakable horrors. Rob seemed to be fully enjoying my misery.

"What's the matter, princess? Not used to getting your hands dirty?"

I flicked a sudsy sponge at him, and that earned me a genuine laugh. Rob moved to the next stall. "This is nothing compared to the messes I had to clean growing up. Six siblings in one washroom? That's a warzone."

I paused, arm deep in a toilet bowl. "Six siblings?" How did I not know that about him?

"It had its moments." His voice echoed off the tile.

I realized, with a pang of guilt, that I knew next to nothing about Rob's life outside of the Outlaws. "What about your parents? What do they do?"

"My mom works two jobs. At a local bank during the week and then staff at the hockey arena. My dad's not really in the picture."

"So you come by the asshole stuff honestly." I snapped my mouth shut, about to apologize when Rob laughed out loud. I straightened and walked out of the stall, peering past the door into his. "I was kidding."

He turned, his hair falling over his forehead. He was in a washroom stall. In the science building. Wearing rubber gloves. And still, my heart somersaulted. "I laughed."

"That was rude, though."

He raised an eyebrow. "What are you going to do to apologize?"

My throat grew thick, and I swallowed hard. "I'm already cleaning toilets for you. What else do you want?" My stomach swooped, not hearing how that would sound until it left my lips. "I—sorry, that didn't come out the right way." I turned and nearly smacked into the open door.

I rushed into the next stall, my face burning up. We didn't talk much until the washrooms were clean. I wished I had my

Walkman. A little Ace of Base would've gone a long way as I sprayed down the urinals.

We finished, threw away our gloves, and moved to the classrooms. On the fourth one, I had to break up the monotony of wiping down desks and sweeping floors.

"Why did you move in with Logan?" It seemed like an innocuous enough question until Rob didn't answer right away. I glanced up. He reached high on the chalkboard, his shirt lifting above the waistband of his jeans. I quickly looked away.

"I didn't have a place to live."

I frowned, wiping the table in front of me for the third time. "Like your contract ended?"

"Like I was living in my truck."

My hand froze mid-swipe. I lifted my chin. Rob was watching me, still holding his chalk-covered cloth. "Are you serious?" I asked.

He nodded, walking to the next board.

"How did that happen?" I crossed the aisle and started on the next section, my head starting to pound.

"I had money saved up, but then my truck needed some work done. I did some of it myself, but with the parts and everything, plus I had a lab fee I wasn't expecting. I couldn't pay rent."

"They kicked you out?" I had no idea where he lived before, but I couldn't imagine a landlord forcing someone out for a few missed rent payments.

"No, I left."

I straightened. "You left? Why?"

He turned. "Because I couldn't pay."

I blinked, walking down the steps toward him. "Yeah, but you could've waited until you had the money."

He drew a breath and shook his head. "I wasn't going to live on charity." He walked to our cart of supplies, grabbed a clean cloth, and dunked it in the bucket of warm water. "I got this job. Started to save up. Logan found out after practice and told me to move in. They needed painting done in the house. That was my first month's payment."

I stopped in front of him. "Logan didn't tell me that."

Rob wet his lips. "Probably because I asked him not to."

I watched him. The flick of his dark lashes against his cheeks. The tiny twitches of his lips. "Why?"

He exhaled. "Because it's embarrassing."

I shook my head. "No. It's not."

Rob glanced down at the water dripping over his wrist, then back up at the last chalkboard. "One more."

I nodded, then took my dirty rag to the cart. "You didn't qualify for grants? Or loans?"

Rob reached up again. That time, I didn't look away. "My dad used my name to push off some of his oil royalties in '93 and save on taxes." He wiped the cloth over the slate, leaving perfect, clean streaks across the cloudy board. "On paper, it looks like I'm loaded."

"Will you see any of that money?"

He let out a puff of air. "Not likely." He finished with the top corner, then walked back to the cart.

"I'm sorry. About what I said earlier. I didn't mean it."

Rob dropped his rag in the cart. He adjusted his shirt. "Yeah. I know."

After washing our hands and restocking the cleaning supplies, we crossed the square. It was ten-thirty, and I was starting to feel it. I yawned as Rob slipped his key into the lock on the front doors of the arts centre.

I stepped inside, my footsteps echoing in the empty foyer. The building felt different at night, the familiar spaces transformed into something dark and eerie. The perfect site for a futuristic dystopian novel.

I hurried through the atrium to the open rehearsal space, my heart pounding. But as I approached the table where I'd left my violin, my stomach dropped. It wasn't there.

"No, no, no," I muttered, frantically searching the

surrounding area. "It has to be here."

Rob frowned. "Maybe someone moved it?"

"Who would move it?" I planted my hands on my hips, turning in a circle.

"Let's check the other rooms."

We split up, combing through the building with growing desperation. Maybe they'd turned it in? The admin offices were locked, and Rob didn't have a key for those.

I walked down the hall to the concert hall and flicked on the backstage lights, and immediately saw my case. Sitting on the floor next to the podium behind the curtains.

"Rob!" I shouted, rushing forward. He wasn't anywhere near the hall. I grabbed the handle and turned to exit the way I came in, when movement made me freeze. Ice slid down my spine, my chest tightening.

"Did you find it?" Rob's voice. *It was Rob.* Of course it was. Nobody else would be in the building this late at night.

I nodded, holding up the case. Rob strode toward me, his hands in his pockets. He appraised my case. "Are you going to play me something?"

My eyes widened. "It's almost eleven o'clock."

He considered this. "You asked for your Christmas gift. This is mine."

My mouth fell open. "That's not fair." My heart felt like it was pumping up a full-to-the-brim beach ball.

He gestured at the black, empty hall. "It's only me."

"That's so much worse." I walked forward to the front of the stage. "Normally, lights are blinding me so I can't see anything."

Rob ducked behind the curtains. "There. I'm not even here."

"Rob—" The curtain rustled. I waited for him to appear, but he stayed hidden. "I don't have my music."

"There's some on the stand." His voice was muffled, and I couldn't help but grin.

"I'm tired. This won't be my best."

"Excuses are for losers."

I laughed and dropped into a crouch, opening up the clasps on my case. My hands were already clammy. *Play for Rob?* The idea was both thrilling and terrifying. I'd never played for anyone outside of rehearsals and concerts, not even Logan.

But there was that feeling again. The flip in my stomach at the idea of Rob's attention on me. Of him noticing. Wanting to know more.

I shrugged off my coat and pulled out my violin, lifting it to my chin and checking the tune. Not too bad. I adjusted the G string and tried them all again, then rubbed rosin over my bow.

I wasn't doing anything wrong. Nothing that had happened tonight was anything I'd be ashamed to tell Logan. On paper. It was the flipping of my heart that I had to keep to myself.

I positioned the bow, momentarily forgetting to breathe, then closed my eyes and started to play.

I chose one of my old recital pieces, and just like in the practice room, the notes poured out of me, filling the empty auditorium with a hauntingly beautiful melody. Within seconds, I'd forgotten that Rob was in the curtains, and the music flowed through me like a river, each note clear and resonant.

I finished at the end of the second A section without the repeats and stood there, letting the silence wash over me. After a few seconds, I lowered the violin. Only then did I see Rob in front of me, his expression unreadable.

I forced a smile. "There. Merry Christmas." I dropped to the floor, nestling the violin back in its case.

"What's this thing?" Rob pointed to a black piece of plastic in my case.

I glanced up. "Oh, that? It's a mute."

He crouched down, picking it up like it was some alien artifact. "And... what does it do? Is it, like, a silencer for a violin?"

I laughed. "Kind of. You put it on the bridge—here, like this." I took it from him, slid it onto the bridge, and plucked one of the strings to demonstrate. The note came out quieter, more subdued. "See? It softens the sound and changes the tone. It's more delicate, less intense."

Rob nodded. "It looks like a weird plastic comb."

I snorted, tucking the mute back into the case. "Well, this one kind of it is. I got it at a random music shop a couple years ago when I realized I'd left my old one at home. It does the job, but it's nothing special."

Rob stood and stepped back.

I continued, "Lily—my friend in orchestra—has this amazing handmade one. It's carved out of this dark walnut, with tiny engraved details on the sides. It's polished so smooth it almost looks like glass. And the sound it creates? It's so warm and rich, it's like . . . I don't know, playing through honey."

Rob tilted his head. "Sounds messy."

I rolled my eyes. "It's hard to describe, okay? But it's gorgeous."

"Do you think Lily would play for me?"

My jaw dropped, and he dodged my arm as I tried to smack him. I clutched my case and walked toward the curtains.

"Hey." Rob's voice sent a shiver through me. "Can you look at me?"

A swoop low in my gut made my head spin. I slowed and turned back.

Rob hadn't moved. His lips parted, and then he spoke in a rush. "I was kidding. That was incredible."

A blush crept up to my cheeks. "Thanks."

He ran a hand over the back of his neck. "I'm serious. That was . . ." He trailed off. "Transcendent."

I raised an eyebrow. "That's a big word, Thompson."

He didn't laugh. Didn't smirk. "Not big enough."

Again it felt like I'd hit the peak on a swing and was plummeting back toward the ground. I pulled my coat on one arm at a time. "We should probably go," I said, breaking the spell. "It's getting late."

Rob nodded, but he didn't take a step forward. For a long

moment, we just stood there in silence, our eyes locked on each other. And in that moment, something shifted. After everything Rob had told me that night, this was the minute—the second— that I would never be able to see him the same way again.

I forced my legs to move, walking toward the exit. Rob followed, his steps slow. I flicked off the light, my hand hesitating on the door knob. *I could stop. I could turn. I could—*

I twisted and forced myself out into the hall, sucking in a lungful of air. We walked back down the hall and through the atrium. I frowned when Rob turned off in the opposite direction of the front doors.

"Be right back."

I waited a moment, then followed and peered down the hall. Washrooms. He'd gone to use the washroom.

My ribs suddenly felt a size too small. I worried my lower lip until he reappeared. "You don't have to do that," I said when he got closer.

Rob shrugged. "Not a big deal."

I put out a hand and stopped him. My fingers slid over his coat and snagged on his wrist. I quickly pulled back, my skin tingling. "You can use my washroom. Put your toothbrush in there. I'll be fine."

Rob circled his fingers over his wrist where I'd touched him. "I don't want to—" He stopped. "I'm not going to make you feel that way again."

I opened my mouth to protest, but Rob was already walking toward the tunnel. I hurried to catch up and matched his stride. He unlocked the door, and we walked through the long hall to the GRB, then climbed the stairs and exited into the night.

When we passed the bookstore, Rob asked. "So, what's your big plan?" His hands were shoved deep into his pockets. At least he wasn't only wearing a T-shirt this time. "With the violin, I mean. You're obviously talented as hell. Are you going to go pro or something?"

I let out a short laugh. "This isn't hockey."

"Whatever you call pro then."

I shrugged, feeling a sudden wave of uncertainty wash over me. "I guess I've never really thought about it. Music has always been a part of my life, but I never considered it as a career."

He chuckled, but didn't respond.

I looked over. "What?"

He shrugged. "Nothing." I shot him a look, and his grin widened. "That's just interesting."

"Interesting how?"

Rob picked up his pace and looked both ways down the road, then waited until I pulled up even with him to cross the street. "I just remember someone telling me I was a coward."

I scoffed. "This is different."

"Mm. So different."

I smacked his arm, instantly regretting the contact with the way my heart jolted. I folded my arms across my chest. "It's crazy competitive." He turned, his face lit up like a Christmas tree, and I realized my mistake. "No, I didn't—"

"Ah, the exact same words." He mimed a chef's kiss.

"Shut up."

"Hell, no. That was too perfect."

I groaned. "It's late. That wasn't fair."

"Sharla, are you afraid to go after your dreams?"

I let out an exasperated sigh. "I helped you clean toilets!"

He laughed and walked up the path to the front door and turned the key in the lock. "The toilets were for the violin. You have nothing on—"

He stopped mid sentence, and I ran into the back of him. "Rob, what—" I froze when I caught sight of something—someone—over his shoulder. "Logan?"

CHAPTER
Seventeen

I STEPPED through the front door, dirty and dishevelled. Logan sat on the couch, arms crossed, face stormy. My stomach dropped.

"Where the hell have you been?" he snapped. "I've been waiting for hours."

Logan was here. In our house. I blinked, wondering if all the cleaning chemicals had gone to my head. "How—I'm sorry, you've been here for hours?" I glanced down at my grimy clothes, suddenly self-conscious. Great first impression after not seeing him for weeks. Rob brushed past me, kicking off his shoes.

Logan tensed. "So you two are just hanging out now?"

I motioned to my clothes. "Does it look like we were hanging out?"

"She left her violin in the arts centre. I had a key," Rob explained with a shrug before ducking into his room.

I hung up my coat and took off my shoes. "I helped him with his shift because he was doing me a favour. The Outlaws have conditioning assessments tomorrow."

Logan barely acknowledged our explanations, his jaw working.

I walked closer and stopped in front of him. "I'm sorry, I didn't know you were coming. You should have told me." I tried to keep the accusation out of my voice. Apparently not very well.

"I wanted to surprise you!" Logan threw his hands up in exasperation. "I got in late last night, had stupid press releases all day, then showed up here at eight o'clock to an empty house. Surprise!"

The sarcasm stung. I bristled. "Well if you'd let me know, I would've made sure to be here." I put out a hand, resting it on his shoulder. "I love surprises. I'm sorry I was an idiot and left my violin on campus."

Rob made a noise behind us, but thankfully, Logan didn't notice. The room to his door was still open.

Logan ran a hand through his blond hair, deflating slightly. "I just missed you so much, Shar. I couldn't wait to see you and now . . ." He gestured vaguely.

My anger faded, replaced by guilt. Here he was, so eager to please. And I welcomed him by picking a fight.

"I missed you too." I slipped my hands around his waist. He wrapped an arm around me, pulling me close. I breathed him in, but couldn't fully relax. Not with Rob standing right there.

Rob reappeared and shuffled around the living room, obviously trying to make himself invisible. When he crossed behind us toward his bedroom again, Logan cleared his throat.

"What, no warm welcome? Afraid you'll miss your beauty sleep, Thompson?"

Rob paused, his jaw clenching. I rested my cheek on Logan's chest and braced myself for a dig. To my shock, he simply shook his head.

"Conditioning at the crack of dawn. Then an exam in physics." Rob's tone remained neutral. "Sorry I can't be around."

"Sure, man. You do you." Logan wrapped his hand around the back of my neck, and I almost flinched.

Rob's eyes flared, his jaw tightening. "I'm assuming press means you didn't get cut."

I shot him a sharp look. *Was that really necessary?* He just shrugged, unrepentant.

Logan chuckled. "Nope. We leave for Europe on the third." His energy returned like he'd just gotten a jolt of caffeine. "Can you believe I get to play there?" He ran his thumb over my skin. "Insane."

Rob was so still, I forgot to breathe. "Insane." He scrubbed a hand over his jaw. "Congrats, bud. Glad it's working out." He turned and stalked to his bedroom, and I exhaled, finally sinking against Logan.

"You didn't have to snap at him like that," I chided gently once Rob's door clicked shut. "He's been helping me out. Cut him some slack."

Logan at least had the grace to look chagrined. "I know, I know. I'm sorry." He took my hands in his. "It's just been a stressful trip and I wanted everything to be perfect and now it's all . . . not."

I softened, squeezing his hands. Logan was back, his blue eyes pleading. But something felt different. Like I was looking at him from the other side of a pane of glass. Like if I tried to push through, everything between us would shatter.

He leaned into me, a tired smile playing at the corners of his mouth. "Have I mentioned that I missed you? Because I did. A lot."

"Once or twice." I grinned as his lips found skin. "But feel free to keep reminding me."

He pulled me to our room, our fingers intertwined. He flopped onto the bed with a groan, burying his face in my pillow. "Mmm, smells like you."

I chuckled, settling beside him. "I hope so. It is my pillow."

He rolled over, pulling me into his arms. I nestled against his chest, breathing him in. I frowned. "Did you change your cologne?"

Logan tipped his chin. "Different deodorant. Why, you like it?"

I nodded. "It's nice." I didn't like it. It was too . . . sharp. In your face. I reached up, threading my fingers in his hair. Something inside of me was pushing away from him, and I needed it to stop.

"Let's just stay like this forever," he mumbled. "Screw Europe. Screw everything else."

My heart clenched. If only it were that simple. "As tempting as that sounds, I don't think your coaches would appreciate our life choices."

He huffed a laugh. "They'll live." His arms tightened around me. "At least we have all day tomorrow. Just you and me. No interruptions."

I stiffened, my hand stilling in his hair.

Logan pulled back, frowning. "What? Don't tell me you have plans."

"I . . ." I bit my lip, averting my gaze. How could I put this without sounding like a complete jerk? "I have to prepare for my audition on Wednesday. And the Christmas concert is coming up."

His frown deepened. "Seriously? I'm only in town for one day, Shar. One day before I'm gone for who knows how long."

Guilt gnawed at my stomach. He was right. What kind of girlfriend was I, prioritizing rehearsals over our limited time together? But the piece Ms. Franck had given me was insanely difficult. I needed every spare second to practice if I wanted to nail it. Him being here meant I was losing out on tonight.

Rob's words from the other night echoed in my mind. *Logan Kemp always gets what he wants.*

I'd brushed it off then, chalking it up to Rob's general dickishness. But now, with Logan's expectant gaze boring into me, I wondered if there wasn't a kernel of truth to it.

Logan sighed, his handsome face pinched with frustration. "Fine. Whatever. I guess I'll just entertain myself."

Okaaay. That stung. I felt the pull to drop into our normal pattern. Stage one: Logan tells me what he wants. Stage two: I adjust my life to make it happen for him. Normally, I wouldn't have even hesitated. I would've cleared my calendar without telling him I'd done it. But tonight, for whatever reason, giving up everything tomorrow made me want to stab a fork into my eye.

I swallowed hard, my pulse rushing. *Open up. Tell him the truth.* "You know how important this is to me." Saying it out loud felt like stripping down and standing in front of him naked.

"More important than me, apparently," he muttered.

A door slammed down inside of me, and he felt it. My body tensed. My skin flashed cold.

Logan slumped. "Shit, Shar, I'm sorry. I didn't mean that." He scrubbed a hand over his face. "I'm just . . . I'm just really damn tired."

I swallowed past the lump in my throat. "I know. It's okay." Even though it wasn't, not really. But I plastered on a smile anyway, determined to salvage what was left of the night.

"Come here." He shifted me higher on his body, his hands going up the back of my shirt. He kissed me, his fingers finding the clasp on my bra.

If I couldn't give him the time he wanted, I could at least give him this.

———

The sounds of a garbage truck outside our window roused me from a fitful slumber, my head fuzzy and thoughts muddled. I blinked blearily in the morning light filtering through the blinds. Logan's arm tightened around my waist, tugging me closer.

"Morning, beautiful," he mumbled into my hair, voice gravelly with sleep.

I tensed, the events of last night rushing back in stark clarity as I stirred, my legs tangled with Logan's under the duvet. He stretched beside me, his arm grazing my shoulder, and pressed a lazy kiss to my bare skin before rolling out of bed.

I sat up slowly, rubbing my eyes, still cocooned in warmth, reluctantly slipping out from under the covers. Logan was already up, rummaging through his small carry-on suitcase on the floor. His clothes were neatly folded, his toiletry bag perched on top from using it last night. It was so strange seeing his things packed up and not settled next to mine.

We moved through our quiet morning routine, brushing our teeth side by side in the washroom. His arm grazed mine as he rinsed his brush, and for a fleeting second, things felt normal.

I thought of Rob. How I told him he could use the washroom if he wanted, then realized I'd never actually talked with Logan about the plumbing situation. How long had it been? I'd completely forgotten about it since Rob was doing his level best not to intrude.

"D'you know what's crazy?" I said with a mouth full of toothpaste. "Rob's washroom is broken."

Logan frowned. "What do you mean, broken?"

I shrugged, spitting in the sink. "There's a leak. It's been off-limits since you left. He had to phone your dad to get the plumber out here. They came, but they're still waiting on a part to fix it."

The furrow in Logan's brow deepened. "He's been using *your* washroom? Like, coming in here to shower?"

I nodded. "I never see him. He never even leaves his towel in here." Truthfully, the only evidence of his presence was a damp bath mat every once in a while. And the scent of his body wash.

Logan's jaw tightened as he fumbled with his belt, muttering something under his breath.

My patience frayed. "Are you seriously pissed about this? What did you expect him to do—bathe in the Bow?"

Logan exhaled. "I just don't like the idea of him being in our space."

"It's a washroom, Logan. Not sacred ground."

He peed, then repositioned himself in his boxers. "Are you two friends now?"

I scrubbed my face, then dried it with a towel. I didn't know how to answer that. Were we friends? We weren't enemies anymore, I was fairly sure of that. "I think he's being nicer. I thought we talked about this? That you asked him to lighten up?"

Logan washed his hands. "Yeah. Right." He slipped past me and back into our bedroom, pulling on his pants and a clean shirt.

I put on moisturizer and exited the washroom. Even though I knew it wasn't my job to improve Logan's mood, I still wanted to. "I could help you make pancakes." I walked up behind him, pressing against his back and curling my arms around his middle.

He didn't hug me back. "I was thinking we could grab lunch and hit the German Christmas Market. They've got that mulled wine you loved last year."

I dropped my arms as he moved toward the bed to grab his watch off the nightstand. I turned and walked back into the washroom, picking up his bracelet from the shelf and attaching it around my wrist.

"I'm not sure I'll be able to do the market, but lunch sounds great." Logan paused, holding his toiletry kit. I swallowed hard. "I thought we talked last night . . . I need to rehearse today. I have an audition tomorrow morning."

His expression darkened. "It's our one day."

A belt seemed to tighten around my chest, and air refused to fill my lungs. "I know. But you keep making plans without asking what I need."

His eyes flashed. "So, this is my fault now? I'm supposed to just . . . what? Sit around while you play violin all day?"

The words hit me like ice water, cold and cutting. I'd never been short with him, and now here I was ready to spout off. *It's our one day.*

Ugh, I wanted to scream at him. Why was he doing this? Making me the bad guy?

I needed air.

I pulled on my joggers and a long-sleeved T-shirt.

"Shar—"

"Don't." I jerked my hand back when he tried to grab onto me, then I picked up my violin case and stormed out of the room.

CHAPTER
Eighteen

I STRODE DOWN THE SIDEWALK, my violin case clutched in one hand and my backpack slung over the opposite shoulder. A gust of wind cut right into my coat. Should've grabbed a scarf, but that would've ruined my dramatic exit.

I heard his footsteps before he called out.

"Shar, wait up!"

So Logan wasn't a total idiot.

I didn't slow my pace. He caught up to me, his blond hair ruffled from running, cheeks flushed. "Babe, I'm sorry."

I pursed my lips, walking faster.

"Hey." He clamped a hand down on my shoulder and pulled me to a stop. "I said I'm sorry."

I jutted out my chin, my eyes flashing. "For what?"

He wet his lips. "For . . . forgetting that you had a routine—"

"It's not a routine. It's my life! Music is important to me. Doing well in my classes is important to me. Could you imagine if I called your hockey practices a 'routine?'" I used air quotes.

Logan blanched. "I'm sorry, I didn't think—"

"Exactly, you didn't think." The words came out harsher than I intended. Guilt stabbed at me but weeks—probably months—

of frustration and hurt were bubbling over inside of me like toxic waste.

Logan put his arm around my shoulder, and we walked in tense silence for a minute, our breath puffing out in white clouds. Another gust of icy wind swept over us and I couldn't suppress a violent shudder. Goosebumps prickled my arms.

Logan pulled me closer, trying to shield me.

"I'm fine," I said through chattering teeth.

He ignored my protest, pulling a toque from his pocket and stretching it over my head.

"Thanks," I murmured.

He walked me to the arts centre, and by the time we passed the bookstore, the anger had drained out of me. I stopped in front of the steps. "I can do a condensed practice. Then we can grab lunch, and maybe we'll have time to hit the market." I pointed to the glass windows of the atrium. "There are couches in there, or you could go back to the house."

"Why don't I just come with you?"

I raised an eyebrow. "To the practice room? They're small."

"If you don't want me to—"

"No, that's fine." I nodded, my heart picking up speed. Logan wanted to listen to me practice? Or was he just doing this to hammer home his apology? Because he thought it was the right thing to do?

I couldn't tell how I felt about it as we claimed an empty practice room and I unpacked my violin. Logan sat in a chair, long legs stretched out as he leaned back, watching me.

As I tightened my bow and applied rosin, a sense of déjà vu washed over me. On stage. With Rob hiding in the curtains.

I glanced over at Logan and pulled out the sheet music Franck had given me, then started tuning my strings.

My blood wasn't rushing in my ears. My hands weren't trembling. Playing for him felt as natural as breathing. Zero butterflies. I wasn't sure what that said about us.

I launched into my warm-up, scales and arpeggios flowing from my fingers. Logan watched raptly at first, but fifteen minutes in, his leg started bouncing. He fiddled with the zipper on his coat. Restless energy rolled off him in waves.

Usually I got lost in the music, the outside world fading away. But Logan's presence nagged at me like an itch I couldn't scratch. Each sigh and shift in his chair snagged my focus, made my bow wobble.

I gritted my teeth and repeated the second line, then stopped and went over it again, annoyed that the bracelet was slipping down my wrist.

"Everything okay?" he asked when I took a longer pause.

"Fine." I blew out a breath. "Just need to drill this one part."

"Oh. Okay, cool." Logan pasted on a smile, determined to be supportive. But I could practically hear him screaming internally, desperate to be anywhere else.

I played a few distracted measures, the notes mechanical and soulless to my ears. Logan grinned. "It sounds great."

Frustration rippled through me. He meant well, but Logan didn't know the first thing about music. In general. That was why the mix tape he gave me was so meaningful. He'd gone way out of his comfort zone to make something that I loved even when it didn't connect with him the same way.

I glanced at the clock, my stomach sinking when I saw how much time had passed and how little I'd accomplished. I ran the middle section of the song a few more times, then played through the whole thing at half speed so I could nail the sixteenth notes.

Blowing out a harsh breath, I lowered my violin. "I think that's enough for today."

Logan practically leaped out of his chair. "You sure? I don't mind waiting longer if you need to keep going."

"I'm sure." I managed a smile as I packed up.

"Yes!" Logan pumped his fist. "I'm starving. I heard about this new place . . . "

And just like that, he was back to his energetic self. He chattered on as we left the practice room behind. We walked back to the house, I dropped off my stuff and changed my clothes, then got into the passenger seat of his truck.

We ended up at a cozy Italian place just off campus, the kind with fabric tablecloths and garlic-infused wood moulding.

"So. Tell me more about your team." That was all I had to say to get him talking. He told me about Coop, the guy who biffed it when we were talking on the phone that first time. About a kid who was barely fifteen and so fast, he was giving all of them a run for their money.

By the time I finished my pasta Logan had barely gotten through half of his. I waited and listened, and then we went to the market. We tasted the wine, Logan bought two bottles, and then we hurried home for him to grab his things so he could head to the airport.

The house seemed empty, but Rob's door was shut. He never closed it unless he was home.

At the door, Logan turned to face me, hands jammed in his pockets. "I don't want to miss everything. The invitational, the holidays."

"Yeah. Kind of crappy timing." I rocked on my heels.

Logan stepped closer, reaching for me. I folded into his arms. "I'll see you in the new year."

I pulled back, tilting my head up to look at him. "I can drive you. If—"

"No, I already called a cab."

I tried not to look too relieved. I was already planning rehearsal number two the second he left the house.

"Love you, Shar." He pressed a kiss to my forehead.

"Love you, too." I meant it. I did love him. But hearing those words come out of my mouth when my insides felt like minced meat left me hollowed out.

And then he was striding down the steps to wait on the sidewalk. I waited until his ride came and he climbed in the back, then blew him a kiss and closed the door, slumping against it. I hated this. I hated that a couple of weeks ago, I would've chewed off my own arm to have Logan next to me, and now? I couldn't suck it up and be happy for twenty-four hours?

Shaking my head, I pushed off the door and headed for my room. I needed to practice, to lose myself in the music until everything else faded away. So I could pretend my life wasn't quietly unravelling at the seams.

The phone rang just as I reached the hall, and I jumped. I retraced my steps into the kitchen and picked it up. "Hello?"

"Hi, it's Mom."

She always announced herself. Did she not trust I could tell who she was by her voice? "Hey, how are you?"

"Oh, you know, a little behind. Baking, cleaning, getting ready for the holidays." She chattered on about her famous gingerbread recipe and the new vacuum she'd purchased from the son of a friend of hers. I made appropriate hums and haws, only half-listening.

"So, what about you? Are you finished with your Christmas shopping?"

"Yeah, mostly. Just a few last-minute things." Like . . . for all my friends except Logan. His present I'd found months ago.

"Well, don't leave it too late. The mall's a zoo this time of year." She paused, and I heard the faint clatter of dishes in the background. "Listen, honey, there's something I need to tell you."

"Okay." I leaned against the counter, not sure if I was about to hear about a house renovation or a cancerous mole.

"It's about your dad."

My heart stopped. "What about Dad?"

She took a deep breath. "He had a little thing happen with his heart, so we ran some tests."

"What?" My legs were suddenly wobbly. "Is he okay? Why didn't you phone me?"

"He's fine, he's fine. They caught it early. But he needs a

procedure—they're going to place a stent." Her voice wavered slightly. "It's scheduled for the twenty-first."

The twenty-first. Why did that date ring a bell? I couldn't think past the *oh and by the way, your dad's having heart surgery this week.*

Mom continued, "This was the earliest appointment available. You know how backed up the cardiac unit gets around the holidays."

No. No, I did not know.

She sighed. "I'm so sorry. I know how much it meant to you to have us at your concert."

Ah. The concert. Tears pricked at my eyes, but not because they'd miss a little Christmas music. "This is more important than the concert, Mom. I'm just glad Dad's okay."

"He will be. It's a routine procedure, very low-risk. He'll be home in time for Christmas dinner." She made a valiant attempt at a laugh. "You know nothing keeps your father from my pumpkin pie."

"Yeah." The word emerged as a croak. I cleared my throat.

"Okay, well. We'll talk soon." She hesitated. "Love you."

"Love you too." I hung up before the first tear could fall, the phone sliding from my numb fingers.

A routine procedure. Low-risk. The words rang in my ears. *Was it though?* All I could think of was Dad lying pale and still in a hospital bed, wires snaking from his chest.

I pressed a hand to my mouth, holding back a sob. That phone call was the match to my fuse. Breaking me wide open. The night before with Rob quickly followed by everything with Logan crashed over me like a wave.

I was not going to cry. This was not cry-worthy. My dad was going in for a routine procedure, and everyone had tiffs with their boyfriends. Just because I'd never had one before didn't mean it wasn't normal.

I needed to pull myself together and stop being so damn

fragile. I turned to fill up the glass I kept next to the sink and stilled.

Rob stood on the other side of the island, hands in his pockets. "Hey."

I nodded, trying to swallow the lump in my throat while now also shoving down the surge of adrenaline hitting my system. "Hey."

"Logan's gone?"

I filled up my glass. "Yeah. He took a taxi to the airport."

"I could've taken him."

I took a drink of my water. "I offered. He said Hockey Canada was paying for it."

"So that's what my club fees are going toward."

I laughed. "All for a good cause."

Rob glanced behind me at the phone on the counter. "What was that all about?"

I exhaled. "Not the plumber."

The corner of his mouth lifted. "Well, if the plumber was planning to come to your concert, I want your secrets."

My grin turned into a full smile. "You couldn't handle my secrets."

His eyes dropped to my mouth, then to the counter. He dragged a hand through his dark hair. "Do you want to talk about it?"

The room seemed to go dead silent. Like I'd stepped inside a recording booth with sound treatments. I did want to talk about it. I wanted to open my mouth and let every last thought in my head spill out like ink dumping on a page.

But it couldn't be Rob. Not with Logan's goodbye kiss still lingering on my lips. Not with my head spinning or my nerves sparking like a downed power line.

Because I wanted to do something reckless.

I wanted to give in to whatever tugged at my centre anytime Rob was close.

And I wouldn't be that person.

"I'm okay right now. Thanks." I gave a tight smile and curled my arms around myself, fingers digging into my skin so I knew they weren't reaching out and touching him.

I waited, half-hoping he would push. He didn't. He exhaled, his breath slow and deep, then gave a short nod and returned to his room.

CHAPTER
Nineteen

THE CONCERT HALL buzzed with nervous energy as I sat on stage readying my violin. I glanced over at Caleb and Lily, pursing my lips and crossing my eyes in an exaggerated face. Lily stifled a giggle, and Caleb grinned. Despite the butterflies in my stomach, it felt good knowing we were all in this together. I did want a solo at some point . . . but I also dreaded the day I'd have to play a solo.

Performing was like that. Full of paradoxes. If only I could always play my solos on a darkened stage with my audience hiding in the curtains.

I had not been given that option on Wednesday at my unofficial audition with Franck. I exhaled with relief at having that over with. All I'd gotten were four words. "Begin" and "You may go." Best believe I'd mulled over those last three during every waking moment since.

As people started filing into their seats, a familiar flash of pink hair caught my eye. Crystal and Maddie waved enthusiastically from the third row and my smile grew so big, my cheeks ached. Those two were the best, dropping everything to come support me tonight when I needed it most. I'd been trying hard not to dwell on the empty seats that should've been filled by my family. Especially with Dad. Mom called once to let me know he was out of surgery, but I hadn't received an update after that. I made a mental note to phone Mom as soon as the concert wrapped.

"Hey," Lily stage-whispered. "You good?"

I blinked, realizing I'd been spacing out. I drew a deep breath and nodded. *"Break a leg!"* She held out her right ankle, and I laughed under my breath.

The house lights dimmed and a hush fell over the audience as Ms. Franck strode onto the stage, her vibrant forest green shawl billowing behind her like a cape. She took her place at the podium, paused and straightened her shoulders, then with a dramatic flourish of her baton, the orchestra burst to life.

We moved through the program, enlivened by the applause and palpable energy that a live audience always brought. The small sounds of rustling fabric, a cough, the voice of a toddler. All of it somehow shocked us into an excellence we couldn't achieve in the practice room.

Lily's violin sang during her solo with such purity and grace, the notes shimmered.

Watching her naturally transported me back to my audition, but I tried to shake it off and just be there. Just enjoy and not think about myself for once. Difficult to do, but if I couldn't achieve that at Christmas time, when could I?

As the song ended, I refocused and adjusted my sheet music. The joyful strains of "Sleigh Ride" filled the air and I let myself get swept up in the familiar melody. We played song after song, and then all too soon, the final notes of the concert echoed through the hall and we rose for our bows.

I grinned as the house lights came up a fraction, squinting across the sea of faces and our standing ovation to pick out Crystal and Maddie in the crowd. There seemed to be a family of giants seated directly in front of them. Hopefully, they were still able to see the stage.

I turned my head further, and my gaze snagged like a ring in a sweater. Energy zinged from my head to my toes.

Rob. He stood at the back of orchestra right, waiting for the people ahead of him to exit into the aisle. He wore a crisp burgundy button-down, dark slacks, and *a tie*. Since when did Rob Thompson own a tie?

That tug in my midsection flared, and I wanted to shove my stand out of the way, barrel through the musicians ahead of me and leap off the stage to get to him. To ask why the hell he was there at my concert. To see what that shirt looked like on him up close.

Before I could catch his eye, he turned on his heel and strode out of the auditorium.

"Sharla!"

I turned to see Crystal and Maddie waving at me from the side stairs at the front of the stage. I set down my violin and skirted through the stands to meet them.

"That was incredible!" Crystal enveloped me in a bone-crushing hug, nearly lifting me off my feet with her enthusiasm.

Maddie grinned, her curls bouncing as she nodded in agreement. "Seriously, I got chills during 'Carol of the Bells.'"

I ducked my head, feeling a flush creep up my neck at their effusive praise. "Thanks, guys."

"Are you so glad it's over?" Crystal whispered.

I laughed. "Oh my hell, yes."

Maddie grabbed my face in her hands. "I have instructions. Are you ready?" I grinned and nodded as much as I could with her palms squeezing my cheeks. "Get your shit. Meet us at the front doors. Dinner's on me tonight."

My eyes widened. "Maddie, you don't have to do that!"

She waved away my protests. "Early Christmas present. I insist."

I followed her list to a T—it helped that there were only two items on it—and as we walked to Ranchmans, laughing and rehashing the concert's highlights, I made a mental plan to do my Christmas shopping now that I was a free woman. I hadn't even started, let alone figured out meaningful gifts for Crystal and Maddie. And it was going to take some figuring. They deserved something special, but on my anemic bank account balance, I'd be lucky to afford a pair of fuzzy socks from the dollar store.

But those concerns could wait until tomorrow. This was a perfect night. Juicy burgers, hearing about Crystal's roommate drama involving an ex-boyfriend and a stray cat, messing with Maddie about her irrational anxiety over finals next week, and finally spilling on Logan's visit.

When I walked in the door to the townhouse, I'd almost managed to forget the sight of Rob at the back of the orchestra section.

Almost.

I flicked on the lights and scanned the living room and kitchen. Nothing. I stepped forward until I could see his door.

My heart stumbled over itself. Open. That meant Rob was out. Where would he have gone after the concert?

I checked the time on the microwave. It was already ten o'clock on a Thursday night. Was he—? Did he go to the concert and then start his shift late?

For a brief moment, I considered throwing on my old clothes and running back to campus. Finding him and offering to help clean toilets. But I didn't know which building he was assigned to. And that would be weird, wouldn't it?

I puttered around the kitchen, and numbers, of all things, sprouted in my head. 403-772-7272. Rob's pager. I hadn't meant to memorize it, but it was the easiest phone number imaginable.

I stared at the phone. If he was working, he'd be near plenty of phones to ring me back. I could give a casual, breezy "Thanks for coming tonight. I appreciate the support" sort of thing. Totally platonic. Just general, societally encouraged manners.

I hesitated, my hand itching to pick up the receiver. But I

didn't pick it up. Because my pulse did not feel general or soci-etally encouraged.

I retreated to my room and took my water bottle with me.

———

Morning came far too soon, the sun peeking through my curtains and mocking my groggy, sleep-deprived state. I rolled over and checked the time. 11:30 a.m. Oops. So much for my grand plans of rising early and being productive.

I stumbled out of bed and into the kitchen. Rob's breakfast dishes were in the sink. His door was open.

Right. The Outlaws had an away game in Leduc the next day. Which meant practice in the morning so they had a full day to recover. Then the big invitational meet was next weekend, so Rob and the others would presumably be spending every spare second in the gym or on the ice, grunting and sweating and chugging raw eggs or whatever.

I brewed a pot of coffee and surveyed the living area. Dust on the TV stand. Lint fuzzies on the carpet. The fact that I couldn't remember the sound of our vacuum didn't bode well.

I ate breakfast and channelled my recently discovered inner janitor, and two hours later, the floors were mopped, the shelves were dusted, and I'd even scrubbed the mysterious Pollock-esque stains out of the microwave. Housework complete, I treated myself to a long, hot shower and a fresh outfit before venturing out into the chilly December afternoon.

The boutique-lined street near Douglas University twinkled with holiday cheer, ribbons, and garlands adorning every store-front. I popped into a few shops, admiring the handcrafted jewelry and artisanal candles, but nothing screamed "Perfect Gift for Crystal or Maddie." I was about to call it quits when a small display of handmade soaps caught my eye—delicate squares in intoxicating scents like "Winter Citrus" and "Sugar Cookie." I selected a few bars to tuck into gift bags when inspiration finally struck.

Huffing soap somehow gave me superhuman energy, so I stocked up on groceries, picked up a new pair of warm gloves, and snagged the last box of Crystal's favorite peppermint bark at the campus candy store. By the time I lugged my bags back to the townhouse, the sun was setting, painting the sky in streaks of orange creamsicle and pink cotton candy.

And yet, after all of that accomplishment and distraction, the second I got back into the house, all I could think about was Rob. Had he come home during the day? Had he already showered? Was he working tonight before the game? *Where had he gotten that shirt?*

I put away my groceries and purchases, cycling between "you should be thinking about Logan" and "Is the bath mat wet?" every thirty seconds.

What did it mean that he'd come to my concert? Did he actually love that kind of music? Or was it curiosity?

Another possibility sent warmth spreading through my chest. He'd heard my conversation with my mom. Did he know my family wasn't going to make it? Had he come because he thought I wouldn't have anyone in the audience?

Yes. The truth of it rang through me like a gong. I didn't know how I knew that was exactly why he'd shown up, but I did.

Suddenly my body felt like a lit sparkler, and any thought of sitting down and reading a book or studying for finals was banished. I had to do something. I had to—

I stared at the fresh loaf of bread on the counter. Toast. I could make toast and . . . I opened the fridge and pulled out the package of lean ground turkey I'd just purchased, along with all the half-finished veggies in the crisper and the new block of sharp cheddar cheese.

I set to work, browning the turkey and sautéing the veggies with a medley of aromatic spices. I was just making dinner. For myself, and since there would be extras, Rob could eat, too. That wasn't weird or flirty or anything.

Just as I was sliding the skillet into the oven to melt the cheese, the front door opened. Rob trudged in, looking like he'd gone ten rounds with a pack of wolves. He froze, his eyebrows shooting up as he took in the scene before him.

I'd put out two plates. Filled two glasses of water with sliced lemon. At the time it seemed like a simple, kind gesture, but now that Rob was standing in front of me, I second guessed it.

"Uh, hi."

Rob dropped his hockey bag, took off his shoes and walked in. "What's all this?"

I shrugged, busying myself with wiping spilled cumin off the counter. "I was hungry. Thought you might be, too."

Rob's lips twitched, a hint of a smile playing at the corners. "You didn't have to do that."

"It's nothing."

He rested a hand on the counter, and I turned back to the oven, checking on the cheese. I'd turned it on broil which meant it was already perfectly bubbly. I pulled the skillet out and set it on the stove top.

"It's hot, but you can dish up if you want."

Rob picked up a plate and rounded the island. I skittered back to avoid being too close, then grabbed my own plate off the counter and waited my turn.

We settled into our seats at the island. Rob blew on his food, then took a bite. I did the same, exhaling with relief that it didn't taste awful.

Rob grunted. "This is good."

I swallowed. "Thanks."

Rob shovelled another forkful into his mouth. "Definitely beats what I was going to have."

"Which was?"

"Energy bar. Cereal."

I grinned. "You weren't going to eat a real meal?"

He shook his head. "Too tired."

"Are you excited about the game tomorrow?"

He shrugged. "Not about the driving."

"Yeah. That's a lot."

Rob leaned back in his chair, letting out a long breath. "I might take a textbook with me."

I laughed. "Oh, you'll get mocked so hard."

As Rob ran a hand through his hair and took another bite, explaining how half the guys on the team were at risk of failing a class that semester, whatever jitters I'd felt earlier drained from me like I'd pulled the plug on the bathtub.

We talked about practice, about the invitational, and the stress of finals. All of mine were stacked at the beginning of the week, thankfully, but he had one on the first day of the tournament.

"Don't you think your professor would change that? Thursday is so late." I scraped the last pieces of turkey and pepper from my plate.

"I think you should ask her for me."

I rolled my eyes. "If it's a she, you'll probably have better luck."

"Are you insinuating that my seventy-year-old professor might be tempted by all of this?" He gestured at himself, and a flush crept up my neck. *How could she not be?*

"She'll think you're adorable. Like her sweet little grandson or something."

Rob let out a puff of air. "Oh, I'm not sweet."

The flush crept higher, and I searched for something to look at that wasn't Rob's dark lashes hitting his cheek. "Oh, wow. It's late." I got up from my stool too quickly, knocking my knee on the counter.

"You okay?" Rob's hand landed on my leg. I inhaled sharply, and he quickly pulled it back.

"Yeah. Fine, thanks." I grabbed for our empty plates but Rob was faster.

"Let me. You cooked, so it's only fair that I clean up."

I hesitated, chewing my lower lip. "No, it'll take two seconds. You've been gone all day. Just go shower and relax."

Rob held my gaze for a long moment. "Are you saying I smell?"

I laughed, dropping my eyes. "I mean, you said it not me."

He tapped a finger on the counter. "Thanks for dinner."

I shoved my hands in my back pockets, swaying in a way that was definitely not natural. "You are welcome."

His lips twitched, then he turned and walked to his bedroom to grab his toiletries and clothes.

"You can leave them in there," I said in a rush. Rob turned back. "Your stuff. If you want. Seems silly to have to take it in and out all the time."

His mouth quirked. "Worried I'm using Logan's?"

"No." I rolled my eyes and yanked the dishwasher open. I knew he wasn't. Because Rob's scent was permanently branded in my mind and it was nothing like my boyfriend's.

CHAPTER

Twenty

MY FINGERS CLUTCHED the pen as I stared down at the jazz composition study guide, the scribbled intervals blurring before my tired eyes. Just one more practice test, then I could pack up and meet Crystal and Maddie for Christmas shopping.

After the twenty-four-seven rehearsals preparing for the winter showcase performance, I was drowning in neglected coursework and final projects. Who knew music majors actually had to study?

"Girl, you've been hunched over that desk for hours!" Crystal leaned over the library desk, a bundle of red and green with jangling bracelets. "Time for some retail therapy."

Maddie stopped next to her, planting a hand on her hip. "Get your butt up, Shar. You already know this stuff."

Groaning, I stood and stretched. Crystal was right, I desperately needed a break. Plus, my stress level would significantly decrease once I bought presents for the last few people on my list.

Maddie drove us to the mall, and it was bustling with holiday shoppers. I picked up a soft flannel shirt in hunter green for my dad. I figured he could use something cozy as he recovered from his procedure. For my violin-loving mom, I found an elegant music journal to record her compositions and a set of artisan rosin from the specialty shop.

"Let's split up for a bit. Meet at the food court in an hour?" Maddie suggested with a conspiratorial wink. Damn, I was so grateful for her. I was positive Crystal had already gotten our gifts, and I didn't want to look like the loser who waited 'til last minute. Now Maddie and I could at least look like losers together.

We parted ways, and I wandered into a funky boutique, drawn to their quirky and slightly inappropriate window display. I browsed, grinning to myself. Mugs shaped like boobs. A frying pan with a penis handle.

I almost laughed out loud when I saw a Chrétien toilet bowl cleaner. I reached for it, immediately thinking of Rob, then pulled my hand back. Would it be weird for me to get him something? It wasn't like it was a serious gift. It was a joke. He'd think it was hilarious, and I wouldn't care if Logan saw I bought it for him.

I picked it up and kept shopping, eventually finding a sweatshirt that said "Sometimes I go off on a tangent" for Maddie and a "Staff Meeting" T-shirt for Crystal, complete with a treble clef and animated music notes. Thoughtful and funny, plus I had the soaps to go with them.

I'd already gotten Logan the perfect present last month. A signed hockey puck from Doug Gilmore. Caleb had a friend whose sister married his cousin. He got one for me when he went back home for Thanksgiving, and I was still forever in his debt.

I had the store double wrap everything, and the toilet bowl cleaner was strangely shaped enough, it threw Crystal and Maddie off the scent. I had gift bags at home that I'd saved from parties over the summer. Not Christmasy, but neither of them would care.

We went for cheap, happy hour sushi and headed back to campus. I wrapped and stashed the presents under my bed, all except the toilet bowl cleaner since that was unwrappable and only got a sticky bow.

I slept and woke on Saturday to find that a mammoth blizzard slammed into Alberta, blanketing everything in white. Crystal, Maddie, and I treated our emails like a chat board, messages flying every two seconds.

The Outlaws were in Leduc for their away game, and we hadn't heard a thing from them. Deerfoot Trail was closed between Airdrie and Red Deer, which didn't bode well for the highway further north.

Maddie:

   I'm worried about them. They have finals and then the invitational.

Crystal:

   Are they going to make it back in time for finals? The storm isn't supposed to let up until Sunday afternoon.

I peeked out my window but couldn't see anything. Wind and snow swirled past the glass, making it look like I lived in a snow globe. I sat on the couch, my leg bouncing. Had they tried driving home? Were they stuck near Edmonton for the night?

There was a way I could get answers . . .

I turned and looked at the phone, the numbers already scrolling through my head. This was logistical, wasn't it?

Before I could second guess myself, I stood and punched Rob's pager number into the phone, then typed in our home phone and hung up. I leaned back against the island counter, staring at the receiver in the cradle. All the expressions about pots not boiling and patience being a virtue flooded my thoughts, and after what felt like ten minutes, I was about to force myself back to the computer.

And then the phone rang.

I nearly dropped the receiver as I snatched it up. "Hello?" My voice wavered, and I coughed to cover it up.

"Hey. Is everything okay?" Rob sounded tense.

I could read his tone like notes on the treble clef. It was automatic. Intuitive. "Yeah. No. Everything's fine. I was worried about you—the team, I mean."

"Oh, right." *Disappointment? Relief? Maybe a little of both?* "We're fine. We just can't get back on the road until the plows come out."

"Plows? They have more than one in Leduc?"

Rob chuckled, his breath crackling in the speaker. "You should take that show on the road."

I stretched the cord across the hall and plopped down on the couch. "How was the game? A little embarrassing for you?"

The grin on his face was audible. "No. We were playing Leduc. Remember?"

"Hey. They make 'em tough up there."

"No, that's fair." He exhaled. "They've got a new team this year. Young. Not much experience."

"Well, no match for the wise and weathered Outlaws."

"Do I sound like I'm trying to be cocky here? You asked me a question. I gave you the truth."

I laughed, my skin starting to tingle. "Sorry." It was so much easier to tease. That was what Rob and I had always done. Mess with each other. Mock each other. I didn't quite know how to talk to him normally.

"Don't apologize." His voice was low, rough. No grin anymore.

My heart thudded so loud, I wondered if he could hear it. "Soooo, you guys are staying at the hotel for the night? They had enough rooms?"

"Yep. Surprisingly not a tourist destination."

A voice cut in. "Who are you talking to, Thompson?"

"Hey—"

Something scuffed over the speaker, and then another voice came on the line. "Hello?"

"Hello. Who am I speaking with?"

"Shit, it's Sharla?" Axel crowed. "Since when do you phone Rob?"

"Since he's the only one on the team with a pager. It's not like I had your hotel number."

"I mean, you could've looked it up. It's not like there are that many of 'em."

"Just what I always wanted to do on the weekend—phone a string of random hotels."

"Alright, alright. You're off the hook. What are you guys jabbering about?"

I worked to make my voice sound casual. "Uh, I was just about to ask if there was anything Crystal, Maddie, and I could do for you guys. I know you were planning to be back by tonight, and with the invitational this weekend—"

"Oh, actually, you would save my ass if you went and got me a bottle of wine." Axel breathed heavily like he was getting up from the couch.

"A bottle of wine for the invitational?"

"No. I'm supposed to meet Pam's parents tomorrow night. I was planning to go get something to take as a housewarming gift, you know, make a good impression and all that. But I don't know when I'm gonna get home. I won't have time to go to the store if I wanna shower."

"Yeah. Showering is a must to meet the parents." I got up from the couch and walked back to the kitchen, grabbing my Post-it notes and pen. "What kind of wine do you want, and how much do you want to spend?"

"Keep it around, like, forty bucks, but nothing that looks cheap. Make sure it has a nice label."

I scribbled down the note. "Alright. Got it. Anything else?"

Axel pulled the receiver away from his mouth and polled the group. Were they all in Rob's hotel room?

"No, I think that's it. Here, I'll pass you back to Thompson. Thanks, Sharla. You're the best."

Rob got back on the line, and I could've sworn I heard a muttered *"asshole."* "Hey, sorry about that."

"No, it's all good. I called to see if there was anything we could do to help." I paused, my mouth suddenly feeling like I was chewing cotton balls. "Is there anything you need?"

Rob drew in a breath. "No, I think I'm good."

Hesitation. His voice had lifted a little too energetic. "What is it?" I pressed.

"No, it's nothing."

I leaned back on the counter. "You're a terrible liar."

He blew out a small puff of air. "There's nothing I want you to help me with."

I scoffed. "What? I'm not good enough to run your errands?"

"No, I didn't mean that."

"What is it, Thompson?" Heat lifted to my cheeks.

Another pause, another breath. "I need to wash my home jersey." My pulse quickened.

His jersey. I blinked, then turned my head. That would probably be in his bedroom.

I thought about pushing his door open, walking in and looking around at where he kept his clothes. Where he slept.

I swallowed hard. "Okay. No problem. Where can I find it?"

"I'll probably have time if we get back Sunday night."

"Rob. I'm about to throw in a white load anyway. Where is it?"

"In my room. I think it's in the closet on top of my laundry bin."

"Okay. I'll take care of it. Anything else?"

Rob grunted. "It's kind of a mess in there."

I grinned. "Well, that's embarrassing because my room is always spotless." I meant it as a joke, but he didn't laugh.

He was quiet a moment. "Thank you."

"Yeah. What are friends for, right?"

Silence.

Rob was quiet long enough, I wondered if the call had disconnected.

"I'm not your friend." His voice was so low, I barely heard it.

When my brain caught up, it felt as if someone had their hand over my stomach, and they were starting to squeeze.

"Okay, I—"

"See you tomorrow."

The dial tone made me jump. *I'm not your friend?* I pulled the receiver from my ear and stared at it. What the hell did he mean by that?

Just as I set it down, the phone started to ring, and I yanked it back to the side of my face. "What the hell did you mean by that?" I snapped.

"Uhh, hello to you, too."

Logan. It was Logan's voice on the other end of the line. My face burned. "Oh, hi! Sorry, I—I thought you were someone else."

"Who?"

"Oh, just someone from orchestra."

Logan blew out a puff of air. "That explains why your line was busy forever. I've been trying to call."

Guilt streaked through me. "Sorry, the Outlaws got snowed in at Leduc. I was on the phone with them, trying to help get things sorted for next week's invitational."

"And then the orchestra asshole?"

I laughed a little too brightly. "Yep, exactly."

Logan drew a breath. It was quiet. There weren't a hundred other voices sounding off in the background. "Man, I miss the Outlaws. It's great here, don't get me wrong, but there's nothing like your hometown team, you know?"

"Totally." I wedged the phone between my ear and shoulder, stretching the cord so I could plop down on the couch. "You're getting close to leaving the country." I braced myself, waiting for him to break down and tell me he didn't make it. Was I a terrible girlfriend for hoping he would get cut? I didn't want him to fail, but I wanted things to go back to how they were. Where Logan and I were joined at the hip. When I looked forward to him coming home every day like it was Christmas morning. Where I didn't get annoyed with him when he surprised me by showing up in the house. Where I didn't think about Rob Thompson . . .

"Three days." Pride and excitement crept into his voice. "It's unreal. I can't wait to get out there and show what I can do."

So. Not coming home, then. "You're going to be amazing."

"Thanks, babe." He paused. "How are your exams going? You must be swamped."

I made a face, zipping up my jacket. "Ugh, don't remind me. I have two papers and a test this week. It's brutal."

"That sucks." Logan actually sounded sympathetic for once. "I'm really lucky—most of my profs postponed my finals until I get back in January. I don't even have to take one of them."

Of course he didn't. The bitter thought flashed through my mind before I could stop it. Logan Kemp. Gets whatever he wants.

Immediately, I felt awful. He worked incredibly hard. He deserved the accommodations and opportunities coming his way. What the hell was my problem? "So, tell me about your week."

I settled back as Logan happily dove into every play, every moment he had on the ice. Just like when we did this at home, my mind wandered.

A year ago, Logan and I got together at the invitational. We'd been crossing paths all semester, but I didn't think he was interested in me. Not until we were talking, all bundled up at the bonfire, and he handed me a mix tape.

Unbeknownst to me, he'd been paying attention. When we were at parties with the Outlaws, he noticed my favorite songs.

Almost all of them were ballads. Love songs. I got the message loud and clear.

"Mhmm." I validated at all the right spots in his story, closing my eyes and letting his voice wash through me.

Wine for Axel.

Jersey for Rob.

I pursed my lips at the flash of nervous energy down my spine. It was just laundry.

"Mm, and what happened then?"

CHAPTER
Twenty~One

I DIDN'T TALK to Crystal or Maddie for the next four days. All of us holed up and studied, working late hours in the library where the internet was faster.

Surprisingly, that was when the festive spirit of Calgary finally started seeping into my stressed-out bones. Wandering between home and the buildings on campus, I couldn't help but smile at the twinkling lights and garlands strung along the brick and wrapped around lamp posts.

Through it all, I barely saw Rob, both of us buried in term papers and exam prep. I fought the part of me that wanted to find excuses to sit out in the living area. To accidentally cross paths when it wasn't necessary.

Then finally, we arrived at Thursday. The first day of the invitational. Finals were over, the weight of academic stress lifted like a helium balloon released into the sky. Which I would never do because: sea turtles. But still. An overwhelming contentment settled against my bones as I made my way to the huge student hall for the invitational pancake breakfast.

The aroma of sizzling sausage and pancakes wafted through the air, making my stomach rumble. Long tables covered with checkered cloths stretched across the vast room, outfitted with plates of butter and bottles of maple syrup. Athletes and friends milled about in their team colours, an excited energy buzzing through the hall.

I loved that we did this. Other universities probably had their own traditions, but I doubted they were as over the top as Douglas. The lore was that the invitational started because the coach of the Outlaws back in the eighties was in love with the mom of a hockey player at some school in British Columbia. He started the tournament and pulled out all the stops to make the teams, and especially her, feel welcome. Supposedly they were engaged a few weeks later. The traditions still stood thanks to generous donors and the invitational was a bigger event than any other on campus.

All teams were invited to participate, and against all odds, there hadn't been any incidents with visiting teams. Part of that could have been that the teams who had reputations simply weren't invited. Plus, getting free food tended to make people grateful.

I spotted Maddie and Crystal already seated with the Outlaws, waving me over. Weaving through the jostling bodies, I slid into a chair between them. I pretended not to notice Rob next to Rory. Or at least not notice him more or less than anyone else.

"Well well, look who decided to grace us with her presence," Axel drawled.

I sighed. "What can I say? Some of us actually value our education."

Crystal snorted. "You do know who you're talking to?" She elbowed the hulking defenseman next to her.

Bear sat down, his plate piled high with a leaning tower of pancakes. "It's not that we don't care. We just know our limitations."

Maddie rolled her eyes. "Your only limitation is right here." She tapped her head with her finger.

Bear grinned and held up his hand. "This finger? Definitely not limited." He waggled his eyebrows.

I groaned and grabbed a plate. Crystal pulled me from my seat, and I followed her to the buffet line. Rob looked up, and I briefly caught his eye before pinning my gaze on the back of Crystal's head.

My sunshiny mood clouded over. *Not friends?* I wondered if he thought I wasn't his friend when he saw his clean jersey draped over his chair. Ugh, I wanted to slap him. I thought I'd gotten over it, but maybe my successful avoidance of him over the past week had been masking those emotions that were still very much there if my clenched fists were to be believed.

Rob had held me in the middle of the night. He'd helped me get my violin, albeit with a tad bit of blackmail, but he did it. I made him dinner, and we talked for over an hour that night. Why would he, after all that, go back to being a jerk?

"Hey, you want sausage?" Crystal pointed at the student waiting to drop two links on my plate. I nodded, and we made our way through the line, then sat back with the team, listening to them swap stats and analyze their competition.

I glanced around the room. There were a few teams that were looking good this year, but the Outlaws were favoured. But without Logan . . .

"So Sharla, you coming to the games this year?" Rory needled.

I scoffed. "Why wouldn't I?"

He shrugged. "I don't know, since Logan isn't here—"

"Um, if you remember, I loved this team first. Logan and I got together after I was already a fan."

Axel reached over and put his arm around me. "I'm here for you. If you get lonely with Logan gone."

I laughed, then looked up to see Rob staring at us. He stood and picked up his plate, his jaw tense. "Probably time to go."

Rory glanced at his watch. "We have a few more minutes."

Rob pushed his chair in. "I'm going to head over now."

"Okay, grumpy," Crystal murmured as he walked away from the table.

I nudged her. "He's probably just nervous." I watched his retreating figure. Had I done something wrong? Said something wrong? I'd rehashed our phone conversation a hundred times but couldn't figure it out.

The truth was, I did feel a little bit naked without Logan there next to me. Normally my schedule revolved around his. I was with him between games, worried about getting him food or Tiger Balm or whatever he needed to recoup. But now? I was free as a bird.

The team started to disperse, heading off with Rob, and eventually, it was just us ladies, surrounded by the detritus of a truly epic breakfast. I turned to Maddie and Crystal with a grin. "So, what trouble should we get into while the boys are away?"

Crystal slapped her hands on the table. "Cafeteria streaking."

"Matching tattoos!" Maddie added.

Pam, Rory's girlfriend, snorted. "How about we grab coffees and scope out the competition instead? I hear the team from Saskatchewan has some real hotties." She winked.

"Now you're talking," Crystal agreed, pushing up from her chair. "Lead the way, oh wise one."

We watched the end of a game between a team from Grande Prairie and U of L—total blowout—then bought snacks in anticipation of the Outlaws facing off against the Coyotes from Bayshore College on Vancouver Island.

"I heard their top scorer, Jaxon Reed, is NHL-bound after graduation," Crystal whispered, eyes glued to the Coyotes' muscular captain as he warmed up. "Twenty goals in fifteen games this season."

"Pfft. Logan's sitting at twenty-five goals, and Rory's right behind with nineteen. Plus, we've got Tim in net and Rob mid. The Coyotes don't stand a chance."

Crystal nodded in agreement. "Totally. The Outlaws are going to destroy them." She chewed her lower lip. "Maybe number twelve will need comforting."

I elbowed her playfully. "Down, girl."

She winked, then launched into a discussion with Maddie about who they thought was single. Okay. So it sucked a little that I wasn't single this year. That had been the most fun part last time, and it stung a little that I couldn't in good conscience join in.

The puck dropped, and the game began in a flurry of motion. Rory won the face-off—the Outlaws took possession. They made it look easy, passing the puck between them as they wove through the other team.

It only took three minutes before Axel took the shot, and the puck sailed past the Coyotes' goalie's outstretched glove. The Outlaw bench exploded in cheers as the goal horn blared. Crystal cheered, doing a victory shimmy.

A few minutes later, Tim made an acrobatic save to keep the Coyotes off the scoreboard. By the end of the first period, we were up two nil and flying high. The rest of the game was more of the same. The Coyotes fought hard, but they were outmatched. Our offense was relentless, even without Logan, and our defense was unbreakable. The final score was five to one, Outlaws.

We spilled out of the stands and into the hall to congratulate the team as they came out of the locker room. Eventually. No secret stairwell today.

After grabbing hot dogs in the square, we went back to the rink for the big welcome celebration. Each team made a grand entrance, skating out in full uniform with their school colors and banners held high. I wasn't sure why they had games before the official reception, but if the Olympics could get away with it, I figured Douglas was in good company.

The Outlaws looked dashing in their maroon and gold, Douglas University's crest emblazoned on their chests. They hammed it up for the cheering crowd, playing to the hometown audience.

My eyes locked onto Rob, his dark hair mussed from the air whipping around his face as he circled the ice. He was smiling, and the sight of it was a gut punch. I couldn't remember him smiling since we had dinner together at the house. It felt like a lifetime ago. Seeing it now blew oxygen over the coals that had been simmering in my chest since that phone conversation on Saturday night. Why did he get to decide if we were friends or not? Rob wasn't in charge of my friendships. He didn't get to just flick his asshole switch on and off. We'd proven we could get along just fine, so why would he go and ruin that?

Boos and cheers erupted for the Timber Valley University Grizzlies in forest green and gold, roaring fiercely. They were followed by the Silver Ridge Sentinels in navy and white. Lastly, the Clearwater University Wolves bounded out in green and white, their wolf mascot loping alongside them and howling.

"Is it wrong that I find that costume kind of adorable?" Maddie stage-whispered.

Crystal's eyes widened. "Babe, go for it."

After the last team circled the ice, we followed the throngs through the square and made our way to Ranchmans where the tables were almost all full. But being the home team did have its advantages. We took up residence at the Outlaws reserved table and ordered as fast as we could so we could vacate our seats when the rest of the team arrived.

By seven o'clock it was standing room only, which was perfect timing because now that it was dark, we were on track for my favourite tradition of the weekend. It was the only reason all of us had worn snow boots to the games earlier.

We left Ranchmans in small groups to avoid being completely obvious, then snuck to the back door of the cafeteria, keeping to the shadows. It was completely unnecessary. We did this every single year, and it wasn't like the administration was oblivious. How could they be when they found a stack of water-logged trays in the kitchen the next morning?

"Shit, you almost knocked me over!" Axel laughed, and Rob shushed him.

Effing Rob. He looked like he was having a grand old time. Celebrating at Ranchmans, laughing with his friends. It made me want to punch him in the face.

Rory ran forward, pulling on the door handle. It was open as expected. He, Rob, and Axel ran in, and a few moments later, trays started appearing through the gap in the door.

We each grabbed one, waiting for them to reemerge. My toes still felt like icicles in my boots, but all it would take was one hike up that hill for my blood to get pumping.

The guys tumbled out of the cafeteria, and we slipped and slid our way across the icy square. The sun was out all day melting some of the snow we got last weekend when the boys got snowed in. Thankfully, there was still plenty on the hill.

Crystal grabbed onto my arm. "He's up there!" she hissed.

"Who?"

She pointed, and Maddie and I peered forward, trying to see who she was pointing at.

"Number twelve?" she said slowly, as if we were not only visually impaired.

I grinned. "Ride with him. You have to."

Our group doubled by the time we reached Pratt Hill behind the arts centre. We climbed the side of the hill, leaving the middle as pristine as it could be. There had already been sled-ders on it, but that would only pack down the snow and make some of the tracks more insane.

"Yo, Thommo!" Axel launched a snowball at Rob's head. "Fifty bucks says I smoke your ass!"

Rob easily dodged the icy projectile and smirked. "Make it a hundred and you're on."

I huffed as we crested the top of the hill and paused to take in the view of the snow-covered campus. The moon was nearly full. No clouds in the sky.

Logan would've loved this.

My chest tightened at the thought of him, hundreds of miles away. But not for the right reasons. As I looked out on my hockey family, the thought that made a lump form in my throat wasn't missing him. It was wondering what all of this would look like without him.

We'd built a life together over the past year. Our friends, our social calendar. All of it revolved around him. What he wanted. Who he wanted to spend time with.

Would I lose it all if I wasn't his? It was true what I'd said at breakfast. I'd spent time with the Outlaws before Logan. But could it be the same after?

"Sharla! Get the hell over here!"

I turned to see Crystal and Maddie already sitting on their trays. I hurried over, dropped my tray on a flat patch of snow, and climbed on.

"Bring it, bitch!" Crystal shouted, and we pushed off. The night air bit at my cheeks as I gathered speed, and then Crystal was careening toward me.

"You're insane!" I yelled, laughing as she missed and rocketed to the other side of the hill. I hit a bump and went airborne for a second, landing hard enough to rattle my teeth.

Maddie somehow beat me to the bottom, and I slid to a stop next to her. Her smile said it all. Yeah. We were doing that again.

I grabbed my tray and raced her back up the hill, meeting up with Crystal on the way. We took turns riding down with the others, mixing and matching passengers. Maddie and I managed to stay upright together for a full thirty seconds before tipping into a snowbank. Axel tried to stand up on his tray like a snowboard and immediately face-planted. Rory convinced Pam to ride with him, then dropped his hand into the snow to send them in circles the whole way down. They probably heard her screams in Okotoks.

My legs burned as we trudged back up the hill, breathless and giddy. And then I made the mistake of looking up. Rob stood at the top, watching us. His dark hair was damp with melted snow, his cheeks flushed from exertion and cold.

Damn it. I jerked my eyes away. Why did I care so much what he thought? Why was his non-friendship declaration eating me up inside?

Yes, I liked to be liked. Who didn't? But this felt like . . . more. I couldn't stop thinking about it. Truthfully, I'd been thinking about it since the day I moved in, my brain hovering over the puzzle that was Rob Thompson.

"I'm going to ask him." Crystal jutted out her chin. "Watch this." She climbed the last few meters and beelined directly for number twelve. We couldn't hear what she was saying, but the guy smiled, then nodded his head. And then they were getting onto Crystal's tiny tray, his legs wrapping around her.

"Hell yes," Maddie whispered next to me.

Hell. Yes.

I clenched my jaw, gripping my tray tighter. "Hey, I'll be right back." I changed my trajectory, walking directly toward Rob. He stiffened as I approached, and I wanted to smack him over the head with my cafeteria tray.

"You and me. Let's go." I pointed at my tray.

His lips twitched. "I think I'm done for the night."

"No you're not." I slapped my tray down and got on, positioning myself on the front half.

"We won't fit."

I looked up at him. "If that's a fat joke—"

"It's not a fat joke," he growled.

"Then what? You've ridden down this hill with people you don't even know, so it shouldn't be too hard to last thirty seconds with a non-friend." I winced. "And don't make some joke about lasting longer than thirty seconds. Axel and Rory have truly outdone themselves with innuendo tonight."

Rob's jaw flexed, and I started to sweat. What if he said no?

What if he walked away from me right now, and I had to get up off this damn cafeteria tray and walk back over to Maddie? What if—?

Rob dropped his tray on the snow and stalked toward me. He sat down behind me, nearly knocking me down the hill before grabbing onto my coat. "You're going to have to sit in my lap."

I smirked. "If you want to get up close and personal with my ass, you could've just asked." I pushed up from the tray and dropped on top of him, relishing the soft "oof." Good. I hope I knocked the wind out of him.

"You'd say yes?" Rob murmured, and every thought in my head evaporated like smoke. His arms wrapped around me, and I was transported back to my bed. To his body behind mine. The warmth of his skin. The scent of him.

"It was a joke." My voice was thin. Breathy.

"Don't dish it out if you can't take it." He lifted his legs, supporting mine as he pushed off and gripped onto me. I wrapped my arms around his thighs, sucking in a breath as we dropped over the edge.

My whole body lit up as we flew down the hill. His stubble rubbed against my cheek, his breath whispering over my skin.

"Why can't we be friends?" I shouted, then gasped as we hit a bump and my stomach dropped out from under me.

"What?" he yelled.

"Why? Why can't we be friends? I don't get it. I—" Another bump, and I was latched onto him like a baby sloth.

My breath came in staccato bursts, my heart punching a hole in my ribs as I waited for Rob's answer. He didn't say a word, and I smacked his leg in frustration. "Rob Thompson, I swear—"

We careened sideways, and I toppled down the hill, tangled up with Rob, until we jolted to a stop. My back sank deep in the snow because I was heavier than usual. I opened my eyes and saw the reason why.

Rob stared back at me, his nose inches from mine. "Are you

okay?" I nodded, struggling to draw a full breath. Rob shifted, starting to roll off me, but I grabbed on.

"Give me an answer, Rob." I was suddenly desperate. I was teetering on the edge of a cliff, and I was either going to take a step back or topple off, but I couldn't stand on the precipice like that a second longer.

"You already asked for answers. For Christmas."

I rolled my eyes. "*One* answer, and this one is more important."

His chest rose and fell against mine, and his exhale warmed my cheek. "Then I'll add it to the list."

My eyes narrowed. "Just tell me."

Rob's eyes dropped to my mouth, and my heart stuttered. "Christmas. I'll give you your answers then."

I groaned in exasperation. "This is so stupid! Why won't you just say it? Is it that bad? If I did something terrible, I'd like to know!" The cold from the snow seeped into my back even with my coat on. My jeans were already damp.

"Don't be a brat. I don't have to give you exactly what you want."

I gaped at him. "You think this is exactly what I want?"

He pushed himself off me and kneeled, straddling my waist. When he spoke, his voice was rough. "Obviously not."

CHAPTER
Twenty-Two

THE OUTLAWS WON both games on Saturday, which meant they were heading to the championship Sunday afternoon. As fantastic as that was, it threw a wrench into our party plans. None of the players were allowed out past eight, per their coach's rules. When I tried to convince Maddie to see if she had any sway with her stepbrother, her cheeks had flushed so pink, I wondered if she could give Rudolph a run for his money.

As we strolled across campus, Crystal turned to us with a mischievous grin. "Sooo, my roomie's having this epic bash at a friend's place off campus. And I may have heard through the grapevine that a certain Outlaw or two might make an appearance—"

"What? Hockey players breaking their coach's rules?" Maddie feigned shock and awe.

Maddie pursed her lips, considering. "What kind of party? Is this going to be "everyone's having sex on the available surfaces" or actual fun?"

Crystal laughed. "Only one way to find out." She turned to me, her eyes hopeful.

"Alright, alright, I'll go to your sex party."

Crystal let out a whoop and dragged us off to her place to get ready. We raided her closet, swapping outfits and giggling like schoolgirls.

"Oh hey, I meant to ask," I said, touching up my lipgloss. "What's the deal with you and number twelve?"

"Ooh, yeah!" Maddie perked up. "You were all up in that cafeteria tray."

Crystal ducked her head, fighting back a smile. "His name's Jake."

"Jaaake," Maddie said seductively, and Crystal laughed. "Let me guess, he's going to be at this party?"

Crystal shrugged. "I may have told him about it."

Ah. So that's what this is about. She needed wingwomen.

Maddie clicked her tongue. "I'm all in as long as I don't see your thong."

Crystal turned and pulled down her pants. I tried to slap her bare cheek, but she ducked away just in time.

We finished getting ready, and by the time we arrived at the party, we were riding a giddy high that had nothing to do with the vodka sodas we'd sampled before we left Crystal's. Maddie offered to be the DD, and I gratefully took her up on it.

The house was packed wall to wall. Bass thumped through the floorboards as sweaty bodies writhed to the beat. I spotted some familiar faces from the hockey teams milling about, red Solo cups in hand.

We waded into the fray, letting the music pulse through us. Crystal made a beeline for Jaaake almost immediately, and as I shimmied my way through the crowd, I nearly collided with someone. "Oops, sor—" I started to say, then did a double take. "Lily?"

Sure enough, there was Lily, an all-around goody two shoes, looking decidedly out of her element.

"Sharla, hi!" She grabbed my arm and pulled me to the wall. "This is insane."

I grinned. "No offense, but . . . what are you doing here? Didn't think this was really your scene."

She shrugged, a little self-consciously. "Oh, well . . . It's senior year. Figured I ought to get the full college experience before I graduate. Live a little, right?"

Her words struck a chord, plucking strings that had no business being touched. "Exactly." I pulled her into a hug, then walked into the next room, searching for a quiet corner. Preferably with no couch sex.

I wasn't any better than Lily. She was tied to her violin, but I was tied to Logan. I'd started to realize it at the pancake breakfast, but now the truth of it hummed within me. It wasn't that I didn't want to give some things up for him. I was happy to. That's what relationships were. But having him gone was shining light on just how much I'd sacrificed. It was like wiping layers of dust off an old photograph and not recognizing the face underneath.

All of that discomfort propelled me to the kitchen. I wasn't normally a drinker. I had a sip every once in a while, but I didn't love the pounding headache and roiling stomach the morning after. Even that wasn't enough to stop me now. I grabbed two beers and found Maddie, sticking close since Crystal was in a deep conversation with number twelve.

We kept our eyes on her, making sure she never left the public spaces. That she didn't put her drink down or leave it unattended. She didn't know we were overbearing parents, and that was exactly how we wanted it.

As the night wore on, the party kicked into high gear. The smell of weed wafted in from the patio, and I saw at least three pills exchange hands. I wanted to slap some sense into the guys and girls who accepted them. We'd seen two friends fail out of Douglas because of that shit.

I hadn't planned on dancing, but when Janet Jackson came on, I took Lily's advice. I was going to live in the moment—do what I wanted to do. Logan didn't dance, and I would never force him. But if he wasn't there, nothing was keeping me from enjoying myself.

I pulled Maddie out with me, and we joined the group gyrating in the middle of the living area. I felt the beat, moving my hips and laughing when I nearly dropped my half-empty beer bottle.

The lights moved over us, making Maddie's hair look purple. "It's a good look!" I shouted over the bass. Maddie laughed and spun, and by the end of the song, we were somehow separated by two guys I hadn't seen before.

"Hey." One of them leaned in, putting his hand on my waist, and rolling his hips into me. We moved together for a full three measures before I realized what was happening.

My heart raced. I didn't want to be a jerk, but I also didn't want this guy's hands all over me. "Hey, I actually—"

"Piss off." Someone pushed between us, rolling me away from random dude and against his chest.

I looked up and nearly dropped my beer a second time. "Rob?"

"Hey." His hands were still on my hips, and for a second, that was all I could feel. My hearing dulled, and my vision blurred, my brain only taking input from those two points of contact.

I swayed on my feet, and Rob steadied me. "You're going to be in so much trouble."

Rob stood there, his dark hair tousled and his eyes hooded. "Are you going to tattle?"

I blinked up at him, my head suddenly fuzzy enough, I wondered if I was on beer number four. Familiar voices blasted over the speaker. "I Swear" started, and everyone coupled up, swaying together to the a cappella intro.

"I didn't need your help," I snapped, starting to pull away, but Rob's fingertips pressed into the small of my back. His hands were so big, they reached that far. I wondered if I'd ever known that before.

He started moving, swaying from side to side, pulling me with him. "Just like you didn't need help in the courtyard?"

My eyes flashed. "That was different."

"This could've been different." He dropped his head, his lips brushing my ear. "It's like you're looking for trouble."

I barked a laugh. "Oh, you mean because I have a vagina?" The couple next to us glanced over. Said that louder than I intended.

"Because you're dancing like you want something." Rob's hand shifted, sliding across the bare strip of skin above my jeans. Heat pulsed through me, making my whole body feel weighted. That, combined with the angelic voice of Delious Kennedy, made it impossible for me to be pissed off.

"Well, I don't. Want anything." My voice wavered, and he blew out a breath. Before he could say something else to knock me off balance, I asked, "Why are you here?"

"Couldn't sleep." His answer was instantaneous.

"Nervous?"

He pulled back to look at me, and I realized one of my hands was around his waist, the other against his chest, still clutching my beer. How had that happened?

"For tomorrow?" He frowned. "No."

I pursed my lips, swallowing hard. "Then why can't you sleep?"

He gave me a look. *Because I was lonely. Because I was worried about you. Because I missed you.* My heart ratcheted up another notch as those phrases echoed in my head.

Where the hell had those come from? Not true. Any of them. I was tipsy and making up ridiculous stories.

"Amped up, I guess."

I exhaled, my insides caving in on themselves. Rob didn't say anything else, and I couldn't think of a response. I took a swig from my beer and cleared my throat. "I leave on Monday."

"Yeah. Me, too."

"So, how are you going to do it?"

He frowned. "Do what?"

"Give me my answers."

He blew out a breath. "One track mind."

"You could just answer me. Then I won't bug you about it."

His fingers pressed into my back, pulling me closer. My cheek rested on his shoulder involuntarily. "I'll email you."

My eyelids drooped. "You don't have my email."

"Yes, I do."

My brows furrowed. "Since when?"

"Since you put it on our emergency contact list."

I pulled back, my eyes wide. "You actually looked at that?" He nodded, and I thumped my beer hand against his chest. "You mocked me for that. Said it was a stupid idea."

"I looked at it. I didn't say it wasn't stupid."

My jaw dropped, but before I could call him a name, he reached up and brushed my hair from my forehead, and all thoughts evaporated.

"Did you put my pager number on there?" he asked.

I shook my head. "No, why?"

He wet his lips, and my gaze snagged on that quick flick of his tongue. "How did you know it? To phone when we were in Leduc?"

I opened my mouth and then snapped it closed. He watched me, his eyes drinking in every shadow from the room. *Just say it.* "It's an easy number so it stuck in my head."

My tongue wouldn't work. Because that wasn't the truth. Yes, it was an easy number, but I'd run it through my thoughts like salt water taffy. Pulling it, stretching it. I'd wanted that number, and by the look on his face, he knew it.

The song ended and we stood in front of each other, oblivious to the people moving around us.

"I'm going to head home," Rob said. "I can give you a ride."

I thought about walking out with him. Climbing in his truck. Riding with him in silence. Walking into our house together— "I'll probably stay out with Crystal and Maddie. She's our DD. Wouldn't want her to sacrifice for nothing."

Rob's nostrils flared. "How long are you going to stay out?"

I shrugged, folding my arms over my chest. "As long as Crystal and Maddie want to stay."

Rob clenched his jaw. "You're not a partier."

That set my teeth on edge. "Maybe I am."

He steered me to the side of the room, his hand wrapped around my upper arm. "Do you need attention? Is that it?"

My eyes flashed, and I poked a finger into his chest. "I'm allowed to have a night out. To let loose. I just finished finals, and I've only had a little to drink." I brandished my beer bottle.

He looked like he wanted to argue, but then he just shook his head, his lips twisting into a wry smile. "Whatever you say."

"Yeah. It is whatever I say."

Rob held my gaze long enough that my insides started to liquefy, then turned and walked away, disappearing into the crowd of sweaty, drunken bodies. I watched him go, my heart still racing and my mind whirling with questions.

What the hell was that all about?

When he disappeared down the hall, I pushed my way through the crowd, searching for Crystal and Maddie. The air was thick with the scent of humans and alcohol. I found them near the makeshift bar, laughing and flirting with a group of guys who were probably friends with number twelve.

Crystal caught my eye and waved me over, her cheeks flushed and her eyes bright with excitement. "Shar! There you are! We were just about to do a round of shots. You in?"

I hesitated, the rational part of my brain telling me to slow down, to be careful. But the alcohol coursing through my veins made everything seem fuzzy and distant.

"Sure, why not?" I heard myself say, grabbing a shot from the table. We clinked glasses and tossed back the liquid, the burn of the alcohol making me cough and sputter. Crystal laughed and slapped me on the back.

The rest of the party passed in a blur of laughter, dancing, and increasingly drunken antics. I spotted two guys shotgunning beers on the porch while a group of girls played a sloppy game of strip poker in the living room. Someone turned on a karaoke machine at one point, but I was definitely not drunk enough to take a turn at the mic.

By the time Maddie, Crystal, and I stumbled out the door at four in the morning, I had a throbbing headache and a rip in my shirt. Zero idea how that happened. We piled into Maddie's car, and she didn't bother driving us home.

We crashed at her place, and I didn't wake until well past noon, my head pounding and my mouth dry as a desert. Groaning, I pried my eyes open to find Maddie already up and dressed, holding out a bottle of water and some ibuprofen.

"Rise and shine," she said with a grin. "Let's get you home so you can finish packing. We need to head to the rink soon."

The rink? I blinked, pressing the tips of my fingers to my temples.

Maddie read my thoughts. "The championship game, babe. Just go pee. We can discuss glitter eye shadow and body paint on the way over."

CHAPTER
Twenty-Three

"MADDIE, FOCUS!" I nudged her shoulder at puck drop for the third period. She'd been distracted all night, not just because of the wolf mascot. She would've blamed it on that, but I saw her sneaking looks at the Outlaws bench. Specifically the end with the coaching staff.

The energy in the building was electric, every inch of the stands brimming with fans decked out in school colours. Signs waved frantically in the air, and the pounding of feet against the metal bleachers became a thunderous rhythm that reverberated in my chest.

Crystal leaned over with a grin, adjusting her maroon toque emblazoned with the Outlaws' logo. "Tie game, ladies!"

I squirmed in my seat. Normally, I loved a tight game, but this was the invitational championship. The Outlaws and the Wolves were locked at ones heading into the third period, and I already felt nauseous. With Logan away at World Juniors, the team had been forced to step up, and they had. But Clearwater wasn't backing down.

The puck dropped, and the tension in the rink ratcheted up a notch. Tim, our goalie, crouched low in the crease, his eyes tracking the play like a hawk. Rob took control in the defensive zone, skating backward with precision as he kept the Wolves' star forward at bay.

"Come on," I muttered under my breath as a slapshot sailed toward the net. Tim reacted with lightning speed, deflecting the puck with his blocker, and the crowd roared its approval.

"TIMMIE!" Crystal yelled, pumping her fist.

Bear, Rory, and Axel pushed hard up the ice, their sticks slicing through the air as they passed the puck. Rory broke through the Wolves' defence, setting up Axel for a one-timer. My heart leapt as the puck soared toward the net, but the Wolves' goalie made an unbelievable save, sprawling across the crease to smother it.

"So close!" Maddie groaned, clutching her scarf. "They've got this. They just need to keep pushing."

Time ticked on, and the game remained deadlocked. The Wolves' forwards were relentless, testing Tim again and again, but he was freaking perfect, his saves drawing deafening cheers from the crowd. Then, with eight minutes left, disaster struck. The captain of the Wolves threaded a pass through Rob's skates, and their winger buried the puck in the top corner.

The rink fell silent for a split second before the Clearwater fans erupted in celebration. My stomach dropped. Rob skated to the bench with his head down.

"They'll come back," Crystal said firmly, as if sheer will could make it true. "There's still time."

The Outlaws threw everything they had at the Wolves in the final minutes, but the Wolves defence held strong. With less than two minutes left, the Outlaws pulled Tim for an extra attacker. The crowd was on its feet, screaming encouragement as the puck zipped around the Wolves' zone. Rory fired a shot that hit the post, the clang echoing like a bell through the rink.

The crowd let out a communal groan when the final buzzer sounded. It was over. Clearwater had won, two to one. The Wolves celebrated at center ice while the Outlaws skated back to the bench, their shoulders slumped.

Maddie nudged me. "You okay?"

I'd chewed my lip to a pulp. "Yeah. Fine." *Not fine.* My stomach was twisted up like an old garden hose. I wanted to go down and see Rob, make sure he wasn't beating himself up. Which, of course, he was.

But I couldn't. Rob wasn't my boyfriend. I wasn't going to sneak down the stairs and meet him in the secret hall outside of the locker room.

Instead, I followed Crystal and Maddie out of the rink, the three of us making our way to Ranchmans for our gift exchange. The bar was bustling as always, filled with students blowing off steam and shit-talking after the game. We found a quiet corner and settled in, Maddie pulling out a bag with a flourish.

"Okay, Sharla, you first," she said, handing it to me.

I opened it to find a beautiful maroon scarf with gold accents like the one she was wearing. My throat tightened. "Did you make this?" She nodded, her eyes bright. "Maddie, this is perfect. Thank you."

"Sorry, the surprise is already ruined." Maddie grinned and handed Crystal her gift. I couldn't have been more thrilled that all three of us could twin it up at the games from now on.

Crystal handed over her gift next, a set of fancy sheet-music-themed notebooks and a pen shaped like a violin bow. "For all your musical genius," she said with a grin. Maddie opened hers and laughed at the syringe pen and notebook wrapped in math equations.

I gave them each their gifts next. They laughed at the shirts and loved the soaps. We exchanged hugs, and I was glad we'd saved this for tonight. After that heart-wrenching loss, we all needed a bit of a pick-me-up.

After a few more laughs and some food, Maddie dropped me off at home. The townhouse was quiet and dark as I let myself in. I'd secretly hoped Rob might show up at Ranchmans after the game, but he hadn't.

I frowned. He still wasn't home. After putting my shoes

away and hanging up my coat, I set my new gifts in my room and flopped onto the couch. I ignored my yawns and flipped on the TV. Tomorrow I was leaving to go home and I already had my things packed. I would just . . . stay awake for a while.

I wasn't waiting for Rob. I was winding down.

There was a difference.

———

I jolted awake to knocking. I rubbed my eyes, confused by the sound and the furniture I saw around me. This wasn't my room.

Then I remembered the night before, lying on the couch, watching a movie after the invitational championship game.

Waiting for Rob.

I glanced over. The TV was off, and a blanket was pulled over my body. Had I slept there all night? Adrenaline flooded my system when I realized Rob must have found me like this.

Another knock. It was coming from the front door.

I jumped up, dragged my fingers through my hair, and rushed to the peephole. I cursed under my breath when I saw my mom's face distorted through the glass. I swung the door open and tried to sound like I hadn't just woken up.

"Hey, Mom," I threw out my arms and stooped to give her a hug. "Just a second. I need to grab my things."

She frowned. "I've been knocking for almost five minutes. Did you not hear me?"

"Nope. I guess these walls are pretty thick." I invited her in, then escaped into my room.

I used the washroom first, noticing that Rob's toiletries now sat on the edge of the tub. I wondered what time he was leaving today. After washing my hands, I threw all of my toiletries in my waterproof case and grabbed my backpack and violin from behind the door. My suitcase was already out in the entryway.

Surprisingly, my makeup hadn't smeared during the night, so I didn't bother washing and reapplying, especially since my mom was already antsy. I paused and grabbed Logan's bracelet from the shelf in the washroom. I slipped it in my pocket. I'd put it on in the car.

Mom stood next to the island when I reentered the room. "Have you had breakfast?" she asked. I shook my head, and her face brightened. "Perfect. I was thinking we could stop at a brunch place my friend recommended."

My stomach grumbled. "Sounds great." I grabbed my purse and moved to extend the handle on my suitcase. My mom took it for me out the door.

I probably should have cleaned out the fridge. Didn't even occur to me until right that second.

"Here. Just a second, Mom." I turned back, set down my violin and toiletry case, and rounded the island to grab a notepad and pen. I scrawled out a message to Rob:

Hope you have a good break.

I chewed my lower lip, the pen pausing above the paper. Words flooded my head.

You played amazing last night. I'm sorry about the loss. That call in the third period was bullshit. I'm sorry I fell asleep.

Finally, I wrote,

At least you'll have the washroom to yourself,

but I'm sorry I didn't clean my food out of the fridge. Take whatever you want.

I set the pen down and turned back to the front door. He had my email. If he needed to get in contact.

My mom gave me a look like, "Are you finally ready?" I grabbed my bags and slapped a smile on my face, then followed her out to the car.

I immediately asked her about my dad, and she filled me in as we drove toward the highway. He was tired but recovering well. All of his numbers looked good. The way she was describing everything in such vague terms did not breed confidence that she actually knew what she was talking about.

When I asked her how she was holding up, she gave a small smile and launched into everything she was doing to prepare for Christmas. I started to zone out around cookie tin prices going up, and a shortage of cloves in our local grocery store. Then she said something that made my ears perk up.

"I hope you don't mind. We're going to have you in your old room instead of the guest bedroom."

I turned to look at her. "No. That's fine. Is there something wrong with it?"

Mom kept her eyes trained on the road. Both hands clamped on the wheel, and my heart started to race.

"No. Nothing wrong with it. We just needed to use it for our other guests."

My eyes narrowed. "You didn't tell me we were having other people over for Christmas."

She smiled a little too brightly. "Well, it was kind of a last-minute thing. I got a call from your aunt Rosemary last Wednesday."

Ice slid down my spine. "Aunt Rosemary is coming?"

"No." She waved me off. "This is something I don't want you

telling anybody else, but you know Aunt Rosemary is getting divorced." I nodded.

"Well, it's getting nasty. She's not in a good place."

I frowned, trying to figure out how this had anything to do with extra guests at Christmas. I hadn't talked to my aunt Rosemary since I left the house, and I would have preferred if that vow of non contact would've occurred much earlier than that.

"Anyway, she wondered if we'd be able to have the kids at our house for Christmas."

My body went rigid. My mouth, dry. I couldn't believe what I was hearing. Mom blew out a breath.

"It doesn't have to be a big deal. They're going to stay in the basement bedroom."

Not a big deal. My hands were shaking. I clasped them in my lap. The edges of my vision lighting up.

"Is Eric going to be there?"

My mom opened her mouth and then closed it. I blew out a breath and squeezed my eyes shut, dropping my head back against the headrest.

"Sharla. It's been six years."

"I don't care how long it's been. He abused me as a kid, Mom."

"Well, we still don't know."

"Don't know what? Just because you and Dad don't seem to know exactly what happened, I do."

"Sharla—"

"No." I cut her off, my chest so tight I could barely breathe. "Is he already there?"

"He and Megan drove in yesterday."

He was there. At my house. *With my sister sleeping upstairs.*

I turned my face to look out the window, not wanting her to see the angry tears pooling in my eyes. I couldn't do this. I wasn't going to drive home and spend my entire Christmas break in a house with him—to sit across the dinner table, to wake up on Christmas morning and have him sitting next to the Christmas tree.

I couldn't feel my hands. "You have to tell him to go." How could she not see how dangerous this was? How could she put another daughter in danger?

"Sharla, I'm serious."

"I can't be in the same house as him. You can get him a hotel or something."

"Sharla, we're not going to get him a hotel. Do you know how much that would cost? You'll be on separate floors."

I was going to pass out. My lungs refused to fill. My hands and toes were starting to tingle.

"Stop the car."

"Sharla—"

"Mom, stop the car!"

She pulled over, her tires screeching, as she pulled into the parking lot of a gas station. As soon as the vehicle stopped moving, I threw open the door and stumbled toward the fence, crouching over my knees and throwing up in the gravel. I stood there watching the tears drip from the end of my nose.

A few seconds later, my mom appeared next to me, handing me a napkin. I wiped my mouth.

"I'm sorry I didn't tell you, but I thought it would be better to talk about it in person."

I let out a sardonic laugh. "There is no better time to talk about this, Mom. I can't be there with him."

"Well, then what am I supposed to do? I already told them they could stay."

I stalked back to the car and opened the back seat. I pulled out the gift bag with my parents' present in it and set it on the front seat, then pulled out my toiletry kit and purse and moved to the trunk.

"Sharla, what are you doing?"

"I'm not going to the house."

"You're being dramatic."

A switch flipped inside of me, turning my panic into raw anger. I yanked open the trunk and pulled my suitcase out. I couldn't go back there. I hated myself for it. For not running to Red Deer and yanking my sister out of the house.

"Yep. Super dramatic. How ridiculous that I don't want to spend three weeks in the same house with the boy who shoved his hand in my underwear in the middle of the night when I was thirteen."

My mom's face went white as she scanned the parking lot, gauging how many strangers had just heard that sentence.

"Don't cause a scene."

"Oh. Sure. You're right. Let's just sweep this under the rug and stay one happy family. Right, Mom?"

I dropped my suitcase to the pavement and slammed the trunk closed. "I swear, if you don't tell Isabel to lock her door, I'll —" I sucked in a breath and dragged my things toward the convenience store across from the pumps.

"Sharla!"

"Merry Christmas, Mom. I love you. Give Dad a hug for me," I snapped.

I didn't look back until I was inside the store. A man in yellow coveralls and a trucker hat held the door for me, and I walked to the back near the Coca-Cola products. I watched out the window, my vision blurring. My mom's car sat in her parking spot.

That's when I started to cry. Hot tears streamed down my cheeks. I'd just ruined Christmas. Completely blown it apart. My dad had just gotten out of the hospital, and I wasn't going to go home for the holiday?

I pressed the back of my hand against my mouth to keep from "making a scene." I could walk back out there. Apologize. Tell her I was overreacting and ride with her back to the house.

She'd driven all the way here. She was probably angry and disappointed in me. Annoyed I couldn't just suck it up for a couple of weeks.

But I couldn't.

I couldn't do it.

Just the idea of seeing his face slammed me back onto my grandma's linoleum floor. Leaned over the toilet. Heaving up stomach acid.

Mom got out once and looked at the store. She tapped her foot. Crossed her arms over her chest.

I'm sorry. I'm sorry. I'm sorry.

Then she got in and pulled out of the parking lot.

What was I going to do? I was standing with a suitcase in a shithole of a gas station. Maddie was already at the airport by now, and Crystal was probably on her way to BC. I didn't have Lily or Caleb's number, and it wasn't like I could find a computer and email them.

Then my heart started to slow. My breathing deepened.

I did have one number.

Memorized.

CHAPTER
Twenty~Four

ROB'S TRUCK pulled into the parking lot of the gas station, and I gripped the handle of my suitcase, suddenly feeling light-headed. Was I really doing this? Had I gotten out of my mom's car and refused to go home for Christmas?

I stood there next to the pop refrigerator where I'd second-guessed myself for the last fifteen minutes. Was I making a big deal out of nothing? It was a long time ago. But the idea of seeing him again, of having to sit in the same space, made bile rise in my throat.

I walked to the doors, ignoring the strange looks the cashier was giving me and my suitcase, and exited to the sidewalk just as Rob got out of the front seat. We hadn't talked much on the phone. Mostly because I didn't want to sob like a baby in front of Chris, the gas station attendant.

Rob rounded the front of the truck and grabbed my suitcase. He threw it into the back seat, then took my toiletry case and backpack and set them in next to it. Then he opened the door to the passenger seat, and I don't know why it was that motion that did it, but the floodgates broke open.

I turned my face away from him as I got in the truck and fumbled for my seat belt. Then turned the opposite direction when he got in and started the engine. He didn't say anything, didn't ask any questions. There was no doubt in my mind that he saw I was upset. I kept swiping my cheeks every five seconds.

I finally got a hold of myself while we waited at a light a few blocks later. "Thank you for picking me up." My voice sounded watery, my nose stuffy and clogged.

"Yeah." Rob adjusted his grip on the steering wheel.

"I wasn't sure you'd call the number. Since you didn't recognize it." He'd made a point about not calling unknown numbers when we played foosball in the basement.

Rob drew a breath. "You did type in 9-1-1."

I pursed my lips. "Yeah." My mom's words came back to me. *You're being dramatic.* "I'm sorry if I messed up your plans. I know you were leaving today."

"No. It's fine. You didn't mess up anything."

I still couldn't look at him. I kept my eyes trained out the windshield, gritting my teeth to keep another round of emotion from washing over me. Standing in the gas station, I hadn't planned on telling Rob the details about why I was going back to the house and not to my parents. But sitting there, it felt like if I didn't get the story out of my body, it would keep looping torturously in my head.

My memories of those nights were like this. Sometimes crystal clear, and sometimes like I was inspecting them at the bottom of a pool. Colours. Shapes. That was when I had to repeat the facts in detail. Otherwise, the whole scene started to slip away from me.

My heart sped. I needed someone else to tell me that I wasn't crazy, that it was reasonable for me to get out of the car and page my boyfriend's best friend in a gas station.

"When I was thirteen, I spent a few weeks of the summer at my grandma's house. My parents were there. It was kind of a summer getaway. I didn't know it at the time, but my grandma was really struggling. My dad went to help her fix some things up at the house so she wouldn't have to hire somebody, and my mom used it as an excuse to take a vacation."

I drew a breath, trying to keep my voice from shaking. "We spent time at the lake, picked wild raspberries, learned how to canoe. It was idyllic. Until the end of the first week when I woke up in the middle of the night. To someone's hands on my body."

I couldn't look at Rob. Couldn't move. I was frozen in the seat. But I heard the twist of his hands on the wheel. The abrupt rev of the engine as we turned onto Center St.

He was pissed. And knowing that gave me the courage to continue. *This was wrong, and now there was one other person who knew it.* My friends knew. Logan knew. But not like this.

"I knew it was my cousin Eric because I opened my eyes when he was finished. I saw his shirt. His buzz cut." My gut clenched, the image of his silhouette against the light from the hall burned on my retina. That was what I saw in my dreams. Light and dark. But the sounds were so much worse.

I blew out a shaky breath. "He pretended nothing had happened. The next day I was sick. Throwing up. He offered to bring me soup. He sat with me while we watched a movie—to this day, I can't watch Hook."

Rob made a sound in his throat. I turned my head to the side and pressed my forehead against the cold glass as shame washed over me. Why had I pretended? Why hadn't I said something then?

And then I told Rob something I'd never said to another person. "I let him be my friend." The last word died on a sob. "He was doing all these nice things for me, and I let him. I watched movies with him, I baked cookies—" My hands clenched into fists.

Six nights he came into my room at night, touched me while he touched himself. And for six days I pretended I was fine with it. I acted like I was friends with him. No wonder my parents didn't believe me.

I hated my cousin, but I hated myself more.

Rob pulled the truck up to the curb in front of our townhouse, the engine rumbling softly before it shut off, leaving us in silence. I stared out the windshield, my face streaked with tears, my throat raw. I didn't know what I'd been expecting, but now that I'd said it all, I felt like I'd been ripped open, bleeding out in his passenger seat.

Rob unbuckled his seatbelt and got out of the truck. I shivered as cold air seeped in, then he was there, opening my door. He reached across my lap and unbuckled my seatbelt, his body brushing against mine.

He didn't leave. Rob wrapped his arms around me and pulled me to the sidewalk, enveloping me in his arms. I burrowed into his chest, his hand cradling the back of my head as I somehow found new tears to cry.

His shirt was soft and smelled like fresh laundry, and I closed my eyes, letting the warmth of his body seep into me.

"I'm sorry. I'm so sorry," Rob murmured, his lips brushing the crown of my head.

Rob didn't say anything for a long time. He just held me there, in the cold, with his thumb stroking my back. My tears slowed, and my breaths became more even.

"He's there. At my house for Christmas. I couldn't go back." I became hyper-aware of his body against mine. The way his chest rose and fell. The way his fingers gripped my hip. The way his thumb brushed against the skin on my neck.

"I knew there was something," Rob said, his voice low. "That night when I was using the washroom."

I exhaled against his now-damp shirt. "Yeah."

"I'm sorry. If I would've known—"

"It's okay."

"It's not okay. You shouldn't have to be afraid at night." He inhaled, my head rising with his chest. "You shouldn't ever have to be afraid again."

I blew out a breath. "I don't think that's how life works."

"Well it should. For you."

My skin lit up where I touched him, my hands threaded through his coat. I could feel everything beneath his cotton shirt, and my pulse thudded like a drum.

"What's your address?" Rob's voice resonated through me.

"Pretty sure you know my address."

He chuckled. "Your home address."

I lifted my chin and blinked up at him, my eyes burning from crying. "Why?"

"So I can go beat the living shit out of your cousin."

I shook my head. "I don't think Douglas would be pleased if you got arrested over Christmas break."

"Then just give it to me for fun."

A laugh of all things bubbled out of me. "I'm not going to give it to you." I eased out of his arms, and Rob dropped his hands to his sides. "But I appreciate that. More than you know." I pulled my coat closer around me, shivering at the loss of his warmth. "We should go in."

He nodded, his jaw tight, and opened the back. I grabbed my purse from the front seat, and he threw my backpack over his shoulder and grabbed my suitcase. I followed him to the front door of the townhouse, and he unlocked it.

Warm air washed over me as I stepped inside, and I needed a minute. Or several. I hurried to the washroom and turned on the light, then grabbed a cloth from the cupboard. After wetting it with cold water, I wiped up my tear-streaked face.

I turned off the tap and set the cloth on the counter. I sat down on the closed toilet seat, glancing up at the edge of the tub. Rob's shampoo and body wash stood beside my own, and now his toothbrush was sitting out on the sink. Right where mine usually was.

Heat started low in my belly and radiated out like a sunburst. A crescendo. I stood and looked for my moisturizer, then realized it was still in my toiletry kit. I walked out of the washroom and into the hall, hoping I could grab it and sneak back in, when I stopped short next to the kitchen island.

Rob stood in front of my suitcase, his back to me. He was bent over, his hand half inside the main compartment.

I cleared my throat, and he froze. Rob slowly turned his head, then stood and spun around to face me. There was a flash of white before he clasped both hands behind his back. "I, uh, was just—"

"If you're stealing my underwear right now—"

"I'm not stealing your underwear."

I walked forward, my pulse kicking up a notch as I waited for an explanation.

He did not disappoint. "I was looking for floss. Since you were in the washroom."

I raised an eyebrow. "In my suitcase?"

He shrugged. "Seemed like a logical place to start."

"For floss."

"Yup."

I pointed at my toiletry kit. "Didn't want to start with that?" I stopped in front of him, and his cheeks heated. I glanced around the living room and frowned. "Aren't you leaving today?" I didn't see a suitcase, and there wasn't one in his truck.

His throat worked. "The plumber's coming in the morning." My eyes widened. "I called him, and he said he could be here around ten."

I nodded. "Well, since I'm here, I can let him in. You won't have to wait."

Rob shifted on his feet. "Yeah, uh . . . " One of his hands reappeared to nervously scrub his jaw. "I'm not exactly going home for Christmas."

I blinked. "But you said you were."

"I lied."

My blinking became morse code. "Why?"

"I didn't want it to be a thing."

"A thing?" I repeated. "What kind of thing?"

Rob's jaw tensed. "It's embarrassing. I didn't want anyone to feel sorry for me." He flicked his eyes to the floor, then back to me.

Realization dawned, and my internal organs flipped positions. "So you're going to be here? Over the break?"

Rob nodded. "Yeah. I guess so."

Okay. This was fine. It was what we'd been doing all along, nothing had to change or get more complicated. Sure, I might not have hugged him as long if I thought I'd have to be alone with him in our house for the next three weeks—

This was not fine. My mouth was already dry, my heart trying to shove its way up my throat. I hadn't heard from Logan. My friends were out of town. It was just me and him.

Rob tried to skirt around me, but I stepped out, blocking his path. "Did you find floss?"

His brow furrowed. "What?"

"In my suitcase."

He wet his lips. "Ah, no—"

"Then what are you holding behind your back?"

He stilled, then pulled it out. A white envelope. "It was just mail."

I raised an eyebrow. "From my suitcase?" The wheels turned in his head, and before he could spin another lie, I said, "I've never told anyone that. What I said in the car." I let it sink in before continuing. "I've told Logan and my friends parts of what happened but not what I did. How I . . . reacted."

Rob's breathing quickened. His jaw tensed. Then he flipped the card over.

My name. It was written on the front. My pulse felt like it was pushing through a crazy straw. "You got me a Christmas card?"

Rob scraped his teeth over his lower lip. "Not exactly."

"Then what is it?" I reached out, but he pulled it back.

"Your answers."

All the air seemed to suck out of the house, the empty space suctioning to my skin like plastic wrap. "You wrote them down?"

I finally managed, my voice barely a whisper. He nodded, his expression tense. I couldn't tear my eyes away from the envelope. "Are you going to give it to me?"

Rob's hand tightened around the paper. "Not while I'm standing here."

I frowned. "Why not?"

"Because."

"Because . . . " I motioned for him to continue.

Rob exhaled sharply. "I thought I could put it in your suitcase and you'd find it over the break. By yourself. Without me there."

The open zipper. I had left my suitcase closed. Rob had opened it and slipped in the card. I worried my lower lip. "But we're both going to be here over the break."

He nodded. "Exactly."

I reached for the envelope again, my fingers brushing against his. Rob didn't let go. "I want to read it."

His grip tightened, and my frustration flared. "I'll just take it and go read it in my room. Problem solved."

He shook his head, his gaze locking onto mine. "No."

I threw up my hands. "What the hell, Rob? You wrote it for me, right? It's got my name on it. Why are you being an ass about this?"

Rob's pupils dilated. "New Years."

Somehow we'd gotten closer during our argument, both our hands still locked on the envelope. "What about it?"

"You can read it then."

I could smell him. Feel the heat from his body. "What's the difference?"

Rob swallowed hard. "I won't be here when you open it."

My eyes narrowed. "You're not going to be here?"

"Right."

"But I thought you weren't going home for Christmas."

He hesitated, then shook his head. "I'm not."

I drew in a breath. "So, what, you've got some hot party you don't want to tell me about?"

Rob dragged his free hand through his hair. "Something like that."

Why was he being so damn cryptic? "Just spit it out! If it's an Outlaws party or something and I wasn't invited—"

"I'm moving out," he blurted, and my arm went slack, my fingers releasing my side of the card.

"What?"

Rob's expression hardened. "I won't be here after New Year's because I'm moving into the house with Brayden and Rory."

CHAPTER
Twenty-Five

TUESDAY MORNING, I sat on a stool in the kitchen, the room dimly lit by the grey light seeping through the window. More snow, finally. Not that I loved bad weather, but Calgary was so much prettier in the winter when it was white.

I stared at my hands, fingers entwined, resting on the smooth, cold countertop. My eyes were red-rimmed and sandblasted. I was theoretically all cried out, but sitting in an empty kitchen when I was supposed to be at home drinking wassail nearly started another round.

The phone rang, and the sound sliced through the silence like a knife. I flinched. It couldn't be Logan. Possibly a friend, but doubtful. Most likely my parents. Did I want to talk to them? I definitely didn't want to explain myself because I shouldn't have to.

The plumber.

Damn it, I had to pick it up.

I stood and rounded the counter, then reached for the phone. I lifted the receiver to my ear, bracing myself for whatever was on the other end of the line. "Hello?" My voice cracked.

"Hello, Sharla." *Not the plumber.* Mom's voice was soft.

Reserved. The one she always used when she was trying to avoid conflict.

"Hello." I'd already said that, but I didn't know what else to lead with. Silence stretched between us for a moment. I stared at Rob's card still sitting on the counter. He'd just left it there, trusting me not to read it.

Mom clicked her tongue. "We were planning to go ice skating at the mall today."

Fantastic. A guilt trip. "I guess you still can."

She let out a slow breath. "We don't want to go without you."

I clenched my teeth. "Who's we?"

"Sharla, everything you told us . . . it was a long time ago. You've both changed since then."

My hands balled into fists at my sides. "It doesn't matter how long ago it was! It still happened, and nobody has ever acknowledged it. Nobody has ever apologized."

Her voice wavered. "I know, sweetheart. But it's not that simple. They're family."

I wanted to scream. To throw the phone across the room. Family. Of course. Why wouldn't that take precedence over their own flesh-and-blood daughter?

"Why can't you tell him to leave?" The words tumbled out of me, hot and angry.

My mom's breath hitched. "Sharla, I can't just kick them out. It's Christmas."

I drew in a shaky breath, my chest heaving. "I see." My voice was barely a whisper. "Well, I guess that tells me everything I need to know."

I moved to hang up the phone when I heard, "Sharla? There's something I need to tell you." I pursed my lips, placing the receiver back against my ear.

Mom cleared her throat. "We got a letter in the mail from the Alberta Heritage Fund. They awarded you eight hundred dollars."

My mind went completely blank.

"It looks like it's an academic award or something," she continued. "I deposited it in your bank account this morning."

"Oh." The word escaped with a breath. "Thank you." An academic award? I got good grades, but when had I been submitted for something like that?

"You're welcome." After a few moments of silence, she said, "I need to go get groceries."

I forced my lips to move. "Okay. Talk to you later."

"Love you, Shar."

I hung up the receiver. I didn't say it back. I knew I should've, but I couldn't drag the words out. It didn't matter how long ago it had been. My parents still didn't get it. I knew they loved me. I knew they wanted what was best for me, but in that moment, it didn't feel like enough.

And eight hundred dollars? What kind of insane conversation did I just have?

I stared at the receiver, the dial tone echoing in my ears. My chest felt hollow, like I'd been carved out with a soup spoon. I leaned against the countertop, my legs shaking as the guilt set in.

I shouldn't have lashed out.

I'd almost hung up on my *mother,* and I didn't say "I love you."

"What a bitch."

My head snapped up. Rob stood on the other side of the island, his hair dishevelled. "That's my mom you're talking about."

He walked to the cupboard. "Still stands."

The corner of my mouth lifted. "You and my fifteen-year-old self would've gotten along."

"Hmm. She sounds hot. Was she already a big Bryan Adams fan?"

I snorted, then turned so he wouldn't see my flushed cheeks from his comment. I pulled a banana off the bunch.

Rob pulled out a bowl and grabbed a spoon from the drawer. "I'm sorry, by the way."

I frowned. "For what?"

Rob poured himself a bowl of Fruit Loops. "For eaves-dropping."

I grabbed the milk for him and passed it across the counter. "Yeah. That was a dick move."

He shrugged, sitting down across from me. "Not quite as dickish as talking loud at nine-thirty in the morning." I feigned indignation as he poured his milk. "I'm sorry you're not going home for Christmas."

"That's a lot of apologies for one morning."

Rob chuckled, then pushed the Fruit Loops box toward me. "This morning calls for more than a banana."

I hesitated, then nodded. "Thanks." I grabbed a bowl and spoon.

Rob started eating, and I followed suit. I couldn't remember the last time I'd had something that tasted like literal childhood. Like Buckshot and Benny with Saturday morning cartoons.

We sat there in silence, the only sound the clinking of our spoons against the porcelain bowls. When I finished my cereal, I set my spoon down and looked up to find Rob watching me. "Thanks for this."

He took his last bite and swallowed. "For calling your mom a bitch?"

I grinned. "Exactly."

"Anytime." His mouth quirked, and he dropped his eyes.

I took my bowl to the sink, then reached for Rob's. He pushed it forward but didn't let go. "I changed my mind."

I frowned. "About what?" My heart flipped. About moving out? I hadn't been able to stop thinking about it. So ironic. It was all I'd wanted for the past year, and now that it was happening, I felt like my stomach was on a merry-go-round.

"Maybe we can be friends." Rob let go of his bowl and the handle of his spoon skittered along the edge.

I rinsed both our dishes and put them in the dishwasher just as a knock came at the door. Was it possible for a plumber to be early?

Rob stood and answered it. The plumber walked in with a bucket and tool belt, and Rob smiled, making easy small talk as he led him into his washroom.

I walked back into my room to get ready for the day, then stopped. There was nothing to get ready for. I took in my rumpled bed and, before I could question it, crawled back in and pulled the covers up to my chin.

———

When I woke, afternoon light slanted through the window, bathing the room in a honeyed glow. *How long had I slept?*

I jumped out of bed and cleaned up in the washroom, then put on fresh clothes and brushed my hair. I walked out to the living room and found Rob sitting on the couch with a book. *Rob read books?*

He glanced up and smiled. "Ready to go?"

I opened my mouth, then closed it. Normally I would ask what he was talking about, but then Rob grinned and stood from the couch. He walked to the front door and grabbed his coat.

Okay, then. Apparently, we were going out.

We walked to his truck and drove. I stared out at the campus as we drove past. The trees were bare, their branches stretching like fingers against the grey sky. Fresh snow already dusted the sidewalks.

Rob parked at the A&W and turned to me. "I was craving a Teen Burger."

I grinned. "And poutine."

We crossed the parking lot, and Rob held the door for me. The warm smell of root beer, onions and fries enveloped us. We ordered, and I insisted on paying for Rob's food to thank him for picking me up at the gas station.

Normally, an added expense like that would've stressed me out, but with that award, my bank account was flush.

We collected our tray and sat across from each other in the corner booth. I unwrapped my Teen Burger carefully, the paper crinkling in my hands. The first bite was perfect—charbroiled beef, crisp lettuce, and that tangy, mustardy sauce.

Rob lifted his burger, his elbows on the table as he leaned in, focused. "I don't know if there are enough pickles."

I laughed, spearing a gooey forkful of poutine. The cheese curds stretched as I lifted the fork to my mouth. "You should probably complain." He took a big bite. "What's the verdict?"

He held up a finger while he chewed and swallowed. "It's good."

I snorted. "Excellent recommendation." I took another bite, then washed it down with a gulp of root beer. "This doesn't feel like Christmas."

Rob raised an eyebrow. "What does Christmas *feel* like?"

I rolled my eyes. "You know what I mean."

Rob shrugged. "We didn't have many traditions growing up."

I set my burger down. "Why aren't you going home for Christmas?" I'd wanted to ask him since yesterday, but there were too many distractions. Rob was from BC, I knew that much, but I had no prior knowledge of his family situation.

He hesitated, his fingers brushing the edge of his tray. "It's complicated."

I stayed quiet, giving him space to continue like he'd done for me.

"My mom died when I was nine," he said finally. "She had cancer. It was fast. One day she was there, and then she wasn't."

My heart clenched. When we told me about his dad screwing him over for taxes, I'd just assumed his mom was still there for him.

He nodded, not meeting my eyes. "After that, it was just me and my dad. But he wasn't the kind of guy who knew how to be a parent. He worked long hours at the mill, and when he wasn't working, he was drinking. By the time I was in high school, he'd pretty much checked out completely."

I swallowed hard, the warmth of the food in my stomach replaced by a cold knot. "That sounds . . . really hard."

He wiped his mouth with a napkin. "Hockey got me through. I spent more time at the rink than I did at home. My coach—he kind of stepped in, you know? Made sure I had rides to practice, helped me apply for scholarships. He was the one who pushed me to leave BC and come here."

"And your dad?"

Rob shrugged, leaning back in the booth. "We haven't talked in years. Last I heard, he sold the house and moved up north somewhere. I don't even know if he remembers I exist half the time."

I blew out a breath. "Welp. I think I'm the asshole."

Rob laughed out loud. "That's what you took from that?"

I fell back in my chair. "Absolutely. For the past month, I've been complaining about my boyfriend being gone, and then I made you come pick me up and told you my sob story—"

"Yes, let's rank our sad childhood histories." He smirked.

I watched him momentarily, then leaned forward and popped a fry in my mouth. "We need to make this Christmas magical."

Rob's grin faded, his brow pinching. The air between us seemed to thicken. "And how do you suggest we do that?"

"I don't know, but we don't even have a tree. Or lights. Or anything."

Rob's lips twitched. "You want a tree?"

I shrugged. "Maybe? I don't know. It just feels weird to have nothing."

He nodded, his expression thoughtful. "We could put up some decorations."

"Do you have any?"

Rob took a drink of his root beer. "I've got something that could work."

CHAPTER
Twenty-Six

WE CROSSED onto the Douglas University campus, and I had to work to keep up with Rob's long strides. We passed the bookstore and arts centre, then stopped in front of a brick building I didn't recognize. He used his keys to open the door, and I stepped into a long corridor.

The air smelled faintly of concrete and cleaning solution. The place was deserted.

"Why does this feel like the beginning of a horror movie?" I asked.

Rob glanced over his shoulder. "At least it's not the climax."

That word sent a shiver through me. *Boyfriend. Logan.* I hammered that into my head. He was going to be home in two weeks.

We walked farther into the dark with only the emergency lights glowing at equal intervals along the hall. "You have to admit, this would be a perfect place to—"

Rob turned sharply to face me, his expression shifting from sarcastic amusement to something more sincere. More intense. "To what?"

I swallowed hard. "To murder me." My breath caught, and I felt my skin prickle beneath my jacket. "I was kidding."

His jaw flexed. "Hurting you isn't a joke to me."

I couldn't move. My limbs were frozen in place as I stared into his eyes. His skin was darker than Logan's, and in the dim light, he looked like a sculpture, shadows drawing out the lines of his cheekbones, the curve of his bottom lip.

My mouth went dry. "I think it's easier to joke about it than accept that it could happen." Rob knew better than most since he'd come to my rescue in the square.

"I would never hurt you."

"I know."

He stood still for a moment, then nodded once. "Good."

Rob led me into the room at the end of the hall. "Janitorial perks," he said, pushing the door open.

He flicked on the light, and I was hit with sensory overload. The room was packed to the brim with junk. Not just any junk, though. It was like a graveyard of university history. Costumes, banners, float pieces, and decorations from events past.

I stepped inside, accosted by the smell of old fabric, paint, and dust.

The first thing that caught my attention was a mangy mascot costume. It looked like it used to be a bear, but now it was more of a sad, matted rug. The head was propped up on a shelf, its eyes staring blankly at me. "Wow. Not creepy at all."

Rob grinned. "We used that for a prank once. On one of our coaches."

"Okay, speaking of coaches, who's the new guy?"

He thought for a moment. "Coach Wilson?"

"Is that his name?" I moved past the nightmare bear and saw a piece of a float that had clearly seen better days. It was painted to look like a giant slice of pizza, but the colours were faded, and there were chunks of foam missing. "Please tell me that was for a parade and not some weird engineering project."

Rob shook his head. "I have no idea." He lifted an old sign and inspected the lettering.

"So Coach Wilson, what's his job?" I tried to be nonchalant

even though I was dying to get something juicy for Maddie. We'd seen him a few times during the invitational, but she still hadn't gathered the courage to talk to him.

"Defence. But mostly compliance."

I frowned. "Like academics?"

Logan nodded. "A lot of guys are failing."

"Hmm. Is he married?"

Rob raised an eyebrow. "Why, you interested?"

I scoffed. "No, I just wondered if he had a family here. If he'd be sticking around."

I unrolled what looked like an old concert poster. It was from a musical production put on by the university's drama department. The edges were tattered, and the signatures from the cast were faded, but I could still make out a few names.

"He hasn't mentioned anyone, but it's not like I interview my coaches about their relationship status."

I shot him a look. "I don't know why not."

Rob flipped me off, and I gave him a cheesy grin.

I walked to a clothing rack with hangers full of costumes. "This room is like a time capsule. I feel like there has to be a magical wardrobe."

"Doubtful, but come over here."

I crossed the room to find the Mecca of holiday cheer. Over the next twenty minutes, we dug through the clutter, unearthing plastic bins filled with garlands, ornaments, and wreaths. Rob found a bag, and we started filling it with our finds.

"Check this out." He held up a string of old-fashioned lights, the kind with huge bulbs.

"Retro chic." I laughed. "Perfect. Now all we need is a Charlie Brown Christmas tree."

Rob's eyes lit up. "Hold on." He disappeared behind a stack of boxes and emerged a moment later, holding a four-foot pink tree.

"No. Way." I clapped my hands. "That's amazing."

He grinned. "It's either this or a fig tree I spotted over there." He pointed to the far corner.

"This'll do." We loaded up our bag, then hauled everything back to the house. By the time we were done decorating, the living room looked like Christmas had exploded. Garlands draped over the mantle, ornaments hung from the tree, and the retro lights made it all look a little bit like a festive patio cafe.

I stood back and admired our handiwork, a smile tugging at my lips. "It's perfect."

Rob didn't say anything. I turned to find him watching me. I clapped my hands behind my back. "Well, I should get to bed."

"Yeah, me too." He started to turn, then paused. "Wait, can I —?" He pointed to my room.

I started nodding, then did a double take toward Rob's room. "Wait, I slept through the plumber action. Is it not fixed?"

Rob stepped past me. "It's fixed. Which is why—" He stopped mid-sentence and ducked into my room, then returned a few moments later with his hands full. "I needed to grab these."

He held all his toiletries. His body wash, shampoo and conditioner, and his toothbrush and toothpaste. "I'll officially be out of your hair."

"Hmm. Finally."

Rob gave a half smile, then walked to his room. I waited until his door was closed to release the breath I was holding.

———

For the week before Christmas, I assisted Rob on his janitorial shifts just for something to do. He had optional conditioning for hockey a few times a week, and on his off days he hit the gym. He invited me once, and when I laughed in his face, he didn't bother bringing it up a second time. I wasn't opposed to a good workout, but doing it in front of Rob? Hell, no.

I used my free time to learn some music I'd always wanted to try, but had never made time to do it. Rob would sometimes come to the practice rooms with me and read. It was nice to have an audience. To feel like he actually enjoyed listening and wasn't just there to flatter me.

I also started going to Outlaws practices. I'd bring a book and sit in the stands, but I never got much reading done. It was too hard to concentrate.

On the twentieth, I got an email from Logan. My heart skipped a beat when I saw his name in my inbox along with the constant strings of messages I sent with Crystal and Maddie. I clicked on it, then waited for it to load.

Shar! I've been having a blast here. We just visited the arc of triumph (not sure how to spell it in french) and the view from the top was insane. We hiked up a million stairs to get there, but it was worth it. Also, I tried snails. They were slimy, but when in France, right? Next, we're heading to Switzerland for a week, four bracket tourney. You'd love it here. The food is incredible. The teams play a little different here but it's been good to mix up our defensive strat. I scored two goals in our game last night. Pumped about that! Hope you're loving time with your family. Merry Christmas.

L

I stared at the screen. That was it? One paragraph after radio silence since the third? It had been fifteen days since I'd heard from him.

I pressed the button to reply. My fingers hovered over the keyboard.

· · ·

That's awesome!

I deleted that sentence.

Logan, hey

Delete.

Logan,

Okay. Starting point.

Thank you for sending a note! I'm so happy to hear that you're having fun in Europe!

I paused, biting my lip. I should tell him about my decision to stay at the house for Christmas. He deserved to know. But how much should I tell him? I didn't want to unload everything on him, but I also didn't want to keep him in the dark.

I've decided to stay at the house for Christmas. I can explain more when you get home.

I deleted that sentence, guilt snagging my middle like a

fingernail on pantyhose. I'd spilled my guts to Rob, and Logan was my boyfriend.

> *I'm actually spending Christmas here at our house. My cousin is staying with my parents right now. The one I told you about. I still feel so angry with my mom for allowing him to be there over the holidays. I tried to talk with her about it, but she doesn't understand why I can't be there with him. I can't do it. So, we decorated for Christmas and I'm going to make the best of it. Sorry. Don't mean to be a downer.*
>
> *On a better note, I can't wait to hear more about your trip! When do you get back? Do you have your flights? I'll be watching the news for anything World Juniors related!*
>
> *Sharla*

I hesitated, my finger hovering over the send button. Did I really want to send that?

Yes. I exhaled through my nose. I did. If I wanted this to work when he got back, I had to be willing to open up to him. Even if it felt like trying to finish the Saturday crossword.

I hit send, my heart pounding in my chest. It was done.

———

I loved mornings over break, especially when they smelled like pancakes. My stomach grumbled. It was a Pavlovian response.

The last time I had pancakes, Logan made them. My heart picked up speed. Why was Rob making pancakes? I kicked off my covers and walked into the washroom. My eyes were still not quite back to normal. I had a new crease showing up between my brows.

I washed my face and brushed my teeth, then threw on a sweatshirt and joggers and walked out to the kitchen.

Rob stood at the stove, flipping the last pancake onto a plate. He looked up. "Morning."

I took in the carton of blueberries and the zested lemon next to the cutting board. "You made . . ." I trailed off, my eyes shifting to the stack of pancakes. They were perfect. Golden brown. "Did Logan give you the recipe?"

Rob's brow furrowed. "Recipe? I didn't use a recipe. I just made them the way I always do."

I stared at him, my brain trying to process the information. Rob made blueberry pancakes? The same blueberry pancakes that Logan had made for me the morning before he left?

I sat down on a stool, my thoughts swirling. "What else?"

Rob moved the pan from the burner and turned off the stove. "There's butter in the fridge—"

"No." I placed my hands on the countertop. "What else did you do that I thought was Logan?"

Rob put a pancake on his plate, his brow furrowed. "Logan wanted that morning to be special for you. He asked me to make these—"

"But he never told me you made them. He let me believe it was him."

Rob shrugged. "I'm sure he wanted to impress you."

"Taking credit for something you didn't do isn't impressive." I took a pancake and drizzled it with maple syrup, then picked up the fork next to my plate and cut a piece. I didn't take a bite. Instead, I let the fork rest on the edge of the plate and stared at the table.

My chest tightened. I didn't want to think about it. I didn't want to believe that the things I'd thought were special between me and Logan were just . . . orchestrated.

"You were the one washing out my water bottles."

Rob reached for the syrup. He cleared his throat. "I was doing dishes anyway."

"Yeah, but it meant a lot more to me than that," I murmured, finally putting the pillowy soft bite into my mouth. I sighed, the lemon and blueberry exploding over my tongue. So good.

I wanted it to be Logan. All of it. Because if it was Logan, then the last year of my life made sense. And if it wasn't . . .

I took another bite. "You might as well just tell me now."

Rob shrugged. "He asked for a favour, and I did it. No big deal."

No big deal. I looked up at him, my mind racing. "How many other 'favours' have you done for him?"

Rob set his fork down, crossing his arms over his chest. "You're making it sound like some kind of conspiracy."

"Why would you do it? Just help him like that? When you knew you wouldn't get the recognition?" I stabbed another piece of pancake. "I've been thanking him for the water bottle for the last six months, and he didn't say a word."

Rob swirled a piece of pancake in the syrup, leaving trails of bruised indigo in the maple. "You know why."

I slowly chewed and swallowed. "No, I don't." My eyes landed on the letter again. Still sitting on the counter. *New Year's.*

"He gave me a place to live. Pretty sure I can live with no recognition for my dishwashing."

I considered this, but the twist in my gut didn't go away. Logan wasn't honest with me . . . or was he? I didn't exactly thank him out loud. It had all been in my head, and the one time I did bring the water bottles up, he didn't know what I was talking about.

Maybe he was just that clueless. Or maybe I was making up stories in my head?

I slumped over my plate. "Am I going to find out that Logan doesn't do his own laundry? Or that you would give me a ski lesson, not him?"

Rob chuckled. "I don't do his dirty-ass laundry. But the skiing." He looked up. "You don't know how?"

I waved my hand, dismissing the thought. "Not really. I went once when I was a kid. School field trip. He said he would take me for a lesson this winter." I chewed on the inside of my cheek. "Maybe he still will when he gets back."

Rob's expression said, "Good luck with that."

I leaned back in my chair. "You know something I don't?"

Rob shook his head. "No, but you know what his schedule is like. We'll be up to our necks in practices and games, and Logan has some catching up to do with his classes." He took his last bite of pancake. "Maybe just don't get your hopes up."

Hopes. That word was laughable. They had slowly been crushed one by one over the past month. Add this one to the list.

Rob picked up another pancake. "I don't have any plans today."

I looked up from my plate. "And?"

He poured a bit more syrup on his plate. "I used to be a ski instructor. We could go to COP. It's not Banff, but it's close, and they have rentals. Douglas students get a free one-day lift ticket every semester." He set the jug down and met my eyes. "You could still give Logan credit."

CHAPTER
Twenty-Seven

WE PULLED into the crowded parking lot at Canada Olympic Park. The sun was shining, and the snow glistened under its rays. Families and kids swarmed the area, the dads looking like pack mules hauling all the equipment.

Rob parked, and we made our way to the rental shop. The air smelled of snow and hot chocolate, and I breathed it in deeply. Inside, the chaos was even more intense. People lined up, tried on boots, and selected skis and poles.

My pulse quickened as we waited our turn. "Have you ever skied here?" I asked, trying to keep my mind off the fact that I was about to look like an idiot in front of him.

He nodded. "A couple times. Mostly for the jumps." My face blanched, and Rob laughed. He clapped a hand on my shoulder. "No jumps for you. Promise."

After an hour and paperwork that rivalled signing over my first-born child, Rob and I stood at the top of the bunny hill, surrounded by a sea of first-time skiers and their patient—or not-so-patient—parents. Kids in oversized snowsuits wobbled on their skis like newborn deer while adults tried to explain to them the physics of gravity and friction through food descriptions. "Pizza! French fries!"

"Do kids not understand triangles or straight lines?" I mumbled, and Rob smirked.

"A little testy."

I rolled my eyes and lowered the goggles he'd lent me. Rob wore his sunglasses and a toque. He looked unbearably hot, so I focused on my legs, which currently felt like they were encased in concrete.

I looked down at the slope before us, which didn't seem steep until I imagined myself pointing my skis south. "This is it?" I asked, trying to mask my trepidation.

Rob nodded. "This is it."

I swallowed hard. "Great. So, what do I do first?"

He grinned. "First, you have to learn how to stand up straight." He moved behind me, placing his hands on my hips, and even through my coat and ski pants, I shivered. "You want to keep your weight balanced. Don't lean too far forward or backward."

I nodded, trying to focus on his instructions rather than the fact that his hands were on my waist. He let go and stepped back. "Next, we'll work on your snowplow. Make a V with your skis and press the inside edges into the snow to slow down."

"Thank you for not saying pizza," I muttered, and Rob held back a grin.

I attempted to do as he said, but my skis seemed to have a mind of their own, sliding out from under me. Rob caught me before I could faceplant, his arm wrapping around my middle. "Nice. Good try."

My heart raced, and it had nothing to do with my near-fall. I took a deep breath and tried again, this time managing to create a semblance of a V. "Okay, now what?"

"Now, we practice moving." He positioned himself next to me, his skis parallel. "Just a little push off with your poles, and let gravity do the rest."

I gave a tentative push, and my skis started to slide. Panic set in as I picked up speed, and I instinctively leaned back. Rob reached out, grabbing my arm and pulling me to a stop. "Remember, stay balanced. Trust your body."

"Trust my body?" I muttered, more to myself than him. It was hard to trust something that seemed hell-bent on throwing me to the ground.

After a few more attempts, I managed to glide a few feet without falling. Rob whooped and pumped his fist in the air.

My cheeks burned, and I wasn't sure if it was from the cold or the fact that I was sweating under my layers. "I'm basically a pro."

He laughed. "Irrational confidence. I love it." I snorted, and he moved in front of me. "Now, I want you to try following me. I'll go slow, and you just mimic what I do."

I nodded, my heart pounding. As he started to move, I pushed off and tried to keep up. My legs wobbled, but I focused on Rob's movements. He shifted his weight, and I did the same, my skis miraculously staying under me as we made smooth, wide arcs across the hill.

We reached the bottom, and I tried to stop but ran into Rob instead. He laughed, catching me. "That was awesome."

My breath came in short gasps, but I grinned, the adrenaline rush making me giddy. "I didn't die."

"You didn't die." Rob chuckled. He reached up and lifted my goggles to look me in the eye. "You ready to try it again?"

A few moments later, we sat on the lift, the metal seat cold against my legs. I gripped the safety bar, my knuckles turning white. "This feels like a terrible idea."

Rob laughed, then moved side to side, shaking the chair. I squealed and smacked him, which only made him laugh harder. "Ow! We're not going to fall."

"You don't know that!"

He grabbed my gloved hand. "I do know that. We pulled all kinds of shenanigans on these things when we were kids."

I gripped him like he was my seeing-eye dog. "You said you were an instructor?"

He shrugged. "I taught my friends."

My jaw dropped. "Rob Thompson. Did you lie to me?"

His grin widened. "I promoted a convincing narrative."

I laughed. "Did you think I wouldn't come out if you weren't an expert?"

"I knew you wouldn't." He pointed to my death grip. Fair enough. Rob glanced ahead. "Okay, just remember to stand up when the chair slows."

I turned my head just as Rob started lifting the bar. "Rob—"

"You'll be fine. I've got you."

I tried to stand, but my muscles went into lockdown. My skis wobbled, but Rob clamped a hand around my waist and basically carried me down the small slope, stopping again at the top of the bunny hill.

"Thanks." I tried to ignore the fact that my heart was still in my throat.

Rob turned to me. "Alright, let's do it again."

I nodded, trying to remember everything he'd told me the first time. Snowplow. Knees bent. Weight forward. I pushed off with my poles and followed him

We went up and down the hill a few more times, and by the end of the day, I was able to get off the lift with only mild cartwheeling arms and make it down the hill behind Rob without stopping. I was sore and exhausted, but I felt a sense of accomplishment that I hadn't experienced in a long time.

"How are you feeling?" Rob grinned as we reached the bottom of the hill.

"Tired." I laughed, pulling up my goggles and looking at him superpositioned between the snowy pine trees and the ski lift. *Happy. Grateful.*

He patted my head with his glove. "Now you get to experience the best part." Rob unclipped his skis and set them aside, then got down on his knees to help me out of mine. I stepped out and he showed me how to snap them together, then carried them for me anyway. I grabbed my poles and followed him to the lodge.

We returned the skis, poles, and boots to the rental shop, and I sighed audibly when I put my shoes back on.

Rob watched me. I grinned up at him. "Okay. That's incredible."

He chuckled, then motioned for me to follow him up the stairs. The air inside was warm and smelled like cinnamon and hot chocolate. We found a table near the window and ordered two steaming mugs of cocoa with whipped cream.

I wrapped my hands around the mug, letting the warmth seep into my fingers. "This is perfect."

"Yeah, it is." Rob took a sip of his drink, then looked at me over the rim of his cup. "Just don't tell any of the guys we came out today."

My eyes narrowed. "Are you embarrassed to be seen with me?"

He pulled off the top to his cup. "More like Coach told us if we skied or snowboarded over the holidays, he'd kick our ass."

I gaped at him. "Why didn't you tell me that?"

Rob laughed. "Because I knew I wouldn't get injured on the bunny hill."

I leaned in. "You knew Logan wasn't going to take me skiing." If Coach gave him an order, Logan would never disobey it. Staying in his good graces was too important to him.

He shrugged. "I don't know. Maybe he would've done the same thing."

We both knew it wasn't true. I took a tentative sip of my hot chocolate. "Your secret's safe with me." My stomach swooped. How many secrets did Rob and I share at this point? I was starting to lose count.

We sat in comfortable silence, watching the snow fall outside the window. When we finished our drinks, we walked back to the truck and headed home.

We pulled into the driveway, and I trudged up the walkway. It wasn't until I got out of the car that I realized the full extent of my workout. Rob unlocked the door, then I kicked off my boots and hung up my coat. I felt like a puppet without strings, my muscles deciding to go on strike after the day I'd put them through.

"Shower."

"Good plan." Rob yawned. "I'll get dinner going."

I stumbled to my room and turned on the water to let it heat up, then stripped out of my layers and stepped under the spray. The hot water felt like heaven, and I stood there for a solid ten minutes, letting it wash over me. When I finally got out, I changed into my favourite pair of sweats and an oversized hoodie.

I returned to the living room and found Rob sitting on the couch, flipping through channels on the TV. I turned on the computer and started the dial up, then plopped down next to him, my body sinking into the cushions. "I don't think I've ever been this sore in my life."

He chuckled. "That's what happens when you use muscles you didn't know existed." He handed me a bowl of spaghetti.

I took in the shredded parmesan on top. "You made this?"

"It's not hard. Ground beef and jarred sauce."

I laughed. "Well, it looks amazing."

Rob turned on an episode of Seinfeld and leaned back, resting one arm on the back of the couch. I twirled a forkful of spaghetti and glanced at the screen, recognizing the opening notes of the theme music. I didn't watch much TV, but this was definitely a favourite.

Jerry and Elaine started their banter, and within moments, Rob and I were laughing. I couldn't help it—Jerry's deadpan delivery and Elaine's sharp wit had us both in stitches. Rob's laugh was unrestrained, his shoulders shaking as he leaned back against the couch, utterly at ease.

I found myself grinning more at him than the show. His face lit up in a way that made my chest ache. How had I never noticed how perfectly his smile tilted, just a little lopsided?

Then Jerry and Elaine began laying out their friends-with-benefits rules, and my blood started to rush. Neither of us was laughing anymore. I tried to focus on the TV, but my attention drifted, drawn to the way Rob absentmindedly tapped his fingers on the armrest.

The soft glow of the screen highlighted the curve of his jaw, the way the light caught the faint stubble on his chin. I honed in on the rest of my spaghetti, and when I finished, I set my bowl on the coffee table. The movement brushed my knee against his. He didn't pull away, and the faint contact sent a ripple through me. My body felt taut like I was holding my breath, even though I could've sworn my lungs were working.

I regretted setting down my bowl. At least five seconds ago, I had a prop—something to keep my hands busy. Now, feeling warm and fed, all I wanted to do was sink into him. His arm stretched along the back of the couch, his fingers just inches from my shoulder. Would it be so terrible if I let myself inch toward him? Just enough to . . .

No. I pushed the thought aside. *Logan, Logan, Logan.* Rob and I were friends. That was the deal. Nothing more. Nothing that would make things messy or complicated. But my body didn't seem to care about the rules of boyfriends and loyalty. My chest ached, my skin felt too warm, and every breath I took felt too heavy.

I got up from the couch, thoughts of Logan reminding me why I'd connected to the internet. I cleared the screensaver and opened up my email. When it loaded, I scanned my inbox. Nothing from Logan.

I exhaled and disconnected, then sat back on the couch. I'd poured out real feelings in my last note to Logan, and it had been a full day. How had he not found time to respond?

Rob laughed softly at another joke, the sound low and rough, and my heart twisted. I glanced at him out of the corner of my eye, hoping he wouldn't notice the way I was staring. But how could I not? The way his lips curled when he smirked, the way his hair fell just slightly into his eyes—it was all too much.

I forced myself from the living room and took our dishes to the sink, then sat on the floor. "I need to stretch or something. I can already tell I'm going to be a walking corpse tomorrow."

Rob nodded. "I have some Tiger Balm in my bag. Our trainer uses it after games. I can grab it for you." He pushed up to stand and walked to the door where he'd dumped his gear. "My bag reeks, but I promise the balm is clean."

I laughed. "A glowing endorsement." I was silent as I watched him unzip his bag and start rifling through his things. He walked back with the tin in his hands, then sat next to me, pulling off the lid.

I sat up straighter. "You can just give me the balm."

Rob looked up. "Oh. The trainer usually rubs it in."

My breath snagged. I swallowed hard. "You don't have to do that."

He dropped his eyes. "Where are you sore?"

I knew exactly what he was asking. I thought of all the places aching in my body. So many of them I could reach with my own hands, but that wasn't what came out of my mouth. "My lower back."

Heat flushed my cheeks, and I hoped he didn't notice with the lights turned low. Rob nodded, still not looking at me. He set the top to the tin on the rug next to him. "Just lie down . . ."

I didn't wait for him to finish that thought. I dropped to my stomach, creating a pillow for my head with my hands.

"Do you want a pillow?" Rob asked.

I shook my head. "No, it's fine." I knew this was a bad idea. I knew we were treading a very thin line. I knew what I would feel the second his hands hit my skin.

And I'd underestimated all of it.

The second Rob lifted the hem of my sweatshirt, heat flashed between my thighs. Holy hell. I thought about flipping over. Scrambling up and telling him I'd changed my mind. But then his hands were on me, and all rational thought faded to the back of my mind.

His hands were strong. Firm. I gasped as he pressed into my sore muscles, and he pulled back.

"Too hard?"

"No. It's perfect."

Rob started again, his fingers gliding easily over my skin with the lubrication of the balm. Lubrication. I should not be thinking about words like that.

I never thought about words like that.

When Logan was here, sure, there were times I got turned on, but they were few and far between unless he was actually, you know. There.

I thought about my conversation with Maddie. About having good sex. This had to be something connected to that because what I was feeling—the way my body was igniting from the inside out—that had never happened to me before. Not like this.

The balm started to cool on my skin, and my brain short-circuited. Heat. Pressure. Cold. Damn it, his hands spanned my entire lower back. His fingers wrapped over my hip bones, pressing into the soft parts of my waist.

I bit my lip to keep from moaning.

I shouldn't be enjoying this. I shouldn't be tensing my lower half to keep from rolling my hips into the carpet.

Rob's thumbs dug into the muscles on either side of my tail-bone, and I had to clench my fists to keep from arching into his touch. This was supposed to be functional. It wasn't supposed to feel *this good*. My heart pounded in my chest, and I struggled to keep my breathing steady.

Rob's hands moved up the sides of my spine, and my skin prickled. Guilt gnawed at my insides. I shouldn't want anyone's hands on me but Logan's. I shouldn't be lying there, fantasizing about anything other than relief from my sore muscles.

But I was fantasizing. Rob was naked in my shower. Using the toiletries that sat next to mine. His wet hair falling over his forehead as he looked up and grinned, nodding for me to join him.

When his fingers grazed the bottom of my bra strap, I pushed up from the carpet and quickly pulled down my shirt. Because I was a good person. A loyal person. And I didn't cheat. Not on my schoolwork, not on my friends, and definitely not on my boyfriend.

I scooted forward and sat in front of him, folding my arms so tightly across my chest, I could barely breathe. "Thanks. I think that's good."

Rob sat back on his heels, still holding the tin, his expression unreadable. "Anytime."

I stood, my legs wobbly. "I'm going to get ready for bed."

Rob nodded, his eyes flicking to the rug where I'd been moments before, then back up to me. "Goodnight."

I hurried to my room, my heart pounding. I closed the door and leaned against it, my mind a whirlwind of emotions. I shouldn't have felt that. I shouldn't have wanted that.

I slipped my hands under my shirt, pressing my palms flat against my stomach.

I was officially a terrible person.

I tried to calm my breathing, but when I heard Rob's door click shut, I hurried back into the kitchen for a glass of water.

There was no way I was going to be able to fall asleep. Not without . . . something. I needed to move. I needed to think. I needed to go to confession or talk to Crystal and Maddie, or—

I froze, my eyes landing on the white card on the counter. I set my glass down, careful not to make it clink.

I pulled the letter off the counter, inspecting my name in Rob's handwriting.

I set it down.

Picked it up again.

I sat on a stool, then stood and paced to the window.

New Year's.

But would he even know? He hadn't touched it since he'd set it down. If I opened it carefully . . .

I tiptoed back to the counter and snatched the card, then hurried back to my room, closing the door without a sound.

CHAPTER
Twenty-Eight

Shar,

Not sure if you're okay with me calling you that, but that's probably going to be the least offensive thing you read in the next five minutes, so here goes.

You asked me what you did to make me "think that" about you. I have to say, I lied to you while we were cleaning. I did remember that day. I remember what I said to Logan, and I remember you walking up to us. You looked pissed, so if you were trying to pretend you didn't overhear, you did a shit job of it. Probably don't go into acting.

Sorry, stalling. Because I really don't want to admit this next part. I couldn't say it while we were all still living at the house together, so let me tell you this part first. I'm moving out. When you come back from break, my stuff will be gone, and I'll be living over at the big house. Living the dream. At least I didn't choose Axel, so I won't have to play foosball in that creepy ass basement.

I'm sorry it took so long for me to get out of your hair. I know you hated having a third wheel there.

Okay. Still stalling.

The truth is, I said those things to Logan because I hoped it would change his mind about you. I hoped he'd give up and focus on hockey instead of trying to make you his girlfriend. I don't know why I thought that would work, but it was one of many strategies I tried in those early weeks.

Logan doesn't know this, but the mix tape he gave you that night at the bonfire? I made it. I didn't tell anyone. I'd been working on it for weeks, paying attention to your favourite songs, waiting until they played on the radio. I'd planned to give it to you weeks before the invitational. Since midterms that semester. But we hadn't talked much, and I was too nervous. So I put it in my bag and carried it around like a douche. It must have fallen out because the next I knew, Logan had given it to you that night.

I don't blame him. He didn't know whose it

was and it already had your name on it. I didn't
know you had it till you moved in, and I heard the
songs playing through the walls. At that point, what
was I going to do? You and Logan were living
together. You'd been with him for six months. I
didn't want to be, like you so aptly put it, an
asshole.

But that brings me to your second question. Why
can't we be friends?

You're smart. I'm sure you've already figured
that out by now, but just in case, let me spell it out
for you:

I love you.

I'm in love with you.

I have been since September of that first
semester with the Outlaws. Watching Logan with you
was never bearable, but I managed. I worked out.
Skated harder. Avoided after parties and that damn
stairwell next to the locker room.

Until you moved in. I've been looking for
housing since that first day, and yes. I acted like
an ass. Because every day of my life I had to
watch you touching him and laughing with him. It
felt like my heart was being thrown in a blender
every damn morning.

I had to try and sleep listening to your soft
voices in the other room. That nearly drove me
insane, by the way. It's why I took that janitorial

job. I could be gone at night. Didn't have to obsess over what he was doing with you behind that door.

And trust me. I obsessed.

So. Kind of a weird note to end this on, but there's not much more to say. Now you have your answers, and hopefully you understand why I had to wait.

I get that you love him. I hate it. But I don't hate you. I've never hated you. Not for one second.

I hate when I see him take you for granted. I hate when he buys you shit like bracelets because he doesn't know you hate wearing things on your wrists. I hate that he's never gone to one of your concerts. I hate that he left you alone over the holidays. I hate what that Montana ass muncher tried with you in the courtyard, and I hate that you wake up scared in the middle of the night.

I hate that it's Logan's arms around you. His lips on your skin. His hands on your body.

Most of all, I hate myself for waiting too damn long to say all of this.

Merry Christmas,

Rob

CHAPTER
Twenty-Nine

I BURIED my face in my pillow, my heart pounding so hard I could feel it in my temples. Not surprisingly, I slept like absolute shit. After I refolded the letter and licked the envelope to make it stuck again, I set it back in place on the countertop. Then I tossed and turned all night.

Now it was past ten in the morning. My palms were clammy, and I smelled like stress sweat.

Think.

Why had I done it? Why had I read the letter early? How was I going to look Rob in the eye and pretend I didn't know . . . everything?

"Sharla, you good?" Rob's voice filtered through the door. I could picture him standing there, leaning against the doorframe in the T-shirt I forced him to wear. My stomach did a somersault, and I had a sudden urge to throw the door open and confess everything.

But I couldn't.

We were still going to be alone together for another week and a half. My mind raced, grasping for an excuse. "Uh, yeah, I'm fine!" I croaked, making my voice sound as weak as possible. "Just not feeling well."

"Not feeling well?" Rob sounded concerned. Of course he did. *Because he loved me.*

"Yeah, I think I caught something." I coughed for good measure, hoping it didn't sound too forced. "I don't want you to get sick. You should probably stay away."

The floorboards creaked as he shifted his weight. "Do you need anything? I can run to the store or—"

"No, no! I'm good." I bit my lip, trying to think of something to make my excuse more convincing. "I just need to rest."

There was a pause. "You sure you don't want me to bring you something? I make a mean cup of tea."

I pressed the heels of my hands against my eyes. What was I going to do, sit in here all day and starve? My stomach was already grumbling. "As tempting as that sounds, I don't want to be responsible for your untimely demise if this is something contagious."

Rob chuckled, and I felt a pang of guilt. I was lying to him. I was lying to Logan. "Alright, well, if you change your mind, let me know. I have a conditioning practice this morning, then I'm heading to work later."

I exhaled with relief. All I had to do was wait until he left, then I could eat and get cleaned up. Probably change my sheets. Ugh, what a mess!

Wait, what day was it?

I scrambled up from the bed and checked my desktop calendar. The eighteenth. That meant Crystal was home from her ski trip. Not home, home, but with her family in Calgary. I searched for my address book.

Yes. I had her home number.

I sat next to the door, listening to Rob move around the house. When I heard the front door close, I exhaled. I had a few hours to figure out my next move. I waited five minutes, then peeked out into the hall. I crept forward, scanning for his hockey bag.

Gone.

I ran to the kitchen and ate a banana and yogurt, then showered and put on my robe. The sheets could wait until later when I sequestered myself away again.

With my hair still damp, I picked up the phone and dialled. After briefly talking with Crystal's dad, her voice came on the line. "Hey! I'm so glad you called! How are you?"

"Umm, good?"

Crystal paused. "Here, just a sec." She set down the receiver, and I heard her yell, "Dad, when I get downstairs, can you hang this one up?" A few moments later she came back on the line and yelled upstairs. There was an audible click. "Okay. Spill."

I couldn't hold back the tide of verbal diarrhea. I told her everything. About the water bottles, the pancakes, about Logan's disappointing emails and phone calls. I told her about my mom and my cousin, and the fact that I was still here on campus.

Then I told her about my email to Logan, how I still hadn't heard back, and lastly I dropped the bomb.

The letter from Rob.

When I finished, Crystal was silent.

"I know," I groaned. "What do I do?"

She exhaled. "I mean, I'm not surprised."

"By which part?"

I could practically hear her eyes roll. "Did you not see how he looked at you when you were dancing at that party? Or the way he's always performing for you at Ranchmans?"

I blinked. "What?"

"Shit, Shar. He's always right in front of you. Messing with Logan. Trying to get your attention. You've never noticed?"

My mouth went dry. "He likes messing with Logan."

"Yeah. Because you're there."

"I—"

"Trust me, I've been to Ranchmans when you couldn't come. He's completely different."

I sank to the floor, resting my head against the cabinets.

"You should come stay with me for Christmas," Crystal said.

"Seriously. The second he sees you, he's going to know you read it."

I scoffed. "I have a couple of hours to pull myself together."

"Shar. You're a terrible liar. You're going to get all weird. All happy and creepy."

I laughed. "I am not!"

"That's how you always get. That one time when you lied about missing rehearsal?"

"Franck believed me."

"No, babe. She didn't. She let you off because she likes you."

I spluttered. "Franck doesn't like anyone."

"Okay, whatever, but seriously. You should pack your bag and take a taxi over. Or I can borrow my dad's car and come pick you up."

I chewed on my lower lip.

"Crystal! We're going for lunch!" a voice called in the background.

"Got it!" she shouted back. "I have to go."

I nodded. "Kay. I'll phone you later."

"Think about it."

I sighed. "I will." I stood and replaced the receiver, but the phone immediately started ringing. I tensed, thinking about the last time that happened. Logan.

There was no way he'd be calling from Europe, was there? My heart thudded as I picked up. "Hello?"

"Sharla, your dad had a little complication." My mom's voice. "They had to take him back to the hospital."

My blood turned to ice. "What happened? Is he okay?" I started to pace.

"They were able to place the stent successfully, but there were some complications with his blood pressure. He went in last night."

I pressed a hand to my temple, trying to make sense of her words. "Why didn't you phone me sooner?"

"I didn't want to worry you. I wanted to make sure everything was under control before I—"

"Mom, this is Dad. I need to know what's going on." My voice was shaking. "Is he going to be okay?"

"Yes, he's stable now, but they had to admit him. They're keeping him for observation."

"I'm coming." I didn't wait for her to respond before I hung up and dialled Rob's pager number. Conditioning was typically only an hour, so he was probably finished by now.

I shook out my hair, running my fingers through it. It was getting longer, shaggier. I kind of liked it this way, too.

I jumped when the phone rang and scrambled to pick it up.

"Sharla? What's going on?" Rob was out of breath.

My thoughts were a tangled mess, and I struggled to find the words. "My dad. He had a complication. They had to take him back to the hospital."

Rob's tone shifted. "Where is he? Do you need a ride?"

I didn't want to inconvenience him. He told me he still had work today. "He's at the hospital in Calgary." At least it wasn't all the way to Red Deer.

"I'm on my way."

I hung up and went to my closet, grabbing the first clothes I could find. Rob walked in ten minutes later. He was already showered, so he dropped his gear, and we left the house together.

We drove to the hospital in silence. I stared out the window, my mind and heart completely numb. I paused when Rob parked the truck instead of dropping me at the front. "You don't have to—"

"Don't. I'm coming with you." Pressure built behind my eyes as I pushed my door open. Rob reached out and held my hand as I forced my feet to move, each step feeling like I was dragging my legs through molasses.

I didn't pull back. It didn't feel wrong. It felt like support, and I needed it.

Inside, the waiting room was a sea of sterile white walls and uncomfortable plastic chairs. The fluorescent lights buzzed overhead, and a TV mounted in the corner played a muted news broadcast.

I hated it there. The air was thick with the scent of antiseptic and sickness and dying. My dad shouldn't be there so close to Christmas.

Rob and I walked up to the nurses' station, and a nurse with dark circles under her eyes and a name tag that read "Debbie" looked up from her computer. "Can I help you?"

"I'm here to see my dad. Norman Barnes."

Debbie's fingers flew over the keyboard. "Barnes, Barnes . . . Ah, here we are. Room 312. Just down the hall and to the left."

"Thank you." I forced a smile, then started off with Rob falling in step beside me.

As we walked, I couldn't help but notice the small details. The way the nurses' shoes squeaked on the floor, the soft hum of voices, the pattern on the linoleum tiles. It was all so clinical, so impersonal.

We passed a room with the door slightly ajar, and I caught a glimpse of an elderly woman lying in bed, her chest rising and falling with laboured breaths. A younger woman sat next to her, holding her hand and whispering something I couldn't make out. My heart clenched, and I looked away.

Finally, we reached room 312. I paused outside the door, my hand hovering over the handle.

Rob squeezed my hand, then dropped it. "I'll wait out here."

I nodded, then took a deep breath and pushed the door open.

My dad sat up in bed, his face pale but alert. He looked better than I'd expected, but the sight of the IV in his arm and the wires attached to his chest sent a shiver down my spine. My mom, sitting on a chair next to him, perked up as I entered.

"Hey, kiddo." His voice was raspy, but he managed a smile.

"Dad." I rushed to his side, not quite sure where to stand. "What happened?"

Dad shook his head. "Nothing, really. Just had to get a little medication."

I laughed. Only he would describe staying overnight in the hospital as "nothing, really." I turned to my mom. "What's the truth?"

Her smile wobbled. "He's doing much better now, but they wanted to keep him for observation. He should be discharged in a few hours."

I nodded, my mind reeling. "So he's going to be okay?"

She nodded, her eyes glassy. I exhaled in relief. "Okay."

Dad reached out and took my hand. "Thanks for coming."

I blinked back tears, trying to keep my emotions in check. "I just . . . I don't know what I would do if . . ."

He squeezed my hand. "Hey, none of that. I'm not going anywhere, okay?"

I nodded, but the lump in my throat wouldn't go away. I swallowed hard, my heart pounding in my ears. "When I got the call this morning, for a second, I thought I would never get the chance to tell you." I took another breath, my chest tight. "I know you both love me and want what's best for me. And I know this isn't probably what you want to talk about, but—" My voice caught. I stared down at the white sheets, and my dad squeezed my hand. Just like Rob had in the hall.

I lifted my head and drew a breath. "Back when I told you what happened with Eric . . . I felt like you didn't believe me. You didn't stand up for me, and that hurt. A lot." My voice wavered. "I know you think I should get over it, but I can't. It happened, and as much as I want to be with you for Christmas, I can't be there with him. I'm sorry if that hurt you."

My mom fidgeted with a loose thread on her sweater, and my dad looked down at his hands. He shifted, the bed creaking under his weight.

I hated that they were uncomfortable, but I needed them to understand. My parents were good people. I knew that.

My dad cleared his throat. "I'm sorry, Sharla. We . . . I didn't know what to do. I didn't want to believe it. I wanted to protect you, but I didn't know how."

My mom nodded, her eyes glassy. "We never meant to make you feel like you were alone in that. We just couldn't believe—" She paused, blinking fast. "You two seemed like such good friends. It didn't make sense, but I did a little research." She dropped her eyes. Twisting her hands in her lap. "It seems that's common. And I'm sorry I didn't know that."

My mom had done research? I exhaled, feeling a weight lift off my chest. I knew they couldn't fully understand, but they'd heard me.

"Maybe we could come to Calgary and do gifts and go out for dinner on the twenty-fourth?" My mom's voice was as tentative as a mouse poking its head out of a hole.

I nodded. She still wasn't going to kick my cousins out, but this was something. "I think that sounds good."

My dad brightened at that. "I think that's a lovely idea." He reached out and took my mom's hand. They chatted about where we should go, and I listened, only half invested. I'd come down here and had the conversation I needed to have. The rest of it was just gravy.

My mom glanced at the clock. "You should get some rest. I know they're planning to discharge you, but you should still take it easy."

My dad waved her off. "I'm not an invalid. I'll be fine."

That was my cue. I leaned in to give him a hug. "I'm glad you're okay, Dad."

He squeezed my hand. "Me too, sweetheart. Me too."

I smiled at Mom, then with a round of "I love you"'s, exited to the hall. Rob pushed off the wall and followed me down the hallway and out of the hospital. When we got to the truck, I climbed in, and he started the engine. The warmth from the heater was a welcome change from the cold air outside, and I settled back against the seat.

Rob reached for the gear shift to pull out of the parking lot, and his hand brushed mine. My breath caught, and I jerked back, planting both of my hands firmly in my lap.

My heart hammered in my chest, and I stared straight ahead, focusing on the snowflakes swirling in the headlights. Rob didn't look at me, but he didn't move his hand either. It stayed right there on the console, begging to be held.

"How did it go?"

"Good. He's being discharged soon." I thought about telling him the rest, but the lines of his letter scrolled in my head. *I love you. I'm in love with you.*

This wasn't fair to him. To keep sharing things with him, to keep drawing him closer when I was still with Logan. So I stayed silent.

We stepped inside, and I shut the door, the sound echoing in the silence of the house. I shrugged out of my coat, hung it on the hook by the door, and slipped out of my boots. Rob did the same.

I walked into the room and turned to him. "Thank you."

He stood in front of the door. "You're welcome." He looked like he didn't know what to do with his hands. "Do you want to get dinner? I don't start work until—"

"No." I shook my head. "I mean, thanks, but no. I think I'm going to read or something."

He nodded. "Okay."

I turned to walk to my room.

"Did I do something wrong?" Rob asked.

I froze, my whole body starting to tingle. "No!" I answered too brightly, plastering a smile on my face. Weird Sharla. This was what Crystal was talking about, but I couldn't stop it. "You just drove me to the hospital."

He took a few steps into the room. "Yeah, you just seem . . . I don't know. Mad or something."

I scoffed. "I'm not mad." He watched me unsmiling. "It's just been a long day."

Rob nodded. "Yeah. Seems like you're feeling better?"

I blinked. Right. This morning. I told him I was sick. "Mmm, yep. Didn't last long, thankfully." My eyes dropped to the letter on the counter, and I swung them away, my heart thunderous.

Rob's eyes narrowed. He walked forward, stopping at the island. When he reached out, I jumped.

"Don't—!" I froze, my hand hovering over the card. I almost choked on my own spit.

"Don't what?" Rob's jaw tensed.

I pulled my hand back, shoving it in my pocket. "Not until New Year's, right?" I squeaked.

Rob's throat worked. "Right." He dragged the card toward him and flipped it over. The "V" on the envelope fell open. His eyes flicked to mine, and my heart dropped to my feet.

I swallowed hard. "I'm sorry."

Rob stared at the ripped envelope. "I asked you to wait."

I swallowed the lump in my throat. "I know. I couldn't."

Rob dropped the letter onto the countertop, running his hands through his hair. "Well, now what the hell am I supposed to do?" He turned away from me, bracing himself on the countertop.

"Rob, just—"

He held up a hand, cutting me off. It felt like someone slammed a hammer into my sternum. I'd seen Rob pissed off before. I'd seen him annoyed. Frustrated. But this was something entirely different.

With his head hung low and his back expanding with rapid breaths, he looked broken, tortured. Every one of our memories together over the past month seemed to crumble away, turning to dust in my hands and slipping through my fingers.

"It's fine, really." My voice shook as I tried to sweep it all up and compress it back into something solid.

"It's not fine."

"We can just pretend I never saw it. We can go back to normal. It wouldn't be that hard."

If I was being honest, ever since that night in my room, I'd been lying to myself. I'd been ignoring the truth that was right in front of me. Of course, the possibility that Rob felt something for me had popped into my head.

Because I felt things for him.

It wasn't just physical attraction. I'd gotten good at rationalizing that away, at pretending it didn't exist, at finding a thousand other explanations for what happened inside of my body whenever he was close. And for the things he did that didn't make any sense, I could keep doing that for another couple of weeks. Until Logan got back, until Rob moved out.

I could barely draw a full breath. I didn't want him to be gone, and I didn't know if I wanted Logan to be back.

Rob turned to face me, crossing his arms over his chest. His fingertips pressed so deeply into his skin, the nails turned white. "I can't pretend. I can't go back."

"So what was your plan then? I would read this after you were gone, and you would just never see me again?"

He looked up. "Yeah, exactly." He stalked to the other side of the island, putting the full slab of granite between us.

"Rob, I'm at every game. I go to the after parties—"

"We were pretty good at avoiding each other before."

I wet my lips. The lump in my throat was growing so big I thought I might asphyxiate. I threw out my hands. "So all of this is just gone?" I motioned at the Christmas decorations but I meant *everything*. The conversations we'd had, the things I'd shared with him, the things he knew about me that I hadn't told anyone else.

"Yeah." He nodded once and turned to his room, but I slapped my hand on the counter.

"Yeah? That's all you have to say?"

He froze but didn't turn back. "What else is there to say, Sharla?"

Tears stung my eyes. *I love you. I'm in love with you.* "There has to be some way—"

He whirled. His eyes so dark they swallowed me up. "There's

no other way. You're sleeping with my best friend, and you read the damn letter. I can't live like this anymore. I have to find some way to move on."

His words stung like a slap. I opened my mouth, then snapped it closed. He was right. He was exactly right. *You're sleeping with my best friend.*

I was. I was with Logan. And here I was telling Rob I didn't want to lose him.

Rob kept walking.

I flinched when the door slammed closed behind him.

CHAPTER
Thirty

I TOOK Crystal up on her offer, and the next morning I was sitting in her living room. The Christmas tree bathed everything in a warm glow, the colourful lights dancing across the walls. It was about ten times larger than our pink tree. My heart twinged, and I focused in on the hodgepodge of homemade and nostalgic ornaments.

Crystal bounced over with two steaming mugs of hot cocoa piled high with marshmallows. "One for you, m'lady." She handed me a mug with an exaggerated bow. "With extra 'mallows, just how you like it."

I smiled and took a sip, the velvety chocolate and gooey marshmallows coating my tongue. "Mmm, you know me so well. What would I do without you?"

"Crash and burn, obviously." Crystal flopped down beside me on the couch, propping her fuzzy-socked feet on the coffee table. "So, ready for two days of non-stop MacMillan family holiday cheer? We've got cookie baking, carol singing, board games—"

"Bring it on." I clinked my mug against hers.

And for the next forty-eight hours, I let myself get swept up in Crystal's family traditions. We made an ungodly amount of sugar cookies (eating half the dough), belted out off-key renditions of Christmas songs, and played cutthroat rounds of Monopoly that nearly ripped apart family bonds. It was exactly the distraction I needed. But even through the laughter, my heart still felt like it was in a cage. Squeezed too tight.

On Christmas Eve, duty called. I zipped up my nicest sweater dress and waited for my parents to pick me up. We went to their favourite Italian restaurant in downtown Calgary. The cozy atmosphere wrapped around me like a warm hug as we were seated at a candlelit table. Dad looked healthier than he had the other day in the hospital, his cheeks rosy and eyes bright. That did wonders for my soul.

We sipped glasses of Chianti—well, all of us except Isabel—and nibbled on focaccia as we perused the menu. I ordered the lobster ravioli while Mom and Dad both went for the osso bucco.

"You seem distracted, honey," Mom said, studying me over her wine glass. "Everything okay?"

I forced a smile. "Yeah, of course. Just thinking about school stuff."

Truth was, my mind kept drifting to Logan's latest email. He'd written finally, gushing about how much he missed me and couldn't wait to get back. But nothing in response to what I'd said. I chose to ignore it. I wanted to believe him, to cling to the possibility that he'd come home and everything would magically be perfect between us again.

The waiter arrived with our entrees, providing a welcome distraction. We dug in, savouring each delicious bite. For dessert, we split a decadent tiramisu and exchanged gifts. I gave Dad his flannel shirt, Isabel a silver charm bracelet, and mom some hand-stitched kitchen towels along with the journal. They surprised me with a gorgeous cashmere scarf in a deep plum hue.

After lingering over cappuccinos, we finally said our goodbyes. I hugged my parents tightly.

"We love you, Shar," Dad said gruffly. "Phone us anytime, okay? For anything."

I nodded, blinking back tears. "I will. Love you both."

I gave Isabel a longer hug than I normally would've. She seemed happy, and I prayed it stayed that way.

Back at Crystal's, we had a photo from Maddie in Hawaii waiting for us. It took nearly an hour to download, but then we got to see her grinning in a bikini on the beach, sipping Mai Tai's at sunset. I sighed wistfully.

"Whore." Crystal typed, then pressed send. I laughed and sent a "Jealous, but we're both actually happy for you!" message.

Christmas morning at Crystal's house felt like stepping into someone else's family photo. I sat cross-legged on the floor in my pajamas, holding a stocking that her parents had filled for me. It shouldn't have hit me so hard, but it did.

Crystal's dad gave me a wink as I pulled out little treasures—a pack of gum, a mini lotion, a pair of fuzzy socks. Nothing extravagant, but it was the thought that gutted me. They didn't have to include me. I wasn't their kid, wasn't even family, but they had.

That was also what made me think of Rob. The idea of him sitting alone in our house surrounded by the decorations we'd put up together by himself made me physically ill. I wanted to go back. I wanted to call his pager number. But I could no longer justify doing those things as "just a friend."

On New Year's Eve, Crystal and I went to a club her sister recommended down south. I still wasn't a party person, but I wanted Crystal to be happy, and I needed a distraction. We danced our hearts out, but neither of us drank. Not smart when we were alone for the night.

Even with bass rumbling through me, my mind wouldn't stop obsessing over Logan's return.

Crystal pulled me onto the dance floor as the countdown began. "5...4...3...2...1...Happy New Year!" Auld Lang Syne played as she threw her arms around me. "This is gonna be our year, babe. I feel it." She pretended to kiss me, and I laughed so hard I snorted.

On the second, Crystal's dad dropped us off at our respective houses on campus. I was glad he stopped at my house first. No awkwardness.

I stepped into the house, the cold air trailing behind me as I shut the door. It was immediately too quiet.

My suitcase thudded to the floor, and I looked around, my heart sinking. The pink Christmas tree we'd set up together was gone. The string lights we'd draped, the decorations we'd hung —all of it, disappeared.

I swallowed hard, kicking off my boots. The living room felt hollow. His favourite blanket was gone, the one he'd thrown over me when I fell asleep there. The books and random hockey magazines he left scattered were nowhere to be found.

I walked slowly down the hallway, my socks muffling my steps. His door was slightly ajar, and I pushed it open, bracing myself.

The room was completely empty.

His quilt, the clothes he always piled on the chair in the corner, gone. The closet door hung open, revealing nothing but a few stray hangers. I stood there, numb, barely able to catch the last scent of him.

I sank to the floor, my knees hitting the cold hardwood. My chest tightened, and the tears I'd been holding back spilled over. The sobs came fast and hard, wracking through me until I couldn't breathe.

This wasn't just about the decorations or the empty room. It was about him. About the way he made this place feel alive, about the stupid jokes, the late-night conversations of the past weeks. It was about the way I noticed everything about him— the way he moved, the way his smile could light up an otherwise grey day. *I couldn't believe I was thinking this about Rob.*

And the way I missed him now felt like a betrayal of everything I was supposed to feel.

How could I explain this? That I was gutted over Logan's best friend leaving, that my chest ached every time I thought of Rob's laugh or the way he poured a damn bowl of cereal? Guilt sank into me, sharp and suffocating. This wasn't who I was supposed to be.

But the ache wouldn't leave. The memories wouldn't leave. I hated that I missed him so much it made my skin crawl.

Eventually, I forced myself to stand, wiping at my cheeks. Crying wasn't going to change anything. Rob was gone. Logan was coming back, and I had to deal with it.

I wandered into the kitchen, staring blankly at the counter. The sink had a few stray crumbs, and the fridge still held the food I left.

Cleaning.

I could clean.

That was something I could control.

That afternoon, I tied my hair back and grabbed the spray bottle from under the sink. The countertops were wiped down with precision, every crumb and streak obliterated. I moved to the stove, scrubbing at a stubborn stain until my arm ached.

The living room came next. I vacuumed the carpet, fluffed the cushions, and dusted every surface.

By the second day, the house was spotless, but the hollowness still lingered, gnawing at the edges of my mind. I decided to tackle the closets. Sorting through my own clothes, I bagged items to donate, trying to keep myself busy.

The third day, I grabbed my coat and headed to the grocery store. The aisles were quiet, the post-holiday rush having settled. I filled the cart with everything Logan liked—eggs, bacon, bread, fresh veggies. I threw in some pasta and sauce, planning meals in my head.

Back at the house, I put the groceries away methodically, the fridge slowly filling up. Then I started cooking. A big pot of soup, a tray of baked chicken and roasted vegetables. The repetitive motions kept me grounded, the smells filling the kitchen with warmth.

By the fourth day, I scrubbed the washroom tiles, rearranged the kitchen pantry, and even cleaned out the junk drawer. When everything was finally in order, I leaned against the counter, exhaustion creeping in. The house looked perfect, ready for Logan's return.

I ignored that it didn't feel right.

I ignored that the only person I kept looking for wasn't Logan.

The morning before Logan's flight came in, I walked to campus to meet Crystal at the bookstore. Getting my textbooks for the semester was my last task, and we both wanted to check it off the list.

The walk was good. The sunshine and cool air energized me, but it didn't prepare me for what I would see the second I entered the bookstore.

"Hey!" Crystal waved from down the aisle, but I couldn't look up. I stared at the stand of school newspapers, Logan's face staring back at me from the front page. Unmistakable even from a distance.

But he wasn't alone. Draped over him was a gorgeous blonde, her sequined dress leaving little to the imagination as she played with the medal hung around Logan's neck. He grinned at the camera, his arm around her waist. His teammates and a few other girls crowded around him in celebration.

The caption below read:

DOUGLAS U'S LOGAN KEMP CELEBRATES RECORD-BREAKING WIN AT WORLD JUNIORS.

CHAPTER
Thirty-One

I WAITED at the arrivals curb, parked near the exit where Logan would appear. Travellers streamed out with bulging back-packs and luggage. I tried to ignore the pit in my stomach, but it was impossible. The picture from the paper was seared into the back of my eyelids, and I couldn't unsee it.

After a few minutes, Logan burst through the doors, his face lit up like a kid on Christmas morning. My heart rate spiked. It should've been because I was excited to see him, but as he crossed the sidewalk, my gut twisted into knots.

He grinned when he saw me, then threw his gear and luggage into the back and approached the driver's side. He reached for the handle. I popped the locks and slid over to the passenger seat.

Logan jumped in. "Hey, you." He leaned over the console and kissed me. I let him. I didn't know what else to do. "What? No 'I missed you'?"

"Of course I missed you!" I tried to keep my tone light. "I just thought you'd want to get out of here. It's a zoo."

"Good point." Logan turned the key in the ignition and pulled away from the curb. "So, the Czech Republic was insane. The rinks there are so different. They have a wider playing surface. Some of those guys, I don't even know. Their puck handling is off the charts."

I tried to keep up, but Logan was talking a mile a minute.

He ran a hand through his hair. It was longer, a little wavier then it was when he'd left. "And the fans! I've never seen anything like it. They were chanting and waving flags. The whole place smelled like sausage and beer. I should've asked you to come with me. You would've loved it. I mean, the games were intense, but the city was amazing. You would've loved the architecture. We stayed in this old hotel with these massive wooden beams. The food was a bit of an adventure, like I said. I had no idea what I was ordering half the time. And the coffee? Strong enough to wake the dead."

I stared at the dashboard, nodding at the appropriate moments. I couldn't bring myself to look at him, not when I was replaying the scene from the paper over and over in my head.

"I'm so glad you came to pick me up. It's been torture not seeing your face for the past two weeks." Logan reached over the console again, his fingers brushing my arm. I flinched, and he pulled back, confusion etched on his face.

"Sorry, I'm just . . . tired." I forced a smile and turned up the radio. "Look, Christmas music! It's still technically the holidays, right?"

Logan's eyes softened. "Of course. You must've been busy with finals and your family."

"Yeah, it's been non-stop." I kept my tone casual, even though my pulse was racing.

We stopped at a red light, and Logan leaned in, his eyes searching my face. "I missed you, Sharla. So much."

My heart clenched. I wanted to believe him, but the ghost of that picture stood between us. I turned my head as he came in for a kiss, and his lips landed on my cheek. "I missed you, too." I managed a smile and reached for his hand. "You probably want to get home and sleep."

Logan shook his head. "I'm wide awake. I slept on the plane."

He ran his thumb over my wrist. "Maybe you can help me burn off some energy when we get home?"

I let out a nervous laugh. Hopefully he'd pass it off as flirty? "Maybe." I closed my eyes and leaned back in the seat, letting Logan's voice wash over me as he continued to talk about the tournament.

I wasn't going to bring up the picture. Not yet. For all I knew, it was probably nothing. Just a fan who'd gotten too close, and Logan hadn't wanted to be rude. He was a Canadian boy, after all.

So I told myself to relax. To match Logan's enthusiasm. He didn't seem to notice my internal struggle. He was too wrapped up in his own world, and to be fair, it was a world worth being wrapped up in.

"The tournament level of play was next level. Those European teams, they don't mess around. I mean, I've played against tough competition before, but this? This was on a whole other level. The speed, the skill, the intensity. I had to up my game just to keep up. And the strategies." Logan ran a hand over his jaw. "The way they moved the puck, it was almost like they were reading each other's minds. It was a wake-up call, that's for sure. I knew I had to push myself harder, be more aggressive, more strategic. And it paid off. I scored in every game except the first one. That was just a warm-up, though. Getting used to the rink and the different ice. But after that, it was like something clicked. I was in the zone." He glanced over at me, his eyes alight with excitement. "You would've loved it."

I nodded. "I'm sure I would've."

"And the country itself, Sharla. It's beautiful. I mean, I'd seen pictures and stuff, but being there in person? It was like stepping into a postcard. The architecture, the landscapes, the people. Everything felt so different from here. It was like stepping into a different world, you know?"

I couldn't focus on his words. I tried to pull myself back into the moment, but it was like trying to swim through molasses.

Logan kept talking about the games, the plays, the goals, and I kept nodding and smiling like a bobblehead on speed.

This should've been where the excitement kicked in. Where I imagined this life he was describing. The teams, the fans, the success. In the past, I was always there next to Logan's side. He was thanking me when he signed contracts, coming home to me after he won or lost, talking to me about his goals, waving to me in the stands.

This time, I couldn't see it. The future stretched before me in a blurry mess, and that scared me more than a picture in the paper.

Logan took a breath. "And then, after that game, I checked my email, and there were messages from NHL agents. Coaches. Sharla, they're interested in me."

Hm. Interesting. He checked his email. I wondered if he wrote them back?

I forced a smile. "That's incredible, Logan. I'm so happy for you."

We turned onto Memorial Drive, and the Bow River ran alongside us, its surface frozen and covered in a thin layer of snow. And then in less than five minutes, we were turning onto our street, and the townhouse came into view.

Logan pulled up against the curb and killed the engine. He turned to me, his eyes alight with anticipation. "Home, sweet, home."

We took in his bags and gear, and as soon as we dropped them in the entryway, Logan didn't waste any time. He tossed his keys on the counter and turned to me. "Come here, babe." His hands found my waist, and he pulled me close. His breath was hot against my neck as he kissed me, his lips insistent.

I tried to reciprocate, but my thoughts were a tangled mess. The photo of that girl. The unanswered questions. I placed a hand on Logan's chest and gently pushed him back. "Wait, wait." I forced a laugh, scrambling for some way to stall. "I want to give you my Christmas gift."

Logan groaned. "Couldn't we do that later?"

I shook my head, wriggling out of his grasp. I ran into my room and grabbed his present, then walked back out to find Logan searching through his bag.

"Mine isn't wrapped." He glanced over his shoulder.

"I don't care." I sat down on the couch. Logan walked over, holding something behind his back. Blood rushed in my ears. The last time I'd seen someone stand like that, it was Rob holding his letter.

I thrust Logan's present into his free hand. "Here. I hope you like it."

Logan sat next to me, hiding whatever he had behind him on the couch, then unwrapped my gift. When he saw the signature, he looked up at me. "Is this . . . ?"

I nodded, a nervous smile tugging at my lips. "Doug Gilmore. The real deal."

Logan shook his head, his expression incredulous. "Sharla, this is incredible. How did you even find this?"

"I have my ways."

Logan's grin spread wide as he stared at the puck, his eyes tracing the signature over and over. "Thank you. This is the best." He leaned in and kissed me, then pulled back and motioned for me to stay put. "Okay, my turn."

He set down the puck and pulled my present out in cupped hands. "I got this at one of the Christmas markets." He opened his fingers, revealing a small wooden box. I ran my fingers over the smooth surface. The wood was dark and polished, with intricate carvings that wrapped around the edges. I lifted the lid and was met with the scent of pine and varnish.

"It's for your bracelet," Logan said. "I wanted you to have something special to keep it in."

The bracelet. My heart sank. Where was it? It had been in the pocket of my jeans, but had I ever taken it out?

The box was beautiful. It was kind that he thought of me. But that box could've been for anyone, and the bracelet was more for

Logan than for me. He didn't see me, and for the first time, I wasn't dying to pretend he did.

I closed the box and set it on the coffee table. "Logan—"

"Wait, where's Rob's blanket?" Logan frowned, searching the living area.

I blinked. "He didn't tell you?"

Logan's eyes widened. "Oh, shit. Rob moved out? He's gone?"

I nodded. "He moved in with Brayden and Rory."

Logan ran a hand through his hair. "I guess it's just us, then." He laughed, but it sounded forced. "Damn. Double rent."

It was that statement, that exact moment that the threads unravelled. Just like those seconds with Rob on stage in the darkened concert hall, I knew. I could never look at Logan the same.

I'd spent my entire life pretending. Pretending I didn't care that my mom wouldn't let me wear baggy pants with boxers showing out the top to school. Pretending it was fine that we ate at the Italian place even though I much preferred Asian. Pretending I was friends with Eric in the summer.

I'd become a pro at it. Pretending I didn't have problems so Logan wouldn't be distracted. Pretending that I didn't care if Logan didn't attend my concerts because of hockey. Pretending like I wanted to have sex when I was exhausted, and it didn't even feel that good.

And now I was pretending like I didn't want to scream and cry and throw crap across the room after seeing that photo in the newspaper. I was pretending like I loved this gift and that I was excited for him to put his hands on me when all I wanted to do was shove him into the wall and ask him why the hell he thought it was okay to let another girl drape herself over him like a shawl.

I wasn't a marionette. I was a real, live girl, and I was done pretending. "Logan, who was the girl in the newspaper?" I blurted.

Logan frowned. "What girl in the newspaper?"

I clenched my hands into fists, trying to steady my breath. I didn't want to say it. I didn't want to remember the image, but it was seared into the back of my eyelids. "She was blond. She was playing with your medal, and you had your arm around her waist."

Logan's eyes widened. "Oh. That was in the paper?"

"The school paper."

He laughed and leaned toward me, but I held out a hand. He stilled, raising his hands in surrender. "I think you're talking about Marta. She was one of the translators for our team. We were all at the bar after our match against Sweden."

"Why was she playing with your medal?"

He shifted his weight, his hands flexing at his sides. "I don't know. She was just having fun."

"And you had your arm around her."

Logan's lips pursed. "It was no big deal, Shar. We were just celebrating."

I swallowed hard, my throat tight. "Celebrating."

Logan nodded. "Yeah, we were all buzzing after the win. She was excited for us."

"She was excited and you were . . . buzzing."

Logan reached for my hand. "I missed you, Sharla. I'm here now, okay? Whatever you saw in that picture, it didn't mean anything." I tried to pull my hand back, but Logan held on. "Hey, it's okay." He brushed his lips over my knuckles.

I pulled my hand away. "Logan, I can't."

He frowned. "What do you mean you can't? I've been gone for over two months. I missed you."

I swallowed, my mind racing. What did I mean? I stood and stepped away from the couch. I needed air.

Logan jumped up and stepped forward, putting his hands on my hips. "Babe." He pressed his lips to my neck, and I felt a shiver run down my spine. "I want you."

I pushed him back. "Logan, stop."

He frowned, his hands dropping to his sides. "Sharla, what the hell?"

I drew a deep breath and met his eyes. "Were you with other girls over there?"

"With?" Logan scoffed. "No, I wasn't 'with' other girls."

My eyes narrowed. He wasn't meeting my eyes. "Let me be a little more specific. Did you touch other girls like you did Marta?"

He gave me a look. "I told you—"

"I sent you emails. I told you real, difficult things that were happening in my life, and you never wrote me back. So. Now that you're right in front of me and not busy, I'm asking you a question, and I expect a real answer. Did you kiss her?"

His face blanched. "Babe—"

"Answer the damn question, Logan."

Logan blew out a breath. "Sharla, I was drunk. It was just a kiss."

I blinked back tears. *Just a kiss.*

Logan's shoulders sagged. "I didn't—"

"How many?" I asked. My voice was barely a whisper. I didn't need to ask how it happened or why. That much was obvious. But he was still squirming, which meant I still didn't know the whole story.

He looked up, his eyes pleading. "Sharla, it didn't mean anything."

I swallowed hard. "How many, Logan?"

He groaned. "Two. Okay? There were two."

My heart felt like it was going to burst through my chest. "Two girls." *Did he even hear himself?*

Logan's grip tightened on my waist. "I was lonely, Sharla. I was there for weeks, and after the games, the whole team was pumped, and these girls . . ."

I shook my head. "So it's *their* fault?"

Logan looked at me like I was the one who didn't understand. "I didn't sleep with them, Sharla. It was just fun."

"Fun." I tried to keep my voice steady. It was an impossible task. "Logan, do you think it would be okay if I kissed two guys? To have fun?"

Logan's jaw tightened. "You're not . . . I mean, Sharla, you wouldn't—"

"No, I wouldn't." I slapped his hands away and took a step back, my heart aching. I was lonely, too, but I'd walked away. When I felt *things* with Rob, I made a damn choice.

Logan reached for me, but I stepped back again. "Sharla, please. It was a mistake. It won't happen again. I promise."

Rob's words in the hall outside the locker room came back to me, this time with a completely different meaning. *She doesn't understand the kind of dedication and commitment this takes, bud.*

I didn't understand. If this was what it meant to be dedicated to hockey, then I was going to take away his focus. Because I sure as hell wasn't going to sit at home while my boyfriend travelled to different cities to celebrate and "have fun" with his adoring fans.

I didn't respond. I couldn't. I was afraid if I opened my mouth, I would scream. Or cry. Or both. I turned and walked down the hall.

Logan followed me. "Sharla, please. Let's talk about this."

I stopped in front of my door, my hand on the doorknob. "Talk? You want to talk now?" I turned to face him. "Logan, you didn't even talk to me when you were gone."

Logan looked away. "I was busy—"

"Bullshit." I spat the word. "You were out at bars with your team. You were out kissing random girls. You could've made time for me." My voice cracked, and I hated how weak it sounded. "I made time for you, Logan, and I gave you so much credit, I can't—" I stopped myself, searching for my suitcase.

Logan tried to reach for my hand, but I pulled away. "You can't, what?"

I shook my head. "Nothing. It doesn't matter."

He stepped closer. "What were you going to say?"

I clenched my jaw. "I can't believe you didn't make those pancakes."

Logan looked at me. "You're pissed about the pancakes?"

I pursed my lips. "It's not about the pancakes."

"Well it sounds like—"

"It's about everything, Logan. You didn't wash out my water bottles, you didn't make the pancakes, you didn't come to my concerts, and you sure as hell didn't make me that mix tape."

Logan blinked. "What?"

I forced myself to draw a full breath, then slowly let it out. "Why didn't you tell me about the mix tape?"

Logan sat down on the bed. "I didn't think it mattered."

"Hmm." I nodded once. "It seems you don't think a lot of things matter." I turned and opened up my dresser drawer, grabbing out a few pairs of underwear and socks, then moved to the closet.

I expected the wave of emotions to keep swelling, building within me until the dam broke, but as I pulled out a sweater and a pair of jeans, the opposite happened. The storm inside me calmed.

Logan wasn't any different now than when he'd left.

I was the one who'd changed.

As messed up as it sounded, a little compassion trickled through me. Logan was expecting to come home to the same girl he'd left. The one who shoved everything in her life to the side to make sure every single one of his needs was met. The one who worshiped the ground he walked on. The one who needed his attention to feel whole. To feel special. To feel worthy.

Logan was used to being able to do exactly what he wanted. In no way did that excuse the behaviour he was rationalizing. But it did make sense. He wanted a hardcore fan. I wanted a relationship.

I dropped my clothes in the suitcase and looked up at Logan, resting his head in his hands. "I changed while you were gone." Logan looked up. "I still care about you, Logan. I do." Logan started shaking his head, but I put up a hand. "You are an incredible hockey player, and I know you're going to have every opportunity after all this. I'm so happy for you. But I need to be more than the tagalong."

"Shar, you were never the tagalong."

I zipped up the suitcase and walked into the washroom, scooping my toiletries into my case. I walked back into the bedroom and gripped the handle of my bag. "I'm taking your truck."

I turned and exited the room, walking as fast as I could without breaking into a run. I grabbed his keys from the island counter, then pulled my coat from the hook.

"Shar. I'm sorry. Take a drive, and I'll have dinner ready when you get back tonight. We can talk about this and—"

"I made you a week of dinners."

Logan sucked in a breath. "You did?"

"I did." I gripped the suitcase handle. "I'll come back for the rest of my things once I figure out where I'm staying."

Logan's mouth twisted. He pointed to Rob's empty room. "You could stay there for now. You don't have to leave."

I looked at the open bedroom door, and my heart twinged. No. I couldn't stay in that room. Because the only person I wanted to see right now had moved all of his things out of it.

Logan opened his mouth, but I shook my head. I couldn't give him false hope. There was nothing he could say or do to fix this because it wasn't just the girl in the paper that broke things.

I needed to rip off the Band-Aid. "We're done, Logan." I pulled the door open and dragged my suitcase out into the night.

CHAPTER
Thirty-Two

I GRIPPED THE STEERING WHEEL, my hands ten and two and knuckles white as I pulled Logan's truck to the curb. I stared at the big brick house ahead of me. I turned off the engine, and the sudden silence amplified the pounding of my heart.

This was it. I'd spoken the words, but if I got out of this truck, I would be putting the final nail in the coffin on my relationship with Logan.

It wasn't that I worried I'd change my mind. I knew I wouldn't. But even though I knew it was the right choice, it was still scary as hell. A month ago, I thought I knew what my life would look like. I had it all planned out. Instead, starting with this moment and all the seconds, minutes, days, and months ahead of it, I was staring at a blank sheet of paper.

I slumped forward, resting my forehead on the wheel as tears spilled over onto my cheeks. I grieved the end of that relationship. The end of the life I'd envisioned and the person I thought I was. The end of my living situation with that nice townhouse and my own washroom. That part was petty, but it was still depressing.

Now, all I had was a suitcase and a headache. I had no idea where I was going to live or what I was going to do.

I sucked in a breath and took inventory.

Okay. So I'd stolen a truck. I was homeless. And I was sitting on the curb in front of a veritable party house full of guys who played on every Douglas sports team.

What. Was. I. Going. To. Do.

I jolted at a tap on my window and straightened, swiping the backs of my hands over my cheeks. When I finally looked up, relief swept over me like a winter Chinook.

It was Rob.

His eyes searched mine through the glass, and the tortured expression on his face made my heart ache. He opened the truck door, and I fell into his arms. For the first time I wasn't holding him because I needed comfort. I wasn't questioning whether it was okay to be this close to another guy or berating myself for feeling something for a person other than Logan.

I sank into him, burrowing my head against his chest and drinking him in. His scent, his warmth, his solid muscle and slow breath.

"I'm sorry," I mumbled into his shoulder. "I'm always such a mess when you find me."

Rob tightened his grip, his breath warm against my temple. "Can you stop being so Canadian? Apologizing for things you didn't even cause?"

I laughed, twisting my fingers in his shirt. I wanted to crawl inside of it. To lie next to him, skin to skin. To talk for hours and tell him everything that was running through my head.

I'd never felt such a magnetic pull to strip down. Physically. Emotionally. Spiritually. It was terrifying and intoxicating, and I had no idea whether it was good or safe or smart. All I knew was that I wanted Rob to see every part of me. All the parts I'd hidden. All the pieces I'd pretended away.

"You're in Logan's truck." Rob's voice was low as he ran his hand over my back. I nodded. "But there's no Logan."

I exhaled. "Damn it, you noticed that?"

Rob chuckled, then stilled when he turned his head and looked in the back seat. "You have a suitcase."

I pulled back, tilting my chin up to look at him. "I hoped—"

"Are things with Logan . . . Does he know?"

I reached up and ran my thumb over his brow. "He came home today. We talked."

Rob's throat worked. "You saw the picture?"

I blinked. "*You* saw the picture?"

He grabbed my hand and moved like he was going to press my fingertips to his lips. Instead, he slowly lowered it back to his chest. "Everyone did. Rory had to tie me to a chair to keep me from breaking down your door and kicking Logan's ass."

I blew out a breath. "An hour ago, I would've let you."

Rob wrapped his hand over mine and held it to his chest. "And now?"

I wet my lips. "I think . . . I learned a lot while he was gone. I think I was a little bit grateful to have proof that what I was feeling wasn't just in my head." I met Rob's eyes. "It's easy for me to question my version of reality. To wonder if I'm overreacting, especially when what I feel isn't convenient for other people." Rob listened, his eyes dark, liquid pools, and I knew I didn't need to give more of an explanation. "I told him it was over."

His nostrils flared, and he crushed me to his chest. "Did he believe you?"

I blew out a breath. "Maybe not until I stole his truck?"

Rob laughed, squeezing tighter. "You can stay." His words came out in a rush, his chest rising and falling in quick succession. "Unless you were hoping—"

"With you." The words were a plea, the whispered prayer I'd kept in my heart the whole drive over.

Rob ran his hands over me like he was trying to memorize the shape of my spine, then released me so he could open the back door. I pulled out my backpack, violin case, and purse while he grabbed my suitcase, then we walked up the steps to the house.

The house was quiet, a stark contrast to the chaos in my mind. We stepped into a living room that looked completely different from Halloween. The furniture was back in place, and there weren't people dancing on the coffee table.

I stopped short when I saw a group of guys sitting on the couch and chairs in the living room. Rory and Axel looked up, and their faces immediately morphed from pissed off to concerned.

"Sharla, are you okay?" Rory shot up from the couch. "Where the hell is Logan?"

I swallowed hard. "He's . . . at his house."

Axel shook his head. "So it's true?"

My heart started to pound. Rob hadn't been exaggerating when he said everyone saw that paper. "Logan didn't sleep with anyone, if that's what you're asking." I wasn't going to protect him, but I also wasn't going to throw gasoline on the rumour coals already glowing. "He just has other priorities right now."

They looked down, taking in my suitcase. "You have company tonight, Thompson?" Rory asked, the corner of his mouth quirking.

Rob's grip on the handle of my suitcase tightened. "Yeah. Possibly for longer than that."

Heat rushed to my face. "I don't mean to impose, I just don't have anywhere to go right now, but I'm working on—"

Rory held up a hand and stood, then crossed the living room in three steps and pulled me into a bear hug. "Stay as long as you want, Shar."

I grunted as another set of arms wrapped around us. "Group hug," Axel announced. "Except for Rob. You stay the hell out of this."

I laughed, gasping for breath, then jolted when someone's hand yanked Logan's keys from my pocket.

"I'll be taking those." Rory grinned as they both let go of me.

Axel's eyes widened. He stalked to the window and peered out. "You took his truck? Sharla, you badass." He turned back and motioned for Tim and Bear on the couch to get up. "Let's go, boys. Time for a little chat."

I breathed out a shaky laugh. "Please don't kill him."

"Don't worry, we won't." Rory gave me a mischievous grin. "But we might make him wish we did."

I shook my head. "I'm pretty sure he's already having a terrible night."

Rory clapped me on the shoulder, and I felt like I would crash through the floorboards. "He's called us out on plenty of shit. Our turn to repay the favour." They didn't even bother grabbing coats, just clomped out of the house, the door slamming closed behind them.

The house seemed to exhale, the walls settling around me. Rob reached out and took my hand.

"You okay?" His voice broke through my thoughts.

I nodded, staring out the window as Logan's truck pulled away from the curb. "Yeah. Just processing."

He stepped closer, his presence warm and solid next to me. "Thank you for coming here. I was worried about you."

Something swooped low in my belly. I turned, allowing him to draw me closer. "Thank you for making this the only place I wanted to be."

Rob's eyes grew glassy. He cleared his throat, then nodded toward the stairs. "You want to put all this luggage down?"

"Mmm. Super sexy pickup line. How long have you been working on that?"

Rob smirked. "Since I watched you pack an instrument to and from campus every day for a year."

My face squinched. "With that much time, I feel like it could've been better."

Rob laughed, then tugged me toward the stairs. The house was old, the floorboards creaking under our feet as we walked up one flight of stairs and down the hall to his room. The hallway walls were painted a faded white, and the wood trim was chipped and worn. There were a few framed posters of Calgary monuments, but otherwise, the decor was minimal.

Rob pushed open a door to reveal a small bedroom. His bed was pushed against one wall, a single nightstand next to it. Across from the bed was a dresser with a mirror, and a closet door stood slightly ajar.

"It's not much, but it's home for now," he said, stepping inside and motioning for me to follow.

I walked in and looked around. "It's cozy."

Rob chuckled and set my suitcase next to the wall. "That's one way to put it."

I turned to him. "Where's the washroom?"

He pointed to a door across the hall. "Shared with Rory and Bear. Keeps things interesting."

I laughed. "I bet."

Rob sat on the edge of the bed and looked up at me. "Not quite as nice as our previous accommodations."

I set down my backpack and violin case, then walked over and sat next to him. "The mattress is nice." I ran my hands over his comforter.

"Hmm. Super sexy pickup line. How long—"

I smacked him, and Rob caught my arm, pulling me down on the bed next to him. We adjusted until we lay side by side, his arm under my head, curving around my side.

My hands trembled. My heart raced like I'd downed five cups of coffee, and I had no idea what to do with myself. I wanted to be close to Rob. That much was clear. But I was also emotionally compromised, and I had no idea if this was the right moment to act on my attraction.

"I'm sorry I was rude," Rob said, his hand running up and down my arm.

"You were rude?" I allowed my hand to wander over his chest, electricity flaring against my fingertips as I felt the outline of his pec, the dip before his shoulder started.

"Yeah. I was." Rob drew in a breath. "When I found out you read the letter."

I considered this. "I don't think you were rude. I was the one who broke the rules."

"I regretted walking away from you. And then when you left—"

I smoothed my hand up to his neck, running my hands over his jaw. "I'm sorry you had to spend Christmas alone. I thought of you the whole time I was at Crystal's. But I didn't want to . . . I didn't want to be disloyal to Logan." I pushed myself a little higher so I could see his face.

Rob smoothed the hair from my forehead. "I shouldn't have given you a massage."

"Uh, no. You shouldn't have."

Rob laughed out loud. "I wanted to touch you so damn bad. I was making up excuses."

"I've never been that turned on in my life." I stilled, realizing what I'd just admitted.

Rob's smile faded. "Is that true?"

My heart suddenly felt like it belonged to a bird or a rabbit. Beating so fast, I was sure it was going to short circuit. "It's true."

Rob pushed up on his elbow, laying my head on his pillow and curling his body until he looked down into my face. "I don't expect anything. Just because you're staying here. You know that, right?"

I nodded, my mouth so dry, I could barely swallow. "I think —I might need some time." The second it left my lips, I hated myself for saying it. I didn't want time. I wanted to pull off Rob's shirt and press my face up against every square centimetre of his skin. I wanted to pick up right where we left off in our living room.

But even though I was sure Logan and I weren't getting back together, I wasn't sure what I'd be feeling in the morning.

"Yeah, of course." Rob dropped back to the pillow. "Whatever you need."

I reached up and turned his face to mine. "What about what you need? I don't want this to hurt. I know you've been hurting, and—"

"No." Rob slid a hand over my waist. "Having you here is . . . " He let out a shaky exhale. "More than I ever could've asked for." His fingers tightened against my hip. "But don't take that as me being satisfied. I'm saying I've waited a year, and I'll wait as long as you need. But you know how I feel, and I'm not going anywhere."

Heat flared within me, zinging through my middle and hitting the ends of my fingers and toes before snapping back and humming through my hips and thighs. I wasn't satisfied either. And I was pretty sure we both knew it.

Rob's jaw tensed, and then he forced himself from the bed. "I got you something. For Christmas."

I frowned. "You got me a present?"

Rob sat up and put his feet on the floor. "Yeah. I wasn't going to give it to you and make things weird, but—" He crossed the room, and my curiosity was piqued.

Rob pulled open his dresser and rifled through his clothes. I heard the crinkle of a plastic bag, then he turned and walked back to the bed. He pulled something out. A rectangular black box.

He returned to the bed and sat next to me. When he saw my face, he smirked. "It's not jewelry."

I pursed my lips. *Had it been that obvious that I didn't like the bracelet?* Rob handed me the box. I drew a breath, then opened the lid.

CHAPTER
Thirty-Three

I STARED at the object nestled in the box, the shape unmistakable. A violin mute. I traced the delicate carvings with my fingers, and my mind skipped a beat.

It was just like Lily's and a large upgrade from my cheap one. I stared at Rob, my brain scrambling to make sense of it. How had he found something like this?

I turned it over, admiring the craftsmanship. "How—?" I couldn't finish the sentence. Rob had asked me about my mute in the concert hall. It felt like an eon ago.

He shrugged, a smirk playing at the corners of his mouth. "I have my sources."

"Your sources?" I raised an eyebrow. "You expect me to believe you just stumbled upon a hand-carved violin mute that looks exactly like my friend's?"

Rob leaned back, crossing his arms. "Maybe I have a secret talent for woodworking."

I narrowed my eyes. "Rob."

He sighed. "Fine." He ran a hand through his hair. "I may have done some digging."

"Dug up a woodworker who whittles these things out of their basement?"

"Not exactly."

I folded my arms. "Spit it out, Thompson."

Rob took a breath. "I found your friend. After the concert."

I blinked. "What?"

"I waited. Talked to her and asked where she'd gotten the mute that you were obsessed with."

"Obsessed?" A grin spread across my face.

The corner of Rob's mouth lifted. "Turns out her dad makes them. So I commissioned one."

My heart swelled. I looked down at the mute, turning it over in my hands. Delicate flowers trailed the side, vines winding through the prongs. "Rob, this is . . . how much did it cost?" My eyes started to sting.

Rob shifted on his feet. "It was nothing."

It wasn't nothing. I thought back to the gifts Logan had given me. A bracelet. A box. Also made of wood.

The gift in front of me couldn't have been more different. It wasn't the gifts themselves that were the problem, it was what they represented. Logan's were both beautiful, but they weren't *for* me. They were for him. To look good. Like a check mark on his list of how to be a proper boyfriend.

But this gift from Rob? He'd been paying attention. He'd remembered something I'd mentioned in passing. Then he'd gone out of his way to find Lily and figure out where she got hers so he could use his hard-earned money to buy one for me.

I looked up at Rob, tears filling my eyes. "I got you something, too." His mouth quirked, and I groaned. "Don't get excited. It's so dumb."

Rob laughed. "How could it be dumb?"

I placed the mute back in its box and closed the lid, then flopped back on Rob's bed. "It's so dumb. And then you go and give me something like this—"

Rob grabbed my hands and pulled me up to stand in front of him. "I can't believe you got me something."

"It's a toilet bowl cleaner," I blurted. "With Chrétien's face on it."

Rob laughed, a deep, rumbling sound that sent a shiver down my spine. "Uh, that's amazing."

I dropped my head to his shoulder. "Well, I wanted to get you something better but it felt like it had to be something I could give to a friend."

Rob dragged his hands over my ribs. "And why were you working so hard to make it look like something a friend would buy?"

My stomach swooped. "Because I had to."

His voice was barely a whisper. "Why?"

I drew a breath. *Because I didn't want to admit I had feelings for you.* How hard was it to just admit the truth? "Because I had a boyfriend. And I was feeling things for someone else."

He let out a soft "Hmm" and wrapped a hand around the back of my neck. "So a toilet bowl cleaner was defensible?"

I closed my eyes, moulding to his touch. "Exactly." Rob threaded his fingers through my hair. I breathed, every thought in my head evaporating as my nerve endings vibrated like plucked strings. "Rob," I whispered.

"Mmhmm."

"Will you kiss me?" I forced my eyelids to lift, and my heart stuttered when I realized how close he was.

Rob's eyes dropped to my mouth. "You said you needed time."

"I do." I swiped my tongue over my lips, and Rob's fingers twitched. "But right now, I also need you to kiss me, or I might—"

Rob's lips closed over mine, pulling the breath from my lungs. He kissed like he played hockey. All in. Full throttle.

His fingers tightened in my hair, gently tugging my head back as he dragged his lips over my jaw, down my neck. It was like he'd been studying game tape and knew exactly where my weaknesses were.

He blew through the neutral zone and hit every single one. The hollow between my neck and shoulder. Check. Right below my jaw. Check. Earlobe. *Holy shit, check.*

By the time he made it back to my lips, I was putty in his hands. How was this so damn good? I didn't feel like I was placating him. I didn't feel like he was doing this for him.

Every touch, every push and pull, every flick of his tongue, it was for me. For him. For both of us. He wanted this *with* me. Not just for himself. Not just to look like he was doing it right.

I love you. I'm in love with you.

I flicked my tongue against his, tangling my hands in the neck of his shirt, his hair, anywhere I could grab to pull him closer, to press him tighter.

And then, his lips slowed, his hands still caging me against him. He brushed his tongue over mine, breathing through me, making me a part of him.

His forehead pressed against mine, his lips stilling, connected to mine. He dropped his hands, and grabbed the hem of his shirt, pulling it up, and breaking our connection for the briefest moment as he tugged it over his head and dropped it on the floor.

And somehow I knew. He wasn't doing this because he wanted to push my boundaries, because he wanted to ask for more.

It simply didn't feel right to have clothes between us.

I reached down and pulled my shirt over my head, then dropped my jeans to the floor, stepping out of them as Rob did the same. I straightened, and he caught my hand, leading me to the bed.

I pulled down the sheet and comforter and slipped in, moving toward the wall so Rob could crawl in next to me. He curled around me and pulled the blankets over us, then dropped his arm over me, threading his fingers through mine.

I closed my eyes, feeling his chest rise and fall against my back.

Somewhere between the steps and this bed, all the panic I felt in Logan's truck had seeped out of me. I was safe. I was loved. Rob didn't need to say a word of it.

CHAPTER
Thirty~Four

I STAYED with Rob for a week before moving in with Lily. The guys were more than accommodating, especially with private washroom time, but when Lily mentioned her roommate had left over the holidays, it was an opportunity too good to pass up.

Rob needed his bed back, and as much as I loved spooning him in a twin, we both needed to catch up on some sleep. Plus, it was getting harder not to push our relationship into high gear, and I still wondered if I was ready.

All conventional wisdom pointed to not jumping into another relationship the second after ending a long-term commitment. I couldn't get my brain or my body to buy in. Every time I was with Rob, I wanted to continue being with Rob. But maybe that was what set off alarm bells.

It wasn't until Logan left for those two months that I realized I had been drowning. I didn't want to make the same mistake twice.

I gave myself a few days to settle in at Lily's before I was itching to get the rest of my stuff from Logan's. I felt guilty leaving him with the full rent payment even though I'd already paid my portion for January, so I waited until the Outlaws had practice to go back to the house.

The walk back was surreal, like I was moving through a dream. I unlocked the front door and stepped inside, setting down my broken-down boxes and canvas bags. It looked exactly the same since everything in there was Logan's to begin with. Somehow, this was both comforting and devastating. How had I spent six months of my life here without noticing I hadn't made a mark?

Logan's room looked almost the same, minus the few things I'd taken when I left. I didn't take long to look at it, just folded out a box and started packing.

I stacked my books first, then my pens and stationery. Old letters and stamps. I reached for my clothes next, pulling them off hangers and out of drawers, tossing them in. I didn't bother folding them since I'd just be taking them out an hour from now.

I moved to my nightstand and grabbed my headphones and walkman, the cord tangling around my fingers. I'd missed that little guy over the past week.

I had just barely set it on top of my clothes when I heard it. The front door opening.

I froze, my heart pounding. Who the hell was here? Logan should be at practice. Did he have a new roommate? A new girlfriend? I scanned the room. Had I missed someone else's stuff?

The footsteps drew closer, and my shoulders tensed. I recognized them.

Logan appeared in the doorway, dressed in his hockey base layer and his puffy coat. "Hey."

I half expected him to be pissed that I was there without his permission, but he wasn't. I exhaled, still kneeling on the floor. "Hey."

He shifted on his feet. "I heard you were grabbing your things."

I wanted to ask who'd told him, but I didn't need to. Besides Lily and Caleb, I'd only informed one other person where I was going this afternoon. "Rob told you?"

Logan nodded, running his hand over the back of his neck. "Don't give him shit. I told him I wanted to talk to you."

I turned back to my packing, my hands trembling as I pulled my underwear from the drawer, shoving it in one of the bags fast enough, I hoped he didn't notice what it was.

Logan watched me. I grabbed a hoodie from my chair and shoved it in the box, then reached for my hairbrush on the dresser. Logan took a step forward, and I turned to face him, my heart thudding in my chest.

He looked at me, his jaw tense. "I wanted to apologize."

My throat tightened. I forced a smile. "Okay."

Logan's throat worked. "I'm sorry for what I did. Over in Europe. I know it was shitty, and I shouldn't have tried to defend it."

I nodded once. "Thank you." It felt surprisingly good to hear him say it.

He blew out a breath. "I think it's more than that, though."

My breathing was shallow. I wasn't sure where he was going next.

Logan looked up, his hair falling over his forehead. "I didn't know how to love you." His voice was low, almost a whisper.

I met his gaze. He took a step forward, then stopped, his hand dropping to his side. "I didn't know how to love you because I don't know how to love anything other than hockey. And maybe myself." He dropped his eyes, his hands clenching and unclenching. "I don't know how to be with someone and give a hundred percent to that. I was using you as a support person or something."

Relief rolled through me. *Yes.* That was exactly it. I wasn't crazy for feeling like my full-time job was helping him, pushing him, encouraging him. I spent so much time thinking about how to lower his stress levels, I didn't know what to do with myself when he left.

A tear slipped down my cheek, and the tortured expression on his face activated that old knee-jerk reaction. I wanted to reach out, to hold him and make it better. But that wasn't my job anymore. "Logan, I—"

He shook his head, his eyes glistening. "I know. I know it's not enough. But I needed you to know that it wasn't because I didn't care. It wasn't because I didn't want you." He let out a low laugh, running his hands through his hair. "But I'm not proud of that either."

"Of what?" I planted my hands on my hips, then thought better of it and put them in my pockets. *There was the bracelet.*

He swallowed hard, his Adam's apple bobbing. "I'm competitive. I always have been, and when I found out that Rob liked you, I don't know. I wanted to prove I could win. That I could be better than him."

My mind started to spin, and I had to steady myself against the dresser. "You knew Rob liked me?"

Logan's jaw clenched, and he nodded. "He never said it, but yeah. It was pretty obvious."

I stared at him. "Wait, so you—"

Logan cut me off, his voice strained. "It wasn't just about that. I swear, Shar. I wanted you, but I'm not proud of that part of it. I don't know. I'm just always trying to prove something. To my team, to myself." His voice wavered. "To you."

I stood there, my hands trembling. I didn't know what to say to that.

He took a step closer, his eyes pleading. "I'm not asking for anything. I just needed you to know."

I nodded, my throat too tight to speak. Logan's eyes searched mine, then finally, he exhaled and took a step back. "Can I help you with that?"

Logan not only helped me finish packing, he carried everything to the front door. When I brought my last bag of knick-knacks and half-empty toiletries, Logan motioned to the stereo.

"Did you know it was him?"

I paused, staring at the mix tape in the cassette player. "Not until recently. Did you?"

Logan shook his head. "I swear, if I'd known it was him, I wouldn't have—" He stopped mid sentence, shoving his hands in his pockets. "I'm sorry I let you believe it was me, though."

I slipped on my shoes. "Thank you." I'd never heard Logan apologize so many times in the space of thirty minutes, but I was quickly becoming a fan.

Logan took in the pile of bags and boxes. "How are you getting all this to your new place?"

"I was going to call my friend Caleb." I had to specify because Logan had never met my orchestra friends. One year with Logan, and Rob had already spent more time with them than he had. "He was going to bring his car over and help me load up."

Logan nodded, then reached into his pocket and tossed me a keychain with a single key on it. I caught it. "You can take my truck. I'm not going to need it until tomorrow."

"You sure?"

He gave me a sad smile. "Might be helpful. If you need to grab anything else."

I put the key in my pocket. "Thank you, Logan. This . . . it means a lot."

A flush crept up his neck. "Here. I'll help you load it up."

We transported everything to the truck, and when I'd successfully convinced Logan that I would only be driving it across campus and not on any major highways, he closed the tailgate and stepped back.

I stood in front of him on the sidewalk. "Thanks for your help."

He nodded, kicking a rock back into the landscaping. "We had some good times, didn't we?"

I stepped forward and took his hand. "Logan, we had so many good times."

He looked up, his eyes glassy. "I'm sorry, Shar."

"I know." I stepped forward and hugged him. It wasn't an attempt to fix him this time. It wasn't out of guilt or a misguided belief that I was responsible for his emotions. I hugged Logan because I wanted him to know that I had loved him. That I still wanted what was best for him. That I was grateful for everything I'd learned about love and especially about myself.

When I pulled back, his eyes were soft. He sniffed. "I'm sorry I wasn't better for you."

I pressed my lips together. "I'm sorry we weren't better for each other."

———

An hour and a half later, I sat in front of Rob's house. That's what I called it now. It wasn't the "Guys' House" or the "Halloween Party House." It was all him. After leaving Logan's, I'd dropped my stuff off at Lily's, and then, instead of driving the truck back over, I found myself winding to the west side of campus.

Practice was barely ending, so Rob wouldn't be there for a bit. I popped his mix tape into the cassette player and leaned back in the seat, listening. The music filled the cab of the truck, and I smiled to myself. Each song sounded just a little bit different knowing it was Rob who'd picked them.

I'd realized something during my conversation with Logan. Rob was the one who told him I'd be there. Considering how much he wanted to kick Logan's ass after he heard what happened, I knew he didn't do that for himself.

Once again, he did it for me. He knew what Logan wanted to say, and he knew I needed to hear it, even if the idea of putting the two of us back together—alone—in the house we'd slept in probably created his own personal hell.

As I unpacked my boxes, I realized that two weeks was plenty of time for me to know exactly what I wanted. I wasn't jumping into this with Rob because I was sad or lonely. It had been him that I'd loved all along, even if I didn't know it.

An engine sounded behind me, and I shot up, looking in the side mirror. Rory's car pulled up, his headlights shining through the back window of the truck. Had they ridden together? I hadn't even checked to see if Rob's truck was parked somewhere on the street.

The passenger door opened, and my heart leapt into my throat. Rob stepped out, his hair damp and tousled, his hockey bag slung over his shoulder. I turned off the truck and stepped out, closing the door behind me. Rob rounded the front of Rory's car and stopped in front of me, his eyes locked on mine. For a moment, neither of us moved, even with Rory and Axel's catcalling.

I waited for them to file past us and go inside the house. "I talked with Logan."

Rob nodded to the truck. "Did you get this in the divorce?"

I smirked. "Asshole." I walked forward, stopping when I had to look up to keep eye contact. "Thank you."

Rob's jaw tensed. "He better have been a gentleman."

"He was. He loaded my things and lent me his truck."

"And apologized?"

I nodded. "And apologized."

Rob adjusted the strap of his hockey bag. He was so hot like this. Freshly showered after practice, wearing sweats with or without a T-shirt, his whole body worn out and relaxed.

"I don't care if you wear a shirt anymore," I murmured.

Rob raised an eyebrow. "Amending the rules?"

"Mmhmm. Maybe all of them."

"Don't we need a pen and paper for that?"

My eyes narrowed. "What should we call it this time?"

"I don't know, but you're not choosing the title."

I scoffed, throwing out my hand to smack his shoulder. He caught it and pulled me to him. "I thought it was a very functional title."

Rob's lips twitched. "Okay. What would be your functional title now, then?"

My heart skipped like a kid doing hopscotch. Just like the last time, my emotions were too heightened to be witty. "I was thinking something like 'Sharla and Rob's rules for an exclusive relationship?'"

Rob's breathing slowed. "That is much improved from the original."

"I thought you might like it." I swallowed hard, my pulse rushing in my ears.

Rob stepped forward, pushing me along the truck until I was past the driver's door. He opened it and reached in, retrieving the keys, then closed and locked the door.

"There's something in there." I pointed to the back door.

Rob inserted the key and opened it, then snorted and pulled out the toilet cleaner. "Finally. I've been waiting on this."

I laughed. "Just spreading out the Christmas joy." I was trembling. Not only because I'd forgotten my coat at my apartment, but because I knew what came next. Or at least what I hoped came next.

Rob locked the door and closed it, then handed me the toilet cleaner.

"What—" I let out a yelp of surprise as Rob squatted down and reached an arm around my backside, scooping me off the ground. "Rob, I can walk." When I realized he wasn't going to set me down, I wrapped my legs around his waist, riding him like a baby koala.

Rob walked toward the front door. I reached down and turned the knob, and he dropped his hockey bag in the entry. We both kicked off our shoes, then he insisted on carrying me up the stairs.

I tried to hide my face as we passed the living room, but I wasn't fast enough. "You're late!" Rory shouted, and the other guys hooted and hollered. "I thought for sure you two would've been back at it right after the game!"

"Go give her the Thompson special!" Axel called out.

Rob turned and flipped them off, and I buried my face in his shirt. He laughed, taking the stairs two at a time. He wasn't even winded by the time we reached his door. My heart pounded as he pushed it open and carried me inside.

I dropped the toilet cleaner.

He turned and pressed me up against the door after it closed, then reached down and locked the handle. "You're sure you don't need more time?"

I ran my hands through his hair, and he tipped his head back. "I'm sure." I lowered my head, kissing his cheek, then dragging my fingernails over his stubble.

Rob slowly lowered me, and I let my legs drop, my feet planting themselves on the floor. "Do you have early rehearsal?"

I shook my head. "Wednesday, remember?"

He pressed his hands against my hips. "It always used to be Tuesday."

I arched against him, pulling at the zipper on his hoodie. "New semester. New schedule to memorize." I unzipped it, sliding my hands across his bare stomach and chest. "Do you have anything in the morning?"

Rob grunted. "I'm pretty sure I just came down with the flu."

I laughed, but before I could give him some lecture about being academically responsible, his lips were on mine.

It was like every kiss we'd shared over the past two weeks, but this time, it was amplified. Like the volume had been turned up on a stereo—every note vibrated through my bones. His lips were warm and insistent, and he tasted like mint.

"I love kissing you," I whispered, my hands still trying to memorize every rise and fall on his torso.

"Good." Rob hissed air through his teeth as I toyed with the waistband of his sweats. He pulled me away from the door, fumbling with my shirt. I helped him get it off and goosebumps lifted on my skin. "Are you cold?"

"A little," I admitted.

Rob flicked back his top sheet and comforter, then looped his fingers in the belt loops of my jeans. He undid the button, his hands unsteady. I may have changed into new, lacy underwear I bought with some of my scholarship money. That counted as "educational pursuits," didn't it?

Now that I stood in the shaft of light from his window, Rob took a good look at me. I stepped out of my jeans, trying not to be self-conscious at the way my stomach rolled a little as I bent over.

"I'm going to get a space heater," he said as I dropped to the mattress and slid under the covers. "I don't ever want to stop looking at you."

I leaned forward and tugged on his sweatpants. "I can think of a few things that might change your position on that."

Rob took off his hoodie and pants, then slid into bed next to me. This time, I didn't turn my back to him. He threaded his legs with mine, bending one knee and lifting until it stopped. I let out a puff of air, closing my eyes as pleasure rippled through me at the contact.

Rob's fingers traced lazy circles over my ribs. "What do you like, Shar?"

I swallowed hard, my mind racing. *What did I like?* I'd never been asked that question before. How embarrassing was that to admit?

"I don't know," I admitted, my voice tight.

Rob's eyes softened, and he brushed his thumb over my cheek. "Perfect. We can figure it out together." He leaned in and kissed me softly, then pulled back with a grin. "I like experimenting. Collecting data."

I laughed, my nerves easing. "You and your backup plans."

Rob chuckled, his breath warm on my skin. "You have no idea."

He started with his hands, slowly exploring almost every inch of me. When he heard my breath hitch, he'd say, "Got it," or, "Noted." His voice lit up the inside of my brain like fireworks on Canada Day.

Who knew that a whisper in my ear could send shivers down my spine? Or that having his fingers toy with the ends of my hair could make my heart race?

Every touch, every kiss, every breath was a new discovery, and I thought about that conversation with Maddie in her bedroom.

What made good sex? I didn't have the textbook, but I was pretty sure I'd found it. It was this. All of this. The wanting, the knowing, the anticipation. Feeling safe, loved, listened to.

My body was on fire, but I never wanted it to stop.

Rob pulled away and smiled down at me. "Good so far?"

I nodded, my breath coming in short gasps. "Mmm."

"I'll take that as a yes." He lowered his head to continue, but I pressed against his shoulder, rolling him to his back.

"Can I take a turn?"

Rob's pupils dilated. "You want to?"

I nodded. I'd never done this before, and that set me shivering again. But I'd never been the one in control, the one doing the exploring, and the idea made every part of my body molten.

It didn't take me long to figure out a few things. When I ran my nails over the muscles of his back, he groaned. When I brushed my thumb over his lower lip, he sucked it into his mouth.

How? How had I never known it could be like this?

This was making love. It wasn't about the mechanics, the positions, or the tricks. It was about being this close with someone, this connected, body and soul.

"I love you, Rob," I murmured. "I'm in love with you."

Rob caught my face in his hands. "Say it again."

I grinned, suddenly self-conscious. "I love you. I'm in love with you."

He pulled my mouth to his, no longer slow and patient but

messy and frantic and desperate. His hands found the clasp of my bra, unhooking it. He found the last parts of me, breathing hard, forcing his body to slow down like he couldn't rush a single second.

Rob slid his hand down the flat of my stomach, and I sucked in a breath. He paused, his fingertips brushing the band of my underwear. I ran my hand over his arm, encouraging him.

"Just a second," he whispered.

I paused, kissing his cheek. "Are you okay?"

He nodded. "Yeah. I've just waited so long for this. For you. I think I might pass out."

I grinned, peppering kisses over his face. "I'll make sure you don't hit your head."

"Don't make promises you can't keep." Rob's hand continued on its path, and my head tipped back on the pillow.

"Yes," I said on a breath. I needed him to know this was what I wanted. This was what I liked. Every variation of his kisses, every new motif where his hands were on my body. I wanted to experience all of them.

Every single one.

CHAPTER
Thirty-Five

TWO WEEKS LATER, I screamed at the top of my lungs next to Crystal and Maddie as the crowd roared right along with us.

"Now that was a damn pass!" Crystal re-wrapped her scarf around her neck.

I nodded in agreement. Rob had intercepted the puck and set up the game-winning assist with a perfect slap pass.

Maddie threw an arm over my shoulders and squeezed. We didn't rush up like we used to. Rob and I didn't have a secret meeting place. We didn't want to make things weird. So, I waited with the commoners up in the lobby until he emerged from the locker room, changed and showered. The best part about this was that he drove us all to Ranchmans.

Crystal and Maddie chattered about the game while we travelled the couple of blocks. Enter stage one of our routine, where Rob played devil's advocate and told them why their assessment and suggested strategy adjustments were all wrong.

Then came stage two, where Rob parked his truck and threw an arm around me, walking into Ranchmans and greeting his teammates. Stage three was the awkward glance and head nod Logan and I exchanged, and stage four was my favourite. Where

Rob's hand found the small of my back, guiding me to a booth in the corner.

As the night went on, we laughed and talked with Crystal, Maddie, and a few of Rob's teammates—they came to us.

Rob leaned in, his lips brushing my jaw. "Ready to go? You have early rehearsal tomorrow."

I grinned. "It's okay, we can stay a little longer."

"What if I don't want to stay a little longer?" he murmured, nipping at the skin of my neck.

I blew out a breath, trying to hide how much the feel of his lips and teeth affected me. I pulled back, cupping his face in my hands. "I don't ever want you to miss out on this because of me."

Rob wet his lips and circled his hands around my wrists. "Shar, I love hockey."

"I know."

"But I love a lot of things." I raised an eyebrow, and he dropped his hands, pulling me closer. "I love the way you stretch your legs out when you sleep."

I laughed, but Rob put a finger to my lips. "I love that sound you make when—"

"Rob!" I hissed, pushing him further into the booth.

"Okay, lovebirds. I think we're going to head out." Crystal reached out and gave me a side hug.

Maddie blew me a kiss. "I'm just going to run to the washroom. Be right back."

Crystal nodded and stood, retrieving her coat and walking over to the main Outlaws table to say goodbyes.

Rob waved to both of them then grinned, running his hand over my thigh and slipping it between my legs. "I told you, hockey has never been my only game plan. I love it, and I want to play as long as I can—"

"You'll play, Rob. None of this 'if they think I'm good enough.'"

He picked up a nacho and put it in my mouth. "There. Chew

on this so I can finish my sentence." I feigned indignation, and he laughed. "I love hockey. But it will never come first. You're not my backup plan, Shar."

I swallowed, then took a drink of water, the words sinking into me like water over dry ground. My heart swelled to bursting. "Okay."

"Okay, what?"

"Take me home Thompson. You can't say something like that and then expect me not to want to tear your clothes off."

"My place or yours?" His eyes glinted.

"Lily's gone for the weekend. She's got some gig with her new band."

"Thank you, Lily." Rob reached for his coat, then stood, pulling me up from the bench of the booth.

"Rob, you want one?" Rory held up a shot, but Rob shook his head.

"All you, bud!" He waved, nestled his hand against my back, and walked me to the door.

Epilogue

MADDIE

I HURRIED to the washrooms at the back of Ranchmans. I was Crystal's ride—I'd parked my car on the street earlier—and if I took too long, she was probably going to get roped into some game with Rory and Axel and I'd never get home before midnight.

I wasn't a total stick in the mud, but I was taking advanced calculus, and my professor barely spoke English. That meant a lot more textbook deciphering than I was used to.

I rounded the corner and gasped as I slammed into what felt like a brick wall. My hands shot up to steady myself, and I froze when my brain came back online. Soft cotton. Definitely not wall-ish.

I looked up to find my palms pressed against a firm chest. *A tall, firm chest.* His shirt was baby blue, not that it mattered, except that this specific colour was always the one I chose in my dirty fantasies. And . . . that face? It might have appeared right along with it once or twice.

"Maddie." He said my name like a statement, not a question. *Chase knew who I was?*

I yanked back like I'd touched a hot stove. "Sorry, I—" My words stuck in my throat. What the hell was I supposed to say? I hadn't seen him in over six years. Or, rather, he hadn't seen me. I'd seen him plenty sitting on the Outlaws bench. One could say that was mostly what I'd been *seeing* lately.

"It's been a while." His expression was maddeningly even and composed.

"Yeah." I let out a hopefully-not-obviously-nervous laugh. "I'm surprised you recognized me."

Chase's lip twitched. "You've definitely grown up."

I grimaced, hating that I suddenly sounded like the kid sister I never wanted to be to him. "So have you." Hmm, nope. Based on the sudden furrow in his brow, that was not the right move. I pressed on, hoping to bury that comment with a new one. "You're coaching now?" Damn it. Now he knew that I'd seen him. That I knew he was here on campus and I'd never stopped by to say hello.

"Yeah. I didn't realize you attended Douglas." He shoved his hand into his pocket. "You still a math whiz?"

My eyes widened. *He remembered that?* "I still love it."

"You tutored me, remember? You were three grades below me and knew the material better than my teacher."

I played that off like I hadn't been thinking about our time at the kitchen counter every day since he showed up on the Outlaws bench. Somehow, my brain decided this was the perfect moment to announce this fact. "I had such a crush on you back then."

The corner of his mouth lifted. "You did?"

My cheeks heated. "Yes. You had real cigarettes, a girlfriend, you played hockey, and I was a math nerd."

His grin widened. "Right, who was I dating then?"

"The fact that you can't remember kind of punctuates my point." It was Melody Sanchez. I considered having a voodoo doll made of her over the summer of '88, but didn't have much follow through.

Chase chuckled. "Yeah. Fair point."

I motioned to the ladies' room, and Chase moved to the side. "It was nice seeing you again."

"You, too." I walked past him and was about to push through the door when he said, "Do you always come to the games?"

I looked back. "Do you always come to the bar after with your players?"

Chase looked amused. "Are you judging me, Maddie?"

I held up my fingers, showing just a smidge. He laughed out loud. "Maybe one of these days, we can catch up."

My heart lodged in my throat. Chase was four years older than me. In middle school, that was a veritable lifetime. Now? Twenty-four to my twenty didn't seem all that bad. But dating your sibling? Dating a member of the coaching staff? No matter how progressive people were in the 1990's, I was pretty sure those were still two widely frowned upon scenarios.

"If you need calculus help, let me know." I pushed the door to the washroom open and stepped inside.

NEXT IN THE SERIES —>

Preorder Now!

Find special edition e-books and paperbacks exclusively at www. CindyGunderson.com

About the Author

Cindy Gunderson is a voice actress and award-winning author. Since she has commitment issues, she writes both sci-fi and fantasy, as well as contemporary romance and women's fiction under the pen name, Cynthia Gunderson.

When she is not typing away in a quiet corner of her local library, you can find her traveling with her family, narrating audiobooks, or happily digging in her garden. She loves acting and performing, beating her kids in card games, and playing ultimate frisbee with her handsome husband, Scott.

Cindy grew up in Alberta, Canada, but has lived most of her adult life between California and Colorado. She currently resides in the Denver metro area. Cindy holds a B.S. in Psychology from Brigham Young University.

Cindy's first novel Tier 1 was awarded First Place in Science Fiction at the 2021 CIPPA EVVY Awards and her women's fiction novel Yes, And was honored with the Indie Author Award's first place prize for the state of Colorado, 2023.

Also by Cynthia Gunderson

Yes, And

I Can't Remember

Holly Bough Cottage

The New Year's Party

Let's Try This Again

Sugar Creek Series

One Last Christmas

Love in Audio

Canadian Played Series

Against the Boards

Called for Icing

Stickhandle with Care

On the Power Play

Guarding Home Ice

Offside Attraction

Drop the Mitts

Find signed books and discounted bundles at

www.CindyGunderson.com

Instagram: @CindyGWrites

Facebook: @CindyGWrites

TikTok: @CynthiaGWrites

Printed in Great Britain
by Amazon